AURELIA

Maybe Hiring

ILLICIT LIBRARY COLLECTION BOOK 1

Maybe HIRING

ILLICIT LIBRARY COLLECTION BOOK 1

AURELIA KNIGHT

Copyright © 2022 by Aurelia Knight

All rights reserved.

No portion of this book may be reproduced in any form without written permission from the publisher or author, except as permitted by U.S. copyright law.

All characters and other entities appearing in this work are fictitious. Any resemblance to real persons, *dead or alive,* or other real-life entities, *past or present,* is purely coincidental.

Contents

Dedication	VII
Warning	VIII
1. Chapter One	1
2. Chapter Two	13
3. Chapter Three	23
4. Chapter Four	34
5. Chapter Five	45
6. Chapter Six	59
7. Chapter Seven	73
8. Chapter Eight	84
9. Chapter Nine	94
10. Chapter Ten	104
11. Chapter Eleven	116
12. Chapter Twelve	129
13. Chapter Thirteen	141

14. Chapter Fourteen	154
15. Chapter Fifteen	173
16. Chapter Sixteen	186
17. Chapter Seventeen	200
18. Chapter Eighteen	216
19. Chapter Nineteen	226
20. Chapter Twenty	238
21. Chapter Twenty-One	249
22. Chapter Twenty-Two	261
Also By	276
Afterword	277
About Author	278
Acknowledgments	279

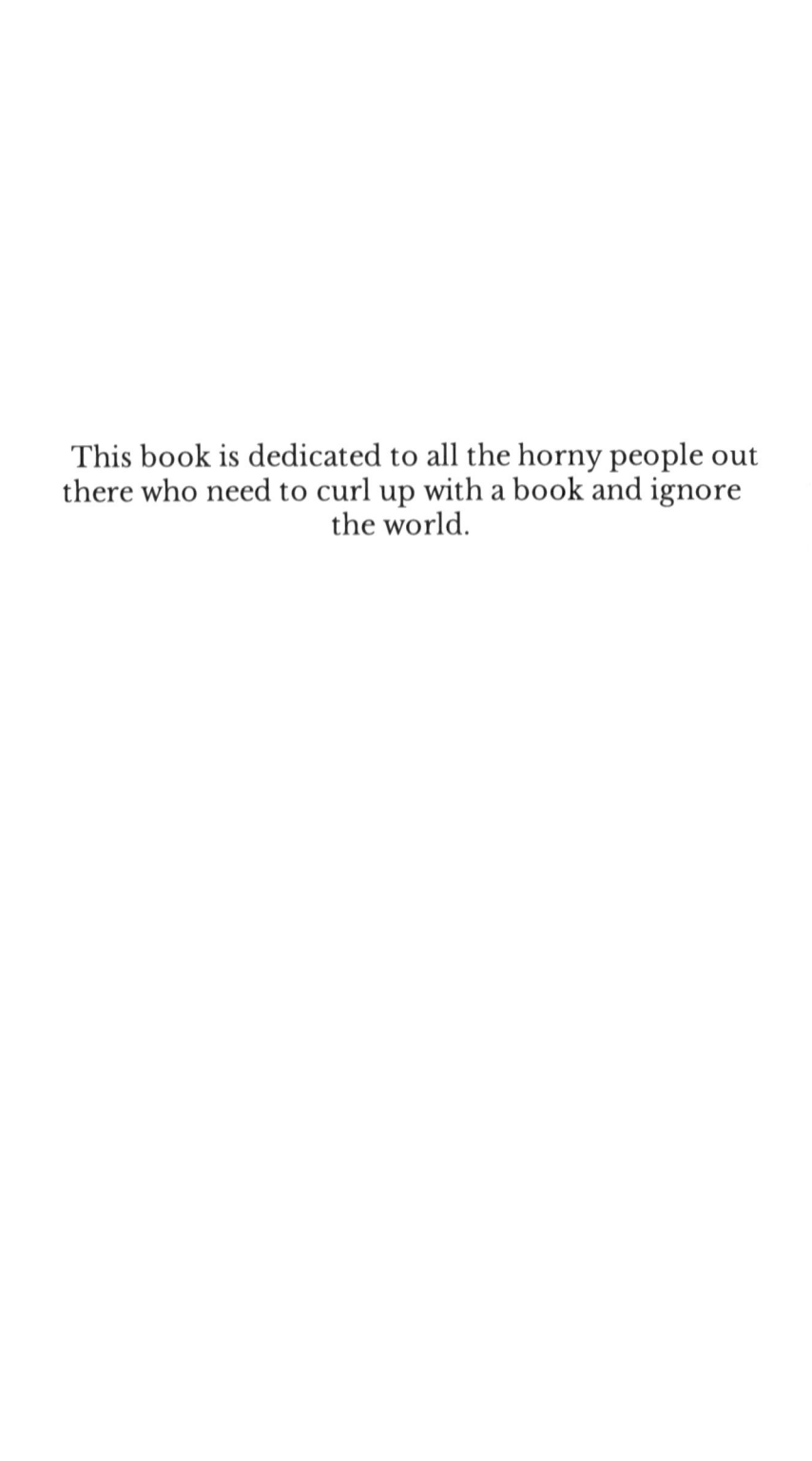

This book is dedicated to all the horny people out there who need to curl up with a book and ignore the world.

Warning

This story contains dark themes that may be unsettling to some readers and is **not** intended for readers under the age of 18.

Maybe Hiring is not a "dark romance", but rather a romance surrounded by a lot of darkness.

If you are triggered by explicit sexual content, graphic violence, or stalking this may not be the book for you.

Chapter One

"I'm so sorry, Claire, but we have to let you go," Anthony, my now ex-boss, had a pained expression on his face that he was trying to cover up with stoic professionalism. He never had much of a poker face, and it was part of what I found endearing about him. His brown eyes matched his ill-fitting corduroy jacket, and it seemed odd that someone sweet like him could smash apart the little peace I'd found in my life, but here we were.

I looked around my makeshift office within the basement of City Hall. The folding chair beneath me was hard and uncompromising, much like the position I now found myself in. It was late afternoon, and the sun lit the room at just the right angle to make the swirling dust motes glow with a golden effervescence.

I would miss this place and the records they hired me to digitize eight months earlier. I only finished that very task an hour before and already started packing up my things to prepare for this moment. "Claire, I want to clarify that this has no bearing on your work ethic or the job you've done here."

I cut him off, knowing this was hard for him, "Anthony, I knew when I took the job it was temp work. I just didn't expect to get so attached." Letting out a pained sigh, I gestured vaguely around myself. This musty, forgotten hole had become my refuge. The smell of old paper filled the air, and the cavern in my chest opened wide.

He fiddled with his tie, a nervous habit. "I'm going to write you a glowing recommendation, and if we ever need help, I'll call." I believed him, but it would never be the same.

"Thank you, Anthony." I knew I would cry later, but for now, I was calm. He didn't want to do this any more than I wanted it done. I was used to trying to make things easier for other people, a task I assigned myself before I could even remember.

"Claire, I know it's probably not my business, but you're overqualified for this job, and any other I could offer you. You have a master's degree, and I don't think you should give up on your dreams. You're only twenty-six and you have all the time in the world..."

I put up my hands to stop him. "Really, it's okay. Thank you for the reference. I packed my stuff up. So, I'll just be heading out." I didn't need a pep talk while he tore my world apart.

"We'll mail your check," he called after me as I forced myself to walk up the stairs instead of running as I truly wanted.

"I get direct deposit," I called back.

The master's degree he was talking about was in library sciences, and sadly, there were no libraries in the city hiring a librarian. I had been working odd office jobs since I graduated two years ago, and this was the first time I actually felt happy. My eyes drifted to the library sitting opposite City Hall. *So close, yet so far.* I stomped off to my crappy apartment and flopped against my worn-out couch.

That's where I stayed for longer than I'd care to admit.

※※※

"You're the man for me," I spoke directly to the actor sudsing his hair on my TV. The water ran through his golden tresses, sweeping the bubbles over his abs, and the camera cut away before it reached the goods. My heart thumped in excitement and disappointment as the news came back on.

"Another young woman found dead in the suburbs of–" I slapped at the remote, turning the TV off. That shit was too depressing, even for me. I shoved another chip into my mouth with the enthusiasm of a limp noodle, overboiled and ready for the trash.

My curly brown hair hung lank. The sheen of sweat covering me made it stick to my neck. I pulled it up into a bun grumbling about eighty-degree weather in May. I wore the same pair of pink bunny pajamas I had for two days straight and I ripped them off, frustrated with the temperature and the fact I failed to be productive yet another day. A bunny slipper flipped over the back of the couch and it landed in a pile of unwashed laundry.

I looked around my apartment, sure the walls were closing in on me. Takeout containers covered my kitchen counters and coffee table, and I needed to take the trash out. The things that didn't need to be done would make for a much shorter list. I flopped back on the couch, feeling the coarse fibers scratching against my skin, and let out a groan. I slapped my hands against my bare chest, remembering the last time I wore a bra, two weeks ago, when Anthony banished me from my post at City Hall.

I checked the time, noting that my favorite Indian restaurant would be delivering. It didn't bother me that three o'clock wasn't a proper mealtime. I had too little to be excited about in my life to care about things like social acceptability. I shoved the containers out of the way until I found my phone. The battery was nearly dead. What else was new? I plugged it into the charger. At only three feet long, it kept me on a short leash.

I leaned against the kitchen counter, enjoying the feeling of the cool tile on my skin. "Hi, Sadar, it's Claire. Delivery, please?"

"You sure you don't want to come in and sit down?" Sadar was a nice guy, and my closest friend, considering I lost contact with everyone else for various reasons. Even my mom was currently not speaking to me, but that was typical of our relationship.

"I'm sure, Sadar. The usual, please?"

He chuckled a little, "One of these days you're going to come in and eat, and I'll get you to try something new."

"Sounds good," I lied.

I closed my eyes for a moment, willing the surrounding mess to disappear. I popped them open, half expectant. So far, no luck. The elaborate monument to destitution I called home wasn't going anywhere anytime soon. Or was it?

I opened my banking app and read over the charges. There wasn't a single credit since my layoff, yet I kept myself in chicken korma. My credit cards weren't maxed out, but they were wheezing, and my savings account was nearly in tears. I needed to find a job before I was out on my ass and the place really disappeared.

I half-heartedly flipped through job listings, observing without surprise that none of the libraries were hiring. It was some elite club I couldn't crack, harder to infiltrate than the NYC garbage union. I'd volunteered at the university library while I was in school as part of my degree program and to meet the conditions of my scholarship, but I couldn't even get an unpaid position at the local libraries.

There were other things I could do with my degree, but most of the options came back to libraries in some way or database configuration and information processing. There weren't a lot of jobs available in my city and none so far fit the bill. Moving wasn't an option. What if I went somewhere with terrible Indian food? I shuddered at the thought.

I slammed my phone down a little too hard, revolted by the state of my life. My mother warned me plenty of times that my chosen career path was stupid, the product of too many dreams and an overactive imagination. There wasn't much I did right where she was concerned and typically, I ignored her. Sadly, her words played in my head now: *dreams are for people who are better than us.*

My entire existence felt like a boa constrictor tightening around me, preparing to swallow me whole. I forced myself to take a breath, and little spots of light burst into my vision as oxygen returned to my brain. The last thing I needed was to pass out and crack my head against the linoleum. Winding up with a hospital bill and a lost security deposit would suck.

At least when I was in school, the structure and having a goal to work toward kept my life in better order. I needed some semblance of a routine. I should at a minimum fill out some applications for the jobs that were available, even if they were light years away from what I truly wanted.

A lot of office positions required a bachelor's degree with no concern for the major, and while the requirement mystified me, at least I had one. Truthfully, all I wanted was to go back in time to my days at City Hall. I wasn't lazy despite the state of my apartment, and I didn't mind hard work. Deep inside, I just knew I would never be as happy or complete as I was sifting bits of history in an undisturbed basement. I was a historian, a small-time, irrelevant one, but I loved it.

A knock brought me out of my misery, "One minute," I called as I pulled my pajamas back on. I walked over to the door and used all my strength to pry it open. The influx of unseasonal humidity swelled the wood tightly.

"Hi, Claire." A smile stretched Sadar's full brown lips, revealing his pearly white teeth and accenting the warmth in his dark eyes. His gaze flicked down my body and, despite my bunny pajamas, he clearly didn't find me lacking. He was handsome and fit, but it's best not to fuck where you eat.

"Thanks, Sadar. You're the best." I took the bags and handed him a generous tip. He invited me to come eat in person one more time before he left me to it. The food tasted delicious, but soon enough the sauce turned cold, and I had nothing but my thoughts to occupy me. I couldn't keep sitting in this cage of an apartment.

I jumped into the shower, cleansing my body and hair. I shivered in disgust as I remembered that I had no clean clothes. Wrapping a towel around myself, I picked through the piles until I found an outfit I was sure I only wore for a couple of hours. I skipped the underwear, unable to bring myself to put on a dirty pair. I shoved a pile of clothes into my laundry basket with the plan to do a load as soon as I got home.

I gave myself a once over in the long mirror hanging on my wall. My tanned skin looked paler than usual, maybe from the lack of sun, or my inner turmoil making its way to the surface. All that mattered at the moment was that I passed for a normal member of society — if no one looked too hard. And why would they? I used to be a pretty girl with nice curves, but I lost the spark that used to draw eyes to me.

This city wasn't cheap, historic buildings lined the streets, and beautiful cultured women were at a surplus. I couldn't compare. Even when I had solid employment, I couldn't afford better than this d-list building or the simple clothes strewn across the floor.

The knobs and fixtures all worked like crap and the ceiling leaked when it rained too hard. *Yeah, I need to get out of here,* I reminded myself as I headed to the exit. Though I'd opened the door only an hour before, it stuck like it had been closed for years.

I yanked and pulled until it finally gave way. The force catapulted me out, and I nearly ran headlong into the door across the hall. I righted myself at the last possible moment, glad I didn't have to explain to mean old Mrs. Jones why I'd disturbed her and her many cats. I often thought of getting one of the adorable little fuzz balls for myself, but feline companionship sounded a lot like tempting fate.

I ran down the hall, ignoring the lure of furry friends. Several of my neighbors roamed around, going about their business. They weren't the friendly sort, and I knew most of them only by the nicknames I'd given them. Keyman, the man with a thousand keys, waved at me with a complaint already waiting on his lips.

I gave him a cheeky wave back and kept moving. His apartment sat directly beneath mine, and it offended him that I needed to do things like move around and shower. My desperation to get away from the scene behind me far outweighed my desire to endure another lecture about "proper showering hours" and "tiptoe walking".

I flew down the stairs, taking them two at a time. The front door slammed behind me and I noticed too late another neighbor coming home with her arms full of groceries. I should have held it open for her. I shrugged away the twinge of guilt. This would be another item on my ever-increasing list of screw-ups.

It was hot for May, but better out here where the breeze kept you from baking. The few trees sticking up from the sidewalk were losing their pale green and taking on the richer tones of summer. The sun beat down on me and the warmth defrosted some of the ice growing in my chest. Thick clouds of pollen hung in the air, turning everything yellow. I sneezed like crazy and my eyes itched, but I still smiled. I didn't mind being without a car this time of year.

The library and City Hall were only three blocks from my apartment. The convenient locale was the main reason I accepted the job in the first place. Well, that and the title of "Fro-yo chef" didn't sit right with me. I rolled my eyes at the naïve girl, who didn't know what she was gaining or losing. *Why couldn't you just serve frozen yogurt?*

The buildings were twins, part of the original city planning with all its historical eccentricities. The municipal parking lot between them had been added years after their construction, covering up a wealth of cobblestones and horse manure. The paint and signage differed between the structures but otherwise, they were identical.

I walked past City Hall, keeping my eyes trained in front of me. It was nearly five, and while the library stayed open until six, Anthony and my former coworkers would be headed out any minute. I breathed a sigh of relief when I made it into the library without having to face them and their good-natured inquiries about my job search.

I found the stairs to the basement, exactly where I expected them. This endeavor was pathetic and a little crazy, but I didn't care. I needed a hit of nostalgia to keep moving forward. I stopped on the landing before I even reached the bottom floor. The striking familiarity held me in place.

The scent matched my makeshift office perfectly. Old paper, dust, and a magical something I could never put my finger on. I descended the rest of the way in a daze, and quickly found a folding chair like the one I sat in for eight months. I took a seat, and closed my eyes, pretending I was back in City Hall.

People seldom used this section of the library. All the new releases and classics lived upstairs under a big round skylight. I didn't think poorly of anyone for the preferential treatment, but I couldn't help empathizing with the basement books. I pushed myself out of the chair to give them some much-needed attention.

Several full collections of no longer published magazines lined the walls, shelves stood packed with outdated textbooks and scientific articles. Poetry books from the seventies and countless things no one looked at in ages sat under a layer of dust. The time slipped by as I investigated the irrelevancy.

I sneezed like crazy as I wiped years of dirt away from the untouched tombs. Filth encrusted me; the dust clung to the slight sheen of sweat on my overheated skin. I lifted my hair into a messy bun to keep the curls off my face while I searched. I was a wreck, but I found my first bit of peace in a while.

I picked up an old book on dinosaurs. They always fascinated me, and I remembered begging my mother to take me to the museum to see them. She never did. I ran my fingers along the tattered edges, gazing at the T-Rex standing upright. Years ago, scientists discovered they didn't stand this way, but I preferred this silly stature. He roared and whipped his head back and forth. I wiped his face clean, speaking aloud without realizing. "No one needs to want you for you to matter. You matter even if you're wrong."

"Odd thing to tell an old book, but true enough I suppose," a warm male voice intruded into the otherwise still space.

I shot into the air from the shock of finding another person in my peaceful sphere. The book hit the ground with a resounding thud, and I let out an unfortunate squeak. "What the shit?!" I spun around, finding a man standing a reasonable distance away. The way his voice reached me, it sounded as if he spoke into my ear.

He towered over me, which wasn't hard to do since I was only five foot four. He buzzed his hair down too short to guess its color. His green eyes met my brown ones and something electric zipped through me, heating my blood and forcing words out of my mouth, "Can I help you with something?"

"Do you work here?" His tightly controlled expression lifted hopefully. I shivered lightly at the sultry sound of his voice. Hot and cold warred for dominance. The heat in his voice warmed me, but the ice in his soft green eyes warned me off.

"No," embarrassment flooded through me, rising a seldom seen blush to my cheeks and clipping my tone.

"Then, probably not." he shot back.

"You know it's rude to sneak up on people." The words came out equally flirtatious and hostile, not sure if I wanted to draw him in or push him away.

Hard, angular lines built the foundation of his face. Soft, wide lips tempted me to kiss him. "I apologize for scaring you." His face puckered as he struggled not to laugh at me before he added, "This is a public library and I'm looking for a book."

My eyes ran over his perfectly tailored gray suit. His broad shoulders begged for me to trace my hands over them. I was sure he was all hard and toned beneath that suit. I worked to soften the edge in my voice, realizing I wanted a reason to keep talking to him. "What book would you want from down here?" I gestured around myself at the mountains of unwanted words.

I watched in stunned amazement as his carefully cultivated control slipped from his perfect face, "It's, uh, something about birds..."

I stared at him, waiting for the punchline. His handsome face and dead sexy body made it hard to think. The scent of cologne and man filled the air between us, interrupting the illusion I'd been enjoying. No one at City Hall ever smelled like that. Frustration filled me and I didn't know if it was aimed at him, myself, or all the forces of nature that combined to form this moment. "Why the hell are you looking for an old book on birds?"

His eyebrows shot up in surprise before they settled, regaining their original stoicism, "I don't have to tell you that." He stared into my eyes, anger replacing the chill in those green depths. My will bent beneath the weight of that gaze, submitting to him without having permitted myself to do so. I leaned toward him, pulled by the force of his presence.

He took a step back, breaking the spell he had me under. My eyes pricked as embarrassment flooded through me anew. This silly attraction was clearly one-sided, and why wouldn't it be? "I," he began speaking, but I needed to escape.

I streaked past him, and my feet cleared the landing before he realized what I was doing. The library blurred as I rushed out the door and let it slam closed behind me. I embarrassed myself enough for one day. *Why did I do that?* My frustration bubbled over onto the empty pavement. Rain fell, and it seemed appropriate. "What is your problem?" Neither I nor the gray skies had any answers.

Chapter Two

My fingers drummed nervously against the plastic arm of the waiting room chair. The secretary shot me an annoyed glance, and I tried to still them. The tight pencil skirt I wore kept my legs together, and my blazer felt like a straitjacket. They both fit me fine, but after weeks spent in pajamas and months in casual clothes, they felt restrictive.

I busied my hands by flipping through a college course catalog, but the words made little sense, and my eyes flitted over the stock pictures of smiling students. A door opened and a small woman in her fifties stepped out, "Good morning, Miss, uh…"

"Green," I told the interviewer as I pushed out of the chair and did my best to walk smoothly in my heels. She held the door to her office open for me. Being the only person in the waiting room gave me a touch of hope that I might get this job. This was the only interview I'd gotten after filling out ten plus applications.

"Please, come in. Have a seat there." I followed her to her desk, taking a quick look around the room. Sandra Whiting was the office administrator for the physical headquarters of a popular online college.

Pictures of small children and various accolades related to her position covered the walls.

Meticulous order prevailed, like dust wouldn't dare settle itself in her domain. Sitting opposite her with her organized desk between us, it was obvious she ran a tight ship. Her small brown eyes darted across my resume and references with crinkled concentration. She looked over her wiry glasses as she read, and I wondered if they were the correct script.

"Yes, Miss Green," she pushed her glasses up her nose as she looked at me. "Why are you interested in this position?"

Truthfully, I wasn't, but the need to not get evicted outweighed the urge to tell the truth. I straightened my back, forcing away the nervousness I felt.

"I have extensive experience with office work and a fondness for education. I'm prompt, hardworking, and detail-oriented. I think I'm perfectly suited for the job." My hands settled into my lap, and I crossed my ankles. The only part I lied about was being detail-oriented, but it seemed like the right thing to say to someone like her.

Her fingers tapped against the desk as she thought. "You're overqualified for the position. Why aren't you working in your chosen field..." her eyes scanned my resume, "library sciences?"

I shrugged my shoulders, trying to look nonplussed. "There are no open positions in the city's library system or local schools. I'm not interested in moving, so I'm waiting for the opportunity to present itself. Given how coveted those positions are, I don't expect that to happen any time soon." I forced a little smile to my lips to validate the idea that it didn't bother me much.

She asked me a few more questions, and I answered them as best I could.

"Well, Ms. Green, I have a few more interviews to complete, but I'll call you either way." I shook her hand and left, feeling good that whether I got the job or not, she wouldn't leave me hanging for an answer.

I rode the bus home, preparing myself for the rejection. To my surprise, she called me the very next day and offered me a full-time, nine-to-five schedule. I went to the mall and bought myself a few new business casual outfits. On my first day there, one admissions counselor, Tyler, took an interest in me right away. Sandy, who gave me the job, was giving me a tour when he popped out of nowhere and insisted he had time to do it.

"So, Claire, how are you liking us so far?" he asked as he led me into the kitchen and poured us each a cup of coffee, "Cream and sugar?" I nodded, and he passed me the one he already prepared.

"In my very limited experience, everyone seems nice." I started there less than an hour before, so I had no idea what I thought of them yet. He watched me as I took a sip of my coffee. He stood on the tall side with neatly gelled brown hair and matching brown eyes. In his dark jeans and blazer, I couldn't help thinking he was handsome, even if he made me a touch uncomfortable. I cut off the thought immediately. If fucking where you eat is bad, fucking where you work is much worse.

"They are nice," he agreed, "but I don't have much in common with them."

"Oh, no?"

He shook his head, "Definitely not. I'm an adventurous person. I like to keep busy," he gave me a moment to respond, but I had nothing to add to that. "We're the only ones here in our twenties, and I'm assuming you're not a grandma."

"No, I'm not even an aunt or a cousin," I commented dryly.

"Are you an only child?" He took a sip of his coffee, but his eyes remained on me.

"Yeah, I am." A little twinge of nervousness tightened my stomach. It was my fault for bringing it up, talking about my family was about as pleasant as a root canal.

"Me too, that's another thing we have in common." *What were the other things? Being in our twenties and not having grandkids?* "You know, another reason we should stick together around here."

"You think?" I tried to keep my answer aloof, not sure where he was going with this.

"Oh yeah, it's always good to have someone in your corner, right?" I took an unnecessarily long sip of my coffee to decide on an answer.

"Of course," I agreed, though I wouldn't know. I had little experience with supportive relationships, but he seemed nice enough, if not a little pushy, "Let's stick together then," I smiled briefly, hoping he wouldn't read too much into it.

"Solidarity, sister." He toasted me with his mug.

"Solidarity," I agreed.

The rest of my first week went by in a blur of meeting people and getting used to the job. The position consisted of a lot of filing and processing applications. It wasn't a love connection, but it paid enough for me to just scrape by, and that had to be sufficient for the time being.

I cleaned my apartment until it was spotless that Saturday afternoon, and I did my best to keep it in order the following week. Since I was low on money, I cooked all my meals, even taking them to work

with me for lunch. It was better for the budg
missed Sadar and the Indian food I would neve.
skilled enough to cook.

Two weeks after I was hired, I sat at a table in the break room eating a chicken salad sandwich with a book open on the table when Tyler plopped down next to me like we were the best of friends. "That looks good. What is it?"

"Chicken salad on wheat bread," I told him after I forcefully swallowed a bite I had not finished chewing. All I wanted to do was keep reading my book.

"Maybe you can make lunch for both of us one of these days?" He flashed me a flirtatious grin.

"I don't know. I'm not sure what you like." I hedged, hoping he would let it go.

"I'm sure I would like anything you made." I smiled a little. It was a cheesy line, but still sort of sweet. "You know, the women around here are all obsessed with their grandchildren."

"I couldn't tell," I deadpanned him and rolled my eyes.

A brief flicker of something flashed in his gaze, but he quickly snuffed it out. "It's actually a game of theirs, even if they'd never admit it. They like to one-up each other on who's the best grandma, which one has the cutest grandkid."

"Really? Who's winning?" the disinterest was obvious in my tone, but he pushed on.

"They all think they are, that's the funny part."

"Hilarious," he didn't notice my sarcasm, which was for the best.

Tyler seemed like a nice enough guy, and handsome too, but he certainly would never be the type who got stuck in my head. I met that person in a library basement and every spare thought I had voted to him. His voice, his face, the ... grace in his body all stuck in my head ... y tune.

... fell into a neat routine. I went to work, p... ..y part, and went home again. When I lay in my bed alone and lonelier than I ever remembered being, I touched myself to the thought of the library stranger. Embarrassment still streaked through me when I remembered the circumstances of our introduction.

The reason those feelings turned me on couldn't be healthy, and I couldn't afford the psychiatric expertise that might explain them to me. He emotionally trussed me up beneath him, and he probably hadn't thought of me once.

"You're pathetic," I told the flushed girl staring at me in the mirror as I cleaned my vibrator and washed my hands. The purple silicone both vibrated my G-spot and sucked my clit and it was by far the best orgasm I ever had. A lot of time passed since I last had sex and my little electric friend had been ridden hard in the meantime.

My college boyfriend, Sam, was the last guy I screwed. I rolled my eyes as I dried off my toy, remembering the poking and prodding he thought of as sex. He was incredibly smart, sweet too—when he wanted to be—but so vanilla he cried after he spanked me the first time. The little pat he gave my ass didn't even hurt. I never asked him to do it again, as much as I wanted rougher stuff. He wasn't comfortable, and it's not right to ask your partner to do things they're not okay with.

Besides that, he couldn't tell a clit from a belly button. The orgasms I had with him were weak, and the majority came from me rubbing my clit while he heaved himself inside of me. I laughed at the

younger version of myself; the way she lov
and how heartbroken she was when he left.

I put the sex toy back in the drawer on my nightstand. The horniness plaguing me was barely dented. I needed some real release, a hot guy who would fuck me hard, and leave. A relationship wasn't what I wanted, or to be in love, but a man who could fuck me hard enough to make me go cross-eyed would do the trick.

I ran over my options, Sadar, Tyler, a handsome man whose name I never learned and likely would never see again. None of them were viable candidates. I could go to a bar. There was one around the corner from my apartment. It was youthful and hipstery, with fancy gin drinks that tasted like potpourri. I could find some guy there to take home for the night, but what would I say, "hey, baby, wanna come back to my place for some pussy?"

I shook the thought out of my head, embarrassed by the mere idea. I ran my hands over my sweat-slicked body. I needed to get an air conditioner before it got so hot I didn't even want to touch myself. A thought occurred to me. There was another option I could try, one that was perfect for a socially awkward, sex-crazed lunatic like myself: the internet.

I went to my computer and opened up a website that had listings for anything and everything. I clicked the section labeled 'casual meetups', and ran over the existing posts. A flutter of nerves filled me at the thought of appearing beside professionals like "Mr. Daddy Fat Cock Seeks a Bottom" and "Mistress Juliette wants to Bleed You Dry".

My hands hovered over the empty template, trying out a few titles before I settled on, "Seeking

...and, Serious Inquiries Only". I rolled .my lack of originality, who would even vith more interesting options available.

.tractive brunette, 26, lots of tits and ass, with a small .aist. What I want is simple: I'm shy, single, and I need to get laid. I would go to a bar and pick someone up, but that's not my style. Seeking a man 25-40, fit, good-looking, and able to do the job right.

If I have to do this twice, I will die of embarrassment. You must chat online with me first and exchange pictures, just to prove to me you are who you say. I'm not trying to date you or see inside your soul. I want to make sure you're not a creep before I invite you over for some steamy, casual sex.

-Tired of Waiting

I waited for a while, but sadly there was no reply. Finally, I crawled into bed, deciding this was just another failed experiment.

I woke up late the next morning and didn't even glance at my email before I rushed through the apartment, dressing in a flurry, and racing out the door to catch the bus. I clocked in at ten after nine and tried to slip in with no one noticing.

Tyler caught me the moment I walked in. A taunting smile spread across his face. "Hey, pal, running late this morning?"

I looked around the office nervously. I despised being late. "Yeah, I overslept."

"Come and see me in my office." I followed him, noticing the way his clothes always seemed to fit him so well. Was I really about to get in trouble? He wasn't my boss, but his position was above mine. "Sit down, Claire." He pointed to the chair opposite his desk. Various pictures of him in places around the world decorated his walls. I noticed there was no one else in the pictures, which struck me as odd.

I ignored the thought and did as he asked while I picked at my nail beds, "I'm sorry, Tyler,"

"Don't be sorry," he interrupted me, smiling with genuine amusement as he took in my nervous posture. "I'm just updating your clock-in to nine on the dot and giving you an excuse for where you were when Sandra asks."

I breathed a sigh of relief, and warmth replaced the cold in my chest. "Thank you so much, Tyler. That is so nice of you."

"It is, but you can owe me one." He winked as he opened the door for me. I walked out to start my day on a much higher note than I expected. I was no longer late and had nothing to explain to anyone. My project for the morning was more alphabetizing and by eleven I was tired enough that I needed a cup of coffee.

I walked to the break room as one of the two Barbaras rolled out from her desk. She shoved a picture of a little blond girl with pigtails into my face, competitive pride beaming from her, "That is my Sophia, my eldest's daughter, isn't she beautiful?"

"She's lovely," I cooed, and satisfied with my answer, she moved out of my way so I could reach the caffeine I so desperately needed.

As I poured the last of the pot into my mug, Tyler walked up behind me, speaking far too close to my ear, "Sophia isn't cute, but you convinced her." He gave me a conspiratorial smile.

I was grateful for the way he helped me that morning, but I noticed a pattern: any time I went anywhere within the office, he turned up too. I tried vince myself it was just a coincidence as I sat and checked my email for the first time that day, I gasped and spluttered on a rogue sip of coffee I inhaled when I saw I had well over a hundred emails in reply to my spontaneous post.

Tyler patted my back gently, and I leaned away from the contact. "I'm okay, thanks."

"Just making sure," he winked as he left.

The rest of the day passed easily. Tyler had back-to-back meetings, so I didn't see him again. I clocked out a little after five, and I spent the bus ride home clicking through the emails, never really minding that people stared at me as I laughed out loud. There were so many responses it made me dizzy and many of them were nothing but images of penises. I know I asked for sex, but it shocked me how many people thought their irregular appendages were a valid resume. None of them caught my interest, and once again I went to bed alone.

Chapter Three

I finished getting ready for work early the next morning. The excitement of looking over the many responses to my ad had me giddy and restless, ready to conquer the day. I sipped my coffee absentmindedly as I scanned through some emails that came in overnight.

I choked on my drink as I read the subject line "Whores Burn in Hell" I hurried over the contents of the email, laughing aloud in shock at his vehemence. I didn't know if whores burned in hell or not, but whoever this random internet crusader was, he didn't seem privy to the inner workings of the universe. Before I let the words upset me, I moved onto another. "A Bit Older than you asked for." I clicked it open with a shrug. I could do a fit fifty.

I choked on my coffee yet again as I took in a smiling picture of a man in his eighties with a message attached.

Don't be fooled, an old bull can be better than a young buck. I would love to show you a wonderful time and take you places you've never been. How about Ibiza?

-Stanley

Well, Stanley, I might accept your offer. I thought to myself as I picked through another few that were nothing but more cock shots. The variety mystified me. I was no virgin, but I'd never seen so many penises in rapid succession outside of porn. Porn stars obviously all fit some criteria because theirs were much more similar to each other than these. Big, small, crooked. There were enough of them that I started seeing penises whenever I closed my eyes. I briefly considered a career as a dick critic.

Aside from the many genitals, there were a lot more genuine responses than I expected; people who commented on aspects of the ad and offered things about themselves in return. A little twinge of guilt passed through me every time I read one of them, because despite their authenticity, they sparked nothing in me, much less desire.

I shared communion with these lonely, horny souls, but I knew I couldn't be the person who assuaged those feelings. I closed a particularly sad email from a widower. He had young kids, and he had not been with anyone since his wife passed. He hoped we could help each other out as he wasn't ready for a more meaningful relationship. Tears filled my eyes but didn't fall as I rode the bus. I wished I could, but that level of pain was more than I could take on.

I arrived at work stuck in my head. I paid little attention to where I went and bumped into Tyler a foot away from my desk. My hands instinctively shot out in front of me, landing on his chest. For a moment, his well-muscled pecs distracted me.

I looked up, stunned, as he wrapped his arms around my back to steady me. I may have accidentally started this, but it felt far too intimate. "Good morning, Claire, funny running into you here," he laughed. *Was he waiting here for me?* I shook my head. *Of course not.* I pushed off of his chest lightly, trying to escape without being insulting.

"Good morning, Tyler," I stepped around him and sat in my chair. "I should start working."

"Absolutely," he agreed with a secretive smile. Leaning forward, he plucked a mug off my desk. It was the same one he offered me on my first day, and I used it a few times since then. "Did you take this out of my office?" There was a teasing note in his voice, but I didn't get the joke.

"No, it was in the break room." I answered at a much lower volume, conscious of the people around turning to look at me.

"*Of course.*" He muttered with a touch of sarcasm as he walked off. Several of my coworkers watched with their own smiles. I dug my nose into my work and did my best to ignore them.

When it came time for lunch, a few of the older women were getting ready to have a meeting of their fiber arts group. A few of them knit and a few crocheted and twice a month they would take a long break and do it together. "Would it be okay if I joined you?" I forced myself to speak up.

Barbara S. eyed me doubtfully. "Do you knit or crochet, dear?"

"No, but I've always wanted to learn." I gave her a smile and a little shrug.

"I have an extra hook and some yarn," a woman whose name I didn't remember offered.

"I would appreciate it." They all nodded to one another, waved me on, and took me to a conference room in the back. We sat around the table as they chatted about office gossip, their grandkids, and showed me how to hold the yarn and use the little hook. It wasn't going well as far as me learning the craft, but it was pleasant to sit with them and be sociable. They warmed up to me a bit and that could only make my time spent with them more enjoyable.

"So, Claire..." Barbara S, the de facto leader, began, "I see you and Tyler have been talking a lot."

"Oh, yeah, I guess. Here at work anyway." I tried to focus on catching the yarn with the little hook and getting it through the hole.

"You seem like you want it to be more." I glanced up at her then, trying to read her expression. She didn't appear to have malicious intentions.

"Well, he's nice but I haven't thought about it." I hoped that would be enough to move the conversation to another topic.

"Really? You looked awfully smitten when *you* bumped into him this morning." I didn't want to embarrass him or cause problems, so I wasn't sure how to respond.

Finally, the other Barbara put me out of my misery. "Leave her alone, Barb. How is Sophia doing in dance class?" That was all she needed to forget all about me and I shot the other woman a grateful smile. I hadn't fully discounted the idea of dating Tyler, but I certainty wasn't pursuing him or seeking his attention. If anything, he seemed interested in me.

Later that night, I sat in front of my computer reading and smiling, *smiling*. I couldn't remember the last time I did it on my own, with no one watching, without trying to act normal. I didn't agree with the practice of sending pictures of your genitals to people who didn't ask for them, but I thoroughly enjoyed the task.

I resigned myself to the fact that this was only an experiment. None of these guys did anything for me other than give me a great way to spend my time. I believed that until I read the next subject line, "If you were brave..." I clicked it open with an odd sense of anticipation thrumming through me.

And this was a bar. What drink should I buy you?

-Able to do any job right

My heart sped in my chest, urging my fingers to the keys. I typed the words before I thoroughly considered what I was doing and pressed send.

Who said I'm not brave? Tequila shot, please.

I couldn't justify my excitement. He might not respond. He might be fourteen or a serial killer. *Don't get too excited.* I reminded myself again and again, but I never took my own advice. I sorted through another ten emails, not seeing them as I waited for him. A little ping told me I had a new one.

Then why are you trying to fuck strangers off the internet if you are brave, and as attractive as you say?

His words stared back at me with accusation. I pressed a few keys, but nothing worthy appeared in my defense. How could I respond? I had scant faith in my attractiveness, but that rarely mattered much when a dude was ready to go.

What kind of creep was he? A normal guy would have asked for a nude, not a verbal defense of my appearance. What was wrong with me, and why did I do this? I stared at the screen with no answers for either of us.

As the week ended, the emails slowed to a trickle. The post became buried so deeply in the feed that very few people still found it, and with it my fun faded away. My life felt empty as far back as I could recall, but that bit of joy made it feel hollower once it passed. I slipped into my old misery, and I needed to change things before the takeout containers started piling again.

I decided to make a scrapbook of the responses I received. It would be good to have a memento to put my hands on and remember the time I'd been spontaneous and the joy it brought me, no matter how fleeting. It seemed wasteful to leave them forgotten, or worse, delete them. My soulmate was certainly not one of the erections marching through my inbox, but each was special and hilarious in their own way.

The following Saturday, I woke up early; the promise of a project fueling me with preternatural energy. I pulled out the four different printers I owned, disgusted that three were broken, and the last had no ink. I headed to the library to print the pages. It was within easy walking distance, whereas getting a new cartridge would require a bus ride and weekend crowds. All I needed to do was forget about my most recent unfortunate visit.

My neighbors regarded me dubiously as I waved at them. Today would be a good day, and their surly attitudes wouldn't dampen my optimism. It was beautiful outside, but too hot for early summer. The sun beat down on me and my skin sizzled lightly. By the time I trudged the three blocks, I was sweating. The library air conditioning hit me like a glacial breeze, and I sighed in outright relief. I peeked around, half hoping to see my friend and half disappointed when I didn't find him there.

My shoes clicked on the tile as I walked beneath the big round skylight and over to the line of ancient computers. I glanced around nervously as I opened my email and pulled up the document I put everything in. The opening page remained blank, so the pictures wouldn't accost any innocent eyes. Thankfully, the printer here was more modern than the computers, and I could insert my debit card directly, avoiding the embarrassment of another person handling my project.

I held the freshly printed pages to myself, savoring their delicious warmth. By the time I finished, I spent twenty dollars. I probably should have braved the crowds and just bought the ink cartridge. I tucked my papers into a manila folder and debated how I would put my book together. A simple hole punch and binder would suffice, but there were so many more elaborate options.

My head was somewhere else, and God only knows where my eyes were pointed, because I had no warning when I suddenly collided with a wall of a person. The heat of his chest brushed through me the instant we touched, just before I bounced off him and fell to the ground, hitting my butt hard on the tile. "I'm so, so-" I said as I glanced up at the man standing over me.

Tall, short blonde hair that had grown some since I last saw him, handsome like no one I'd ever seen, with green eyes resembling springtime and home. He regarded me with amusement as he looked over me and the contents of my folder scattered over the floor. The last of the penises finished cascading over me, a ceremony sealing my fate.

As if our introduction wasn't embarrassing and haunting enough, now I sat beneath him in a flurry of dicks. I imagined being beneath him plenty of times since then, and there was always a dick involved, but this wasn't precisely the picture I had in mind. My brain finished processing the situation we were in and begged for my body to do something: stand up, stop staring, close my mouth. Nothing happened.

He reached out a hand, and I took it after waiting just long enough to make it awkward. He pulled me up to my feet as I focused on fighting off the shiver from the electric current his touch sparked in me. His hands rested on my shoulders, making sure I was steady, before he bent down to gather up the papers. People walked past us and I stared down at the floor, unable to face another set of eyes on me.

I regained control of my body and squatted down beside him, picking up the rest. Tears gathered in my eyes, a response to the embarrassment, but mercifully, they didn't fall. The shock of the whole thing likely kept them inside of me. I couldn't permit myself a glance at him, and risk fueling my fantasies with more of his disapproving stares.

He handed me the pile he collected, pushing the papers directly into my line of vision.

"Thank you," I choked out in a small, defeated whisper. I hoped desperately he would leave me here and not prolong my misery, but where was the fun in that?

"Interesting project," his voice melted over me like caramel, rich and thick. Why did the condescension in his voice speak straight to my pussy? "You thought it was odd I was looking for an old book about birds, but everyone needs a hobby, right?" He chuckled a little, pleased with the vindication implicit in this moment. I stared at the floor carefully, searching for any stragglers.

He picked up one I missed and looked at it longer than was polite or necessary. His eyes traced the lines of an email, clearly reading its contents. I wanted to tell him how rude he was being, but I couldn't force the words out.

He flipped it around, pointing to the text. Amused shock lit his features so beautifully it made me wet. "I guess you are as attractive as you said. Would you like to go for that shot and explain to me exactly where my email is going to end up?" His eyebrow lifted in a flirtatious challenge.

What the actual fuck?! I screamed internally. I had to have some seriously messed up luck for the guy I'd been crushing on and the only email I answered to be one and the same. I wanted to run away in sheer disbelief of this cosmic joke, but I stayed, finding myself desperate to meet or exceed any challenge he set for me. He laughed at the shocked expression on my face.

"Uh, no, thank you." The small, hurt part of me blurted out in response to his laughter. The intrigued majority was overridden and would not be accepting his invitation. There wasn't a single person I'd ever been more embarrassed in front of in my life, and that included getting my first period in school while wearing white pants when I was eleven. I memorized the look on his face for a moment, then ran past him, down the steps of the library, and all the way home for the second time.

I wheezed as I flew down the sidewalk, the hot thick air hard to take in. *Running sucks*, I reminded myself as I jiggled my key in the lock. The door opened, and the air got thicker. *Shit, I need an air conditioner.* I threw the folder on the coffee table, then stripped naked and flopped on my scratchy couch. I didn't deserve the soft comfort of my bed. A few angry tears fell, and eventually I slept.

In my dreams he stood above me like he did in the library, but instead of leaving my eyes cast down in shame, I slipped my curious fingers into the waistband of his jeans and pulled his cock free. I ran my tongue over it, tasting the smooth deliciousness of his skin. Those eyes watched me with the same condescending amusement before they tipped to the ceiling. His face buckled with pleasure. He came down my throat, growling, and twining his fists tightly in my hair. "Your turn."

I woke up panting and unsatisfied. Pulling a couch cushion over my head, I screamed my frustration. I went to the bathroom and flipped the shower on to cold, standing under the stream until I shivered. While it helped with the heat in my apartment, it didn't touch the burning beneath my skin.

As I walked back into my bedroom, I heard the email notification coming from my computer. A frisson of excitement raced through me. What if it was him? I ignored the lure as long as I could, drying off and getting ready for bed. *Who are you kidding? You don't have self-control.* I ran to the computer.

I would like to say I took no pleasure in our meeting today, but I try to consider myself an honest man. When I responded to your ad, I admit I was having some fun. From our rather odd encounter, it seems you were too. I'm intensely curious. I have to know, where will my emails and the dicks of half the city end up?

Oddly enough, the tits and ass are far from your most marketable quality. You provide a goldmine of absurd entertainment. Oh, and your face is pretty great too.

-Able to get the job done right

Pathetic little butterflies filled my stomach as I read his email. I typed out a few responses, but none of them fit. I didn't know what I wanted anymore, and the excitement I felt only a moment before morphed into something dark and hollow. I didn't have the words to make whatever this was possible. I lusted after him, that much was true, but every time I got near him, I was such a wreck it wasn't worth the trouble. There must be something seriously wrong with me if being this embarrassed and twisted up left me aching for him.

This had to be a joke. That made more sense to me than him being interested in me. Maybe he was hanging around with his friends having a laugh. Something deep inside told me this could only lead to more embarrassment and pain if I let it go on long enough. Aversion was the safest option. I deleted the draft, flipped on the TV, and laid on my couch until Monday morning.

Chapter Four

Monday morning came, and I hoped the fresh start to the week would bring me a clear head and simple decisions to make. Considering the X-rated dream I had the night before, the idea was rather silly. The library stranger smacked my ass until my skin reddened, and then fucked me senseless. I still felt his phantom hands on me. The heat beneath my flesh burned so intensely I took another cold shower. I was starting to think this only worked for guys and overheated people with no air conditioning, not horny women.

I spent the morning mulling over how I might respond to the email he sent me, and what that meant about my sense of self-preservation. If I thought with my head, I would let the crush go and never set foot in the library again. Not only did I make a complete ass out of myself whenever he was around, but there was something dangerous about him. He could destroy me if I gave him a chance. Unfortunately, my long-neglected pussy enthusiastically involved herself in the decision-making process.

The bus ride to work went faster than normal, with all my confused, lusty thoughts keeping me busy. The rest of the day followed suit, and I couldn't tell you if I spoke to another person. I must have, since a pile of papers I hardly touched sat in front of me. I glanced up and jumped as I found Tyler leaning against my desk with a smile on his face. *How long has he been there?*

"You're distracted today," he commented with a little smirk. He sipped a mug of coffee and handed one to me.

I smiled appreciatively and took a deep sip. Getting lost in your thoughts is more tiring than you would think. "Yeah, I guess I am. I have a lot of stuff to do." I shrugged and gestured to the papers stacked in front of me.

"You work too hard, Claire. Do you ever relax?" He ran a hand through his brown hair, giving him a tousled look.

The image of me masturbating to my own dirty dreams popped into my head. I coughed to cover the heat rising in my cheeks. "Well, yeah, sometimes, of course." I stuttered.

"You have been doing wonderfully here. I think we should celebrate your success and get to know each other better." His brown eyes crinkled around the edges and his practiced smile revealed straight white teeth. I couldn't help but find him quite handsome, even if he made me nervous.

"What did you have in mind?" I gazed up at him through my lashes, deciding it wouldn't hurt to flirt a little. I could blow off some steam with him, at least enough to stop the need for those too-many-to-count cold showers.

"How about I take you to dinner tonight?" Surprise flitted through me. I assumed he would invite me for a coffee, or lunch tomorrow, but his urgency packed the pressure. It took me a moment to answer, and all the while he smiled at me like the decision to accept was a given.

It was against company policy—and my personal rules—to date a coworker, but he was cute, and my pussy kept making decisions above her pay grade. *It's only dinner. What could it hurt?* My rampant libido whispered in my ear.

"Okay, sounds fun." He asked me for my address and phone number and I wrote them out for him on a sticky note.

"Great, I'll pick you up at six-thirty." I opened my mouth to tell him that wasn't enough time with my bus ride, but he was already strolling out the door. I looked at the clock. Crap, it was past five. I raced to the bus stop, hoping this was not a huge mistake.

As I stepped off the bus down the block from my apartment, my phone buzzed with an incoming text. It was Tyler telling me he would take me to a popular fusion restaurant downtown. I ran inside as quickly as possible, rifling through my closet with superhuman speed to find something that looked nice but not too sexy. I shook my head at myself. My only options were lounging, professional, or smoking hot.

I took out a red dress that fit me snuggly and accented my curves, but at least it showed a limited amount of skin. I paired it with black heels and a matching clutch. A knock on the door interrupted my open-mouthed mascara application. "One minute," I called as I finished applying the product and pulled my hair up.

I grabbed my purse and headed to the door, peeping through the hole to make sure it was Tyler. He looked quite handsome in his fitted light blue suit. He *could* be the distraction I needed. I used some genuine effort to open the door, and when it relented, I grinned at him. He didn't have the panty-meltingly good looks the library stranger did, but it would probably be healthier if I stopped using him as a benchmark for attractive men.

"Well, hi," he purred, as his eyes ran hungrily over my body. "You kept me waiting. Can I come in?"

The expectation in his voice had me questioning myself. Did we agree to a drink here first, or something else I didn't remember? "Uh, sure," I stood aside, and he waltzed in. I expected we were going straight to the restaurant. In the little time he gave me, I just managed to get dressed, never mind ready the place for company. It was not a true mess anymore, but my things cluttered the apartment.

"Can I sit?" He didn't wait for me to answer, sitting on my couch and running his hand over the spot next to him like I should take a seat too. He looked at his palm, cringing slightly at the fabric. His eyes flitted around the room, taking it in with apparent distaste. "Nice place."

"Thanks." I stood beside the door, holding it open, and doing my best to muster up a backbone. "I thought we'd head to the restaurant. It's almost seven."

He leaned back, draping his arm over the couch and spreading his legs in a gesture I think he meant to be inviting. "Let's stay a minute. I've known you for weeks now, and I hardly know anything about you." The look he gave me told me all he wanted to learn was what I looked like naked.

"No, thank you. We can always talk at the restaurant, and I promise to tell you all about myself over dinner." I tried to give him a convincing smile as a pit opened in my stomach.

He must have had some modicum of humility, because he got off the couch and held his hands up in surrender, "Fine, let's go," and he stomped toward the exit. To my surprise, he held the door and gestured for me to go first with an annoyed wave.

As we walked through the hall, he raced ahead of me, jogging down the stairs. He stood by the entrance tapping his foot in irritation as I clung to the railing and maneuvered the stairs in my heels. When I made it to the bottom, he let me go ahead of him again, and I felt his eyes on my ass as he walked behind me, brooding like a sullen teen who had been thwarted in his efforts to steal a playboy.

He led me over to a sleek silver Maserati, and I choked on air. There was no way he afforded that car as an admissions counselor. He opened the door for me and stared down my dress as I slipped in.

"This car is my baby," he began as soon as he sat beside me. I clipped my buckle into place and he took off, darting through the darkening streets, ignoring traffic laws and making me as nervous as possible. "Ever been in a vehicle like this before?" Doubt dripped from his tone.

"No, I haven't." *You saw my apartment.* I stared out the window, rolling my eyes without him noticing. I worked at keeping my polite smile in place as he droned on about horsepower.

We arrived at the restaurant, which was spacious with large glass windows showing the interior decorated in red and gold. Crap, I matched the décor. A young man stood behind the valet stand and greeted us warmly. Tyler flipped his keys at him. "This car is worth more than you make in three years, don't fuck it up." Then smirked at me like he did something impressive.

"I'm so sorry," I mumbled. The valet shrugged and rolled his eyes like I held equal responsibility for standing next to the pig. Inside the restaurant, he was rude to the host about the table he brought us to, which was perfectly fine, but apparently twenty feet from the bathroom was too close. He flirted with the waitress as soon as she asked for our drink order. Her dress hugged her curves tightly and ended mid-thigh, likely for the tips, but I doubted she enjoyed the open-mouthed attention Tyler gave her.

She bent over our table to refill his water and he leaned in, making her visibly shrink away. *Did he smell her?* I discarded the thought. That was too creepy to be true. When she came back to take our orders, I chose a pasta dish. It was the cheapest thing on the menu, and I didn't want him thinking I owed him.

The server brought us posh little salads and a basket of fresh bread. As she placed it on the table, he reached out for a slice, running his hand across the back of hers. She snapped it away as he licked his lips at her. When he turned back to me, he did the same. I surreptitiously pulled up my dress, hating his eyes on me. Was he always like this and I didn't notice, or did he behave better at the office?

He shoved giant forkfuls of his salad into his mouth. He packed it in further with huge bites of bread and then spoke through it. I picked at my plate, though my appetite disappeared entirely.

"I could've gone to med school or something." A little of his spit hit my cheek, and I lifted my napkin to wipe the moisture away without him noticing. "I mean, I'm more than smart enough,"—he picked his teeth— "my IQ is genius level. I won't tell you my score because people find it threatening. Do you know your IQ?"

"No, I don't." I hadn't spoken a word in about ten minutes. His lengthy monologues needed no help. I wanted to smack the superior smile off his face.

He sucked air through his teeth, working out something stuck there. "Yeah, I wouldn't think you would. I could have been an engineer or anything I wanted with my brains. Being an admissions counselor is kind of beneath me, but I'm giving back to the community. I'm a role model molding young minds. Who else gets to do that?" I thought of a few career paths that were directly responsible for molding young minds, but sure, his martyrdom rivaled John the Baptist.

"Only a few people." I buttered a piece of bread I didn't plan on eating.

"I knew you'd understand," he winked. He kept speaking, and I imagined the poor woman whose life he would ruin when he married her. She would need a strong stomach to deal with all that self-adoration, and God help their children. They would either hate him or wind up exactly like him, perhaps a bit of both.

The server took our salads away and replaced them with our entrees. The pasta tasted delicious, and I mourned my ruined appetite. "My favorite part of being on safari is the elephants. They're incredible creatures." I perked up at that. They were my favorite animal, and though this date was a complete wash, I would love to hear about them from someone who had seen them in person. "Hunting them is better than sex, primal, you know?"

"I can't imagine." He didn't seem to notice the revulsion in my voice, and I drifted back to a psych one-oh-one class I took freshman year of college. Nature vs. nurture, was Tyler born this way, or was he spoiled rotten? It must have been amazing to grow up with money. I certainly didn't, but it never bothered me that others were more well off than myself. There were plenty of people in much worse situations too. That's how life is.

I wouldn't want anyone to judge me for my lower-middle class upbringing, but I couldn't help feeling like all that privilege and opportunity were wasted on him. His parents' money gave him a plethora of experiences to use as backdrops for his narcissistic rants. Most likely, they bought him the Maserati he loved so much. I hoped that was the problem, anyway. The idea that someone came into the world screaming and bloody with narcissistic ass as their factory settings was too depressing to accept.

"Would you care for dessert?" I shook my head at the offer and the flirtatious suggestion in his tone. He flagged the server down and winked at her as he ordered the crème brûlée.

Another personal anecdote later, she brought him his desert. He paused his monologue only long enough to crack the brûlée shell. "Do you want a taste?" he purred at me with his custard-filled mouth. I wondered again if he was excellent at hiding his awfulness, or if I was exceptionally unobservant? *Why do our coworkers like you?*

"No, thanks." I trained my eyes on the wall somewhere beyond his head. I would stare at the beige paint all day if it meant I didn't need to see his open mouth. He tucked the spoon between his lips and licked suggestively at it. My stomach rolled as I thought of his lips anywhere near mine. This retired frat boy was the antithesis of what I wanted, not only in a partner but anyone.

"Would you like to come back to my place for drinks?" Unease settled in my chest at the certainty in his tone. He tapped on the white tablecloth waiting for my response. I gaped like a fish searching for divine intervention. This whole dinner was one red flag after another. There were two things I was absolutely sure of. Tyler considered me a forgone conclusion and he made me nervous in a way that went far deeper than a creep I didn't want to screw.

Tyler didn't strike me as the type that took well to being turned down. I imagined him pressing me against the door to my apartment, refusing to leave without a kiss. I shuddered at the thought. Him being my coworker complicated matters further.

I had no means to slip seamlessly away without ever seeing him again. The nausea in my gut inspired me, and I grabbed onto it like a lifeline. My hands wrapped protectively around my stomach and I moaned gutturally.

"I think I'm going to be sick," and before he responded, I ran to the bathroom.

I stared in the mirror over the sink. *God, Claire, you know better than this. You should have never gone on this date.*

"Awful date, huh?" A pretty blonde woman asked as she came to the sink to wash her hands.

"You have no idea," I answered as I stepped aside for her.

"Actually, I do. I come here a lot and that guy is in here with a different girl every other night. He's a real sleazeball." She flipped her hands toward the sink, shaking off the water.

I rolled my eyes. "I figured that out myself, if only it was before I said yes to this date."

She nodded her head at me as she pulled down a few paper towels. "I'm at the table in the back corner. If you want, I'll pretend to be your friend to get you out of it."

"I appreciate it, seriously, but I work with the guy. I'm not getting off that easily." She gave me an apologetic look as she left the bathroom.

Dread settled into my stomach like stone as I went back to my seat. The image of him forcing himself on me outside of my apartment developed into a full-blown horror scene. His lips on mine, his body shoved against me, hands sliding up my thighs, the images wracked my mind with startling clarity. Clearer was the rage that would no doubt follow when I turned him down.

"Are you alright? Your face is bright red." The disgust in his tone gave me my reprieve.

I released the breath I held. "No, I think I'm coming down with a stomach bug." My voice distorted around the word bug, banking on him not being a nurturer. He leaned back, trying to escape the line of trajectory. I nearly laughed but kept it in so he wouldn't call my bluff. I held my napkin over my mouth and moaned, pleased to have a purpose for my dramatic flair.

"I should take you home." He waved our server over and handed her a credit card. I didn't miss the fact he slipped his number inside the bill with it.

He ushered me out of the restaurant, mumbling something about his car's interior. We waited for the valet to bring his "baby" around. My eyes trained on the pavement, trying to avoid a conversation. From the way Tyler watched me climb in, I was sure he would rather I take the bus. For the first time in my life, I wished I had a stomach bug. I mulled over the many things I would trade for the ability to puke all over his car.

He drove me home oscillating between super slow and super fast, unable to decide if it was better to get me out sooner or go easy on the bumps. Neither of us said a word. I held my hand over my mouth like it was the only barrier between vomit and the leather. The traffic thickened, and the trip took much longer than I hoped it would. Eventually, we pulled up in front of my building, and I hopped out. "I'm so sorry, Tyler. Thanks for dinner." I told him with some sincerity. I was sorry it had been so awful.

"You can make it up to me." There was a dark promise in his voice I didn't want to explore further.

My hand smacked over my mouth as I bent forward, then I turned and fled, calling another "Sorry!" over my shoulder. I ran into my apartment as fast as possible, slamming the door and flipping on the lights. I leaned against the wood and slid down to my butt. *What the hell am I going to do about that?*

Chapter Five

The sun rose outside my window, casting a golden glow on my sleeping face, and instead of greeting the day with enthusiasm I groaned and tossed my pillow over my head. "Damn sun," I shouted at the window. *Why the fuck haven't I bought curtains?*

I scrubbed my hands against my eyes hoping the events of the night before were simply an awful dream. The more I acclimated to the day the harder it was to wallow in denial. My bed was the only safe place in the entire world, and it took every bit of my strength to leave its warmth and comfort.

I forced my legs to stand, showered quickly, and looked myself over in the mirror. Darkened bags hung under my eyes like I hadn't slept in days, but really, I just responded poorly to stress. I fought the urge to put makeup on, this look would suit my purposes perfectly. People always asked me if I was sick when I didn't wear makeup, and for once the insulting assumption would work in my favor.

I hopped on the bus; little nerves flipped around in my stomach. I probably should have called in sick to avoid dealing with people entirely, but I figured if they saw me, and believed I was sick, I could spin a couple of days out of this without having to bring in a doctor's note. I walked through the door to the office and, right on cue, Sandra came up to me with professional concern on her face. "You don't look well, Claire."

"I'm not feeling too great." I pouted at her, trying to ham it up, while internally rolling my eyes at her assumption. "My stomach is bothering me. I'm going to put in a few hours and go home early if that's alright with you."

"Yeah, that's fine. Try to finish the stack I left on your desk and you can leave." She smiled at me sympathetically, but she didn't feel bad enough to tell me to go home and not worry about it.

"Thanks," I went to my little station at the back and dug right into the pile. This wouldn't take me too long if I focused. As I alphabetized and checked the corresponding paperwork for the applications, I sensed a presence behind me. I turned, finding Tyler in a button-down shirt and dark dress pants.

His handsome face and flattering clothing did nothing to temper the disgust twisting my stomach into painful knots. He ran a hand through his brown hair, his eyes drifting over my body with obvious lust. "Since you're feeling better, come over to my place tonight and we can pick up where we left off." *That's some good morning.* I used all the strength I had not to gag at the insinuation that I would go fuck him after work because he bought me dinner the night before.

"Thanks for the offer, Tyler, but I'm still not better. I'm going to leave here as soon as I finish," I gave him a little shrug as I gestured to the remaining forms.

"Later this week," he pressed, leaning toward me with a hint of anger in his eyes.

"I don't think I'll be free. My family is coming into town and I'm uncertain how long they're staying," I hoped my apologetic expression wouldn't piss him off further or lead him on. He made me nervous, like walking down the street alone at night.

The fact I was blowing him off clicked, and the faint anger sparking behind his eyes went deathly cold. "Sure, Claire, whatever you say..." he stomped off back toward his office. His gaze bored a hole into me as I worked. A chill constantly raced up and down my spine as I fumbled with the papers. Mercifully, I finished and brought the pile over to Sandy. She flipped through them. "Nice work, Claire, I'll see you tomorrow. Call in the morning if you're not feeling better."

"Okay, thanks, Sandy. Have a good one." My palms were slick with sweat from the nerves as I left the office. I dropped my time card as I tried to clock out and struggled to pick it up. The whole time I felt as if someone was watching. The sensation of eyes on me made me move faster and clumsier. My hands shook, and I tried to tell myself how silly that was as I looked around and saw no one.

I took the bus home as usual, although the crowd was a lot different than the end of work commute I was accustomed to, a lot of moms riding with small children. This route went past the library and there were programs there for kids during the day. The people sitting around me ignored me as thoroughly as I ignored them, and I started to relax a bit. The only eyes I felt on me belonged to a toddler, I was safe.

I settled into the hard plastic seat, watching the city pass in a soothing blur. The tension leaving my body made room for an interesting thought; I wasn't sick and now I had a day off. The proximity to Tyler nauseated me so intensely I almost forgot I faked my illness.

I hopped off the bus, pleased with my new freedom. The building door stood open and my neighbors milled around. A couple of old men played backgammon on a table right outside the door. It was a beautiful day, and even with the sunshine, the heat wasn't sweltering.

I let myself into my apartment, satisfied that for once it didn't require a full body workout. A little bit of mess accumulated, and I picked it up before it had a chance to overwhelm me. I hummed a mindless tune as I washed the dishes, pulled out the trash, and walked the bag down the hall to the shoot.

Leaning back against my freshly wiped counter, I drummed my fingers on the tile. I pulled my phone out of my pocket and flipped through my contacts. The list was a lot shorter than one might expect and the quality of those few connections was lower than I would have liked. All my friendships fizzled out or blew apart for varied reasons. Weeks passed since I last spoke to my mother, but the lack of contact was for the best.

I pulled up my email app and my heartbeat pounded in my ears, deafening me. I had one from a gorgeous stranger I should be forgetting about. *Strange Circumstances* greeted me from the subject line.

I'm certain my emails reached you. The modern age is amazing with these reliable communication methods. With that in mind, I'm not offended you ignored them. You have every right to. Foolishly, I am still waiting for your reply.

-Doer of Jobs

He was right, of course. His emails sat in my inbox tempting me at every turn and making me doubt everything about my self-control. The urge to answer him invaded my thoughts and made my fingers twitch, but I didn't really consider doing it, not until now anyway.

My date with Tyler made me feel like I had nothing to lose. Unless he was a murderer or something else equally sinister, talking to him couldn't possibly be worse than the pompous ass I'd given a date to. My relationship with him thus far had been one humiliation after another. What was one more? Why did someone like Tyler deserve a chance, but he didn't?

Dear Doer of Jobs,

I won't be posting any of the pictures or emails in a public forum. You never had anything to worry about since you never sent me the goods. My extracurriculars should be no cause for your concern.

Regarding the email you sent after I gracefully landed on my ass in a compilation of penises (thank you for the compliments, by the way), I honestly cannot tell you if I intend to follow through or not. Can you help convince me?

-Maybe Hiring

I pressed send and went to my little kitchen to make myself something to eat. I rummaged around remembering I hadn't eaten all day and even though I should be ravenous, nothing inspired me. I settled on toast as it would help with the turmoil pitching in my stomach. The situation with Tyler was far from resolved and the cold look in his eyes spoke volumes. I pushed the lever down on the toaster as I questioned my sanity for even thinking of talking to another guy.

The logic that made so much sense only minutes ago sounded absurd. I should be swearing all of them off. The ping of my email notification forcefully shoved all thoughts of food out of my mind. The knife hovered in midair and I nearly forgot to drop it before racing back to the screen. "*A pleasant surprise,*" greeted me from the subject line.

Ms. Hiring,

I'm glad to hear you're not sharing them on behalf of the poor souls who were much less discrete than myself. You told me not to worry, and now I'm only more vexed. What the hell are you doing with them?

I think too highly of myself, and of you, to persuade you on whether you're interested in what I offer. Helping you pick up a menagerie of dicks off the library floor didn't make me think less of you, and your desires are your own to decide. Tit for tat, Miss Tits and Ass, what gives with the pictures?

-Maybe an Applicant

My body responded to the challenge implicit in his tone before my mind did, but they were both equally tantalized by the prospect of being tested. The sensation was new for me, and utterly thrilling. I wasn't the type of person people tried to compete against, I was never anyone's rival. Not because they thought highly of me or my skills, but rather no one considered me worthy of the effort.

I felt myself rising to the occasion. He made me want to be better, to be more, and that thought alone terrified me. How different could my life have been if someone believed in me?

I thought of the little girl always sitting on the sidelines. The teen and woman that came after her were comfortable there too. Perhaps I spent too long letting the opinions of others cloud my judgment of myself. For as long as I could remember, I'd let other people's whims outweigh my own until I was too quiet and unobtrusive to bother anyone. When would it be my time to have the things I wanted?

Quiet and out of the way was the safest option when I was a child, and throughout my schooling, I accepted and cultivated that camouflage. The few friends I had were superficial and faded easily enough. The only person I ever relied on was my ex, Sam, and he abandoned me like my father, and my mother, in her own unique way. What if my fear prevented me from having better, more lasting relationships?

I wasn't a child anymore, and years passed since anyone had the opportunity to truly hurt me. This man surprised me, turned me on, and made me question things about myself. I needed to read more of his quick wit and find out if I made him feel half of what he did for me. I laughed as I reread his words, and the mission I'd been toying with cemented itself. Despite my fears, I would unravel his secrets and go after something *I* wanted.

If you must know, and I'm not sure why you must, I am making a scrapbook, an honest-to-goodness collage of bits and pieces. It's an homage to the one and only time I said 'fuck it' and asked the world for what I wanted with reckless abandon. You're not in it, by the way.

-Hiring

I hoped he would take the bait. My new friend had an ego, and the idea of how he might defend himself when I prodded at it left me desperate. I thought of Tyler and his sickening narcissism. This gorgeous stranger was nothing like that. He was darker and more controlled. I could see it in the way he held his body, the way he looked at me when I sat beneath him. I would bet money he earned his sense of pride. His reply came a few agonizing minutes later.

I find myself equally torn between a yearning to tease you and to offer you everything you want. In fact, I will mock you and encourage you to ask me for whatever you desire with reckless abandon. Why didn't I make it into your book, not exciting enough of a response?

-Applicant

A silly grin spread across my face, my hands were already on the keyboard to reply. This man could offer me more excitement than I'd ever known.

Mocking seems to be a natural state of being for you. I won't take too much offense. Do you mean it? Should I ask you for whatever I want? What should I do if I don't know what that is? Desires are complicated.

You won't be in my book because you are the only one I answered. Also, because I wouldn't need any help to remember you and our unfortunate meetings.

-Hiring

My stomach settled into the right sort of nerves. The nausea that stalked me all day slipped away like a distant memory. *Tyler who?* I tried to imagine my friend's face as he read my words. Did I make him laugh as he did me? Did he look them over with that imperious gaze that said he owned the world or did he crack a smile for me?

Maybe you're easy to tease. I'd prefer you didn't take any offense at all, but I'll settle for not much. I want you to demand whatever you wish, just as it comes to you. That's what I do, and it works quite well for me.

My sage advice is stop thinking so hard, and quit worrying. Your desires probably aren't half as complicated as you'd like them to be. We're all people. It's a remarkable thing when we think or feel something unique. It might surprise you what the world will give to you if you're willing to ask. Even more, if you're willing to take it.

I'm flattered that of your many options you chose me to respond to. I imagine you had no shortage of alternate choices. I don't consider our meetings as unfortunate as you do. You might not agree, but meeting someone as smart, funny, and beautiful as you, is very fortunate albeit strange.

-Applicant

I stared at the screen for a moment, blinking rapidly. My first response was disbelief, but outrage quickly followed. Did he believe the things I wanted could be so simple? *I am different.* I insisted to myself. I spent my *entire* life as an outsider looking in on the rest of the world. I *had* to be different.

I closed my eyes, trying to temper the anger coursing through me. The heat eventually faded and I thought through his words. Was it possible I was just a person like everyone else, and would that be a relief or a disappointment? I read it over again and wondered if he was right.

My identity as a person who never fit in was part of what made me feel unique. Was my loneliness a self-fulfilling prophecy? I had put myself on a pedestal, no not a pedestal, a rickety tower no one could climb, leaving me inaccessible and alone. Maybe, I forced that image on myself because it was the only thing that made me feel special. If I let go of that, and didn't think or worry myself to death, what did I want? The answer was simple; I wanted him.

If you could have me, what would you do with me?

I sent it before I could change my mind. Tingles rushed through me, softening my limbs and making me giddy and weightless. My pussy throbbed with anticipation, overjoyed that I finally voiced my desires to another person. Not just anyone, but him. I couldn't deny that he was the only person I wanted, his teasing, his hard eyes, and his heat.

My teeth worried my nails as the time stretched on with no response. Was I too forward, and misread the situation? A shower sounded like a better option than sitting there waiting to be rejected. The hot water would thaw my tense muscles and melt the ice forming around my heart. I stripped naked in my living room, shoving my clothes into the hamper.

I stared in the mirror wondering what he could have seen that would make a man like him reach out to me. I climbed into my shower stall, rolling my eyes at myself. *Who knows*. I scoffed as the hot water immediately set to work, calming me. I spread the soap over my hands, ignoring my loofah as my palms skated over my soft flesh.

My stiff nipples tickled my fingertips as I soaped my breasts, pretending someone else's fingers danced over me. My fingers slid between my labia and stroked my oversensitive clit in rhythmic circles. My orgasm rapidly approached when the fact he still hadn't answered me dumped a bucket of cold water on my libido.

I twisted the knob, killing the spray, and stomped out of the bathroom wrapped in a towel. *God, I'm embarrassing.* After drying myself and getting into my pajamas, I brushed out my long brown hair and braided it into pigtails. Sleeping on my hair while wet was a guaranteed way to wind up with a pile of unmanageable frizz.

I climbed into bed holding my phone, notifications turned on. As I relaxed, I slipped into a light sleep, wandering on the edge of a dream, not quite able to make out the face of the man standing beside me. When the alert came, I snapped awake, my heart pounding in my chest. The subject line read "*everything*".

What would I do with you if I could have you? I gather from the tone of your email you want me to explain to you how I would rub every inch of you, kiss, lick, and bite you if you like that sort of thing. Every hair on your perfect body would stand on end as I made you come again and again.

I would do all that and a lot more if you let me. I would also tell you, you're enchantingly awkward, endearing, and sexy as hell. You're unique, gorgeous, and if you were mine, you would never doubt it.

-Highly Motivated Applicant

His words electrified my blood, sending sparks that threatened fire without him there to ground me. I needed him in a way I scarcely understood. If he were here with me, I would be naked beneath him as his teeth sank into my skin and his fists gripped me. I returned my fingers to my overheated pussy. With his advice to stay out of my head still fresh, I typed back a reply.

I'm making myself cum right now to the thought of you doing all of that to me. I am absolutely into that type of thing.

His response came instantaneously.

Prove it.

I had lost my mind. I must have to consider what I did next. Adrenaline coursed through me as I spread myself open and snapped a picture of my fingers working their magic. I took a quick peek at it, satisfied with the final product. My vagina never impressed me outside of what it could do for me, but this surprised me. It was sexy. I sent it, relishing doing what I wanted without worrying. I couldn't explain why, but he made me feel safe.

I guess you're serious. I'm so fucking hard for you.

I was getting close, but I couldn't bear to finish before I got to see the erection he promised. I was so sex-deprived it took very little stimulation to push me over the edge. My virginity was long gone, and yet this game we played was more provocative than any sex I'd had. I slowed my fingers, hoping to drag this out.

Prove it.

About a minute later, the perfect response came. The picture of his cock was striking. Where all the other uninvited appendages failed to lure me in, this one would have succeeded. It was long and thick, remarkably well proportioned, featuring no imperfections or irregular dimples. A smattering of veins stood out from the surface.

Wrapped tightly around his shaft was a strong, masculine hand. I imagined him grabbing me with those hands, hovering over me as he pressed his cock to my entrance. The moment of anticipation before he entered me, so sweet, it made it even more enjoyable when he finally filled me.

I'm stroking this for you. Will you put me in your dick-tionary now?

I never laughed so hard that near to an orgasm, and the combined sensations were difficult to make sense of. He barely knew me and had already mastered my emotions, playing with me in the most delicious ways. My eyes caressed the picture, imagining he was close too.

The image of his handsome face crumpled in pleasure flashed behind my eyelids. His powerful jaw strained as he clenched his teeth and tipped his head back, his cum spilling out of him. I was desperate to taste it. With that thought, my orgasm erupted through me, harsh and shaking.

You won't be in my dick-tionary, but I will keep you in my spank bank. By the way, you're pretty fucking great.

I settled in my bed, panting, slowly but surely coming back to myself. We weren't even together, and the whole thing still felt like an out-of-body experience. I wished he was lying beside me, on top of me, inside of me.

Thinking about your perfect pussy is going to keep me up all night. I appreciate the vote of confidence, sexy girl.

My eyes were heavy, so I typed out my reply as quickly as I could manage.

Go to sleep, baby. Dream of me.

I slipped into an easy sleep. When his reply came, I woke only long enough to read it.

Baby, huh? If orgasming makes you this sweet, I'll have to make you come more often.

My dreams enveloped me and I followed the advice I gave in reverse; I dreamed of him.

Chapter Six

I woke in the morning refreshed, barely recognizing the face looking back at me in the mirror. Everything around me appeared softer and sexier somehow. I sat down at my computer, checking my social media and finally my email. A new message from my friend greeted me with the subject line "A rose by any other name..."

You've shown me such intimate parts of you and I still don't know your name.

I smiled, noting that he didn't include his own.

I prefer to maintain what mystery I have left. Isn't it alluring? If you convince me to meet in person, you'll have my name. I'm sure you can think of things to call me in the interim if you're still interested.

I got ready for work, letting the tight braids I put in the night before loose. My hair fell in waves instead of curls and I tied it up and away from my face. I wore something sexier than I normally would. The skirt stopped at the knee but clung tighter than my typical style. My bright red button-down shirt set off my coloring. I ran my hands down my body, appreciating my soft curves. I rushed to the computer when I heard the notification.

I don't have to convince you. That wet pussy last night told me everything I needed to know. I'm fine with giving you time, attention, and some patience, but I won't beg for it, baby. I think too much of myself for that. If your perfect pussy hovered an inch above my cock, I wouldn't beg. One of these days I'll show that ass who's boss.

How could he do this to me with plain black and white text? My pussy was wet, needy, ready for him in a way that was nearly pathetic. I feared the day he had me in person and realized what a slave my body was to his. I needed to make him want me even a fraction of how much I wanted him.

Are you sure you wouldn't beg? I think highly of you too, so much so that she is already wet for you. She feels so nice and soft and tempting. No one would think less of you for begging for her. The idea of you showing this ass who's boss is titillating. I might need a man who can keep me in line, at least while we fuck.

I had never been in the lifestyle or anything, but I always dreamed of having an incredibly sexy guy take control and manhandle me while we did the deed. Rough sex with a hot, smart, funny, and willing man, one who would fuck me how I liked. It sounded too good to be true. The damp heat between my thighs wouldn't leave.

I might make a begging exception for you, but don't count on it. I always want you as wet as possible, and I have plenty of ways to make that happen. That picture has kept me hard for you longer than I care to admit. I only want to return the favor. I would be more than happy to keep you in line. Tell me everything you like, baby. I need to know exactly what I can do to you.

I ground my thighs together, trying to temper the riotous effect his words had on my body. My mind spun with images of the many things I'd allow.

I would let you do almost anything to me.

I'd let him devour me whole if it pleased him. I left my email alone on that note, grabbed my purse, and headed out the door to catch the bus. Thoughts of him floated through my mind the entire ride. I fell so deeply into my fantasies that I almost missed my stop.

Warm fresh air cleared my mind as I stepped out into the beautiful sunshine. Blue skies, singing birds, and a gorgeous man, everything in the world was in the right place for once.

I walked into the office with a big smile plastered on my face. Tyler stood near the door. "Good morning, beautiful." His tone didn't match his words, and it was clear he was still put out from the day before. I wanted to call in sick again today but decided I needed the money. The look on his face told me I should have stayed home.

"Oh, hey, Tyler, how are you doing today?" I tried to ignore his expression as I made my way back to my desk. I pulled out my chair and adjusted my tight skirt as I sat down.

He followed me, and I caught his eyes tracing my thighs and my hands on them. There was heat in his gaze, along with something else that made my skin prick. He sat against the edge of my desk, tilting his pelvis toward me. "Be straight with me, Claire. This game of cat and mouse has been fun, but when are you going to give in?"

A choked sound escaped me, "I'm sorry, what?"

"Don't play coy with me, it doesn't suit you," he reached out, trailing his fingers along the back of my hand.

I jerked it away in shock. "Look, Tyler, I'm sorry if there's been some misunderstanding, but I just don't think we're a good fit. You're a really nice person, but I don't think we have much in common," the lie burned on the way out; he was a complete asshole. This would have been so much easier if he took the hint that I wasn't interested. While I desperately wanted to tell him that, my gut screamed that preserving his ego was in my best interest and the last thing he wanted was my opinion of him.

His face twisted into something dark and frightening. "Whatever you say, Claire." He made it clear he didn't believe me, and that it wouldn't be the last I heard from him. He got up and stalked off to his office. The interaction made me nervous, but my thoughts quickly drifted back to my friend and our conversation from the night before.

As the day went on, discontent bubbled up within me. All I wanted was to talk to my new friend and be anywhere Tyler wasn't. *Why didn't you just play hooky?* I chastised myself repeatedly. By the late afternoon, I noticed people treating me oddly. I walked through the office to grab a three pm cup of coffee, and sideways glances and whispers replaced the normal friendly conversation and kid pictures.

I opened my email on my phone as I poured milk into my cup. There was a message from *him*.

Just about anything, huh? I'll have to think of something extra special then.

I shivered, and a stupid smile spread across my cheeks.

"What are you so happy about?" a woman named Tanya asked with a judgmental look.

"Oh, nothing really," I smiled at her, disregarding her tone.

"Mm, I'm sure," she rolled her eyes and walked away. *What the hell was that about?*

The rest of the week went the same way, emails with my friend exchanged in every free moment I had, and the small standoffish behaviors grew more and more obvious. My coworkers spoke until the moment I came into the room, and then they were deathly quiet. They could have been talking about anything or anyone. Despite the unsettled feeling in my gut, I tried not to make it personal.

Women whispered to each other while staring at me, but the second I looked their way, their eyes shot down. Their judging voices grew louder and more frequent. I swore I could hear my name occasionally. The women who'd taught me to crochet huddled together talking, "... Claire... slut..."

I turned to them, unable to believe my own ears. "Excuse me, did you say something to me?"

"No, of course not, dear," one of the Barbaras answered with a condescending twist to her otherwise bright voice.

I stared at them for another stupid minute before I muttered, "I could have sworn you called me a slut," and stomped back over to my desk. *What the hell was going on here?* I pulled on the sweater I kept in my desk, trying to hide away from the prying eyes.

It took me an embarrassingly long time to suspect the culprit, even though I frequently felt his eyes on me. Perhaps, I was too caught up in the email exchanges with my new friend, too besotted and turned on from the late night pictures we exchanged while we masturbated to one another to notice the obvious right in front of my face.

One morning, about two weeks after the conversation Tyler and I had as he sat his ass on my desk, I went to the break room for a cup of coffee. No one noticed me as I entered. Two of the admissions counselors, Tony and Jared, were talking and laughing boisterously in front of the refrigerator.

"... and like that..." Tony snapped his fingers, "She fucked him!" Jared noticed me standing there and his mouth dropped open in shock. He threw out his hands, trying to stop Tony from continuing, but he was on a roll.

"She tried to fuck him on the couch before they went to dinner. Can you imagine? He told her he'd be happy to show her a good time, but at least wanted to buy her a meal first," Tony looked at Jared with stupid confusion, "What are you doing, dude?"

Several women from the office stood around them, listening. They watched me with hungry eyes, waiting for me to blow up or cry, anything to make their boring lives interesting. I didn't care about them, and I used all my self-control to plaster a calm look on my face and leave with my head held high. It was fifteen minutes to five. I clocked out early without saying a word and went outside to wait for the bus.

Throughout the entire ride home, I told myself not to worry. Tyler lied, and all I had to do was tell everyone the truth and the matter would be behind me. I would never have friendly feelings for any of them again, but that was okay. I needed a paycheck, not friends. Well, friends wouldn't hurt, but I didn't need any of them. These self-righteous assholes would not make me feel like Hester Prynne without even getting laid.

The next day, I went on the offensive. When I heard the whispers, I faced them head-on, asking what the hot gossip was. When the same group of women were chatting about 'Claire, the slut', I walked right up to them. "You know, I didn't sleep with him. We went on one crappy date and we didn't even kiss. I can't imagine why he's lying about it, but he is."

One of the Barbaras gave me a fake smile. "Oh, dear, that's terrible. I have worked with Tyler for a long time and I've never known him to be a liar. Are you sure you aren't misremembering one of your other dates?" Her cronies laughed at the dig.

"I'm certain." I insisted as I ground my heel into the carpeting.

"The two of you have been awfully comfortable since you started here. Come to think of it, you've been a lot more comfortable than him, following him around like a lost puppy." She shrugged her shoulders and raised an eyebrow at me like it was obvious. "Are you sure your little crush didn't just get out of hand?"

I will not hit an old woman. I will not hit an old woman. I repeated to myself as I stomped off to my desk again. Stomping around this place was going to wear out my heels. I told every single person in that office he lied and most of them had the common decency to act as if they believed me. They were sympathetic but full of shit.

Things only got worse for me. The lie was more entertaining than the truth and entertainment was scarce in that fluorescent tube-lit shit hole. My misery gave them a renewed sense of community and togetherness. Maybe they were jealous that the years crumbled to dust behind them, along with their sexual prospects.

The little comfort I once found there faded. The open friendliness I once displayed folded up, trying to protect my remaining shreds of confidence, like a morning glory closing for the night. I did my best to carry on, arriving on time and leaving at five. I did my work and tried my hardest to tune them out.

My friend tried to email me a few times, but I couldn't bring myself to answer.

I've missed our chats. Where have you been?

I missed them too, but I still couldn't force myself to type the words and send them.

It's quite alright if you're not interested anymore, just let me know so I don't worry.

I was interested, and I knew I wasn't being fair. I didn't want him to worry, but the words remained locked inside of me.

I won't keep bothering you. I just want you to know I deleted your pictures. No one should look at you that way if you don't want them to.

His last message brought tears to my eyes. This wasn't what I wanted. Nothing was going the way I thought it would, but how could I make it right when I couldn't even figure out what I wanted, let alone use the words to make it happen. The thought of sex sapped my joy. It was nothing more than an excuse for people to treat you like shit.

One night, I sat on the floor beside my coffee table looking through the pages of the scrapbook I never finished. Pain and shame rushed through me as I remembered how giddy this used to make me. I couldn't fathom what I would endure if my coworkers or Tyler learned about my little stunt and the many reaching consequences. I cut the pictures out, pasting them into the pages with the corresponding text as I ordered Indian food for the first time in a while.

"Hey, Claire," Sadar called when I opened the door. His face lit with genuine excitement to see me. The tears hovering in my eyes fell. "Hey, what's wrong?" He reached out like he was going to touch me, but dropped his hand when I backed away. We had a friendly relationship, and I'd been his customer since I first moved out of my dorm. Him putting a hand on my shoulder wouldn't normally upset me.

I pulled the door open wider, trying to cover the action. "Everything is fine. Can you put it on the counter?" The pitiful sniffle that escaped me ruined my bluff.

He placed my korma down slowly and I pulled the money out of my purse. "Keep the change," I tried to hand it to him but he wouldn't take it.

He stood there, waiting until I met his eyes. "I know it's really not my place, but I haven't seen you in a while and you don't seem like you're okay. I know we're not that close, but if you need a friend, call me at the restaurant, okay?"

"Thanks, Sadar," I shoved the money into his hands once more.

He handed it back to me and briefly squeezed my hands. The gesture was empty of any flirtation, just friendly concern. "It's on me," he gave me a kind smile as he left.

The caring in his voice and eyes nearly broke me. It's silly to care what others think, right? But what about what you think? What about gossip that is so pervasive it messes with your head and the way you see yourself? I did nothing but fake an illness to escape Tyler, and yet, I felt wrong and dirty. Sadar made me feel like maybe I was worthy of kindness.

The next morning, I talked to Sandy, the office administrator. I waited weeks for this to die out, for them to get bored, or realize it was a lie. It was impossible for me to continue this way. "Why did you need to speak with me, Claire?" She smiled at me warmly from the opposite side of her desk.

It gave me a touch of courage, and I dragged in a huge breath. "I'm being bullied by my coworkers," her eyes trained on me, waiting for me to continue. "Well, it's like this. I went for one meal with Tyler. Nothing at all happened between us. However, he is spreading some pretty awful rumors about me. People are staring at me, talking behind my back, calling me a slut under their breath. I can't work this way."

She gave me a very serious look as she drummed her fingers against her desk. "Were you aware that there is a non-fraternization policy in effect?"

"I was..." my voice trailed off.

"Then I'm not sure what you expected to happen. I would be within my rights to fire you, but you're a hard worker and I don't want to do that."

"Wait, what?" I spluttered, unable to believe my ears. Was she really suggesting this was my fault? I used all my self-control to close my hanging mouth.

She tapped her fingers harder on the desk. "I'm sorry, Claire, but I'm afraid there's not much I can do. Has anyone said anything to your face or prevented you from using facilities necessary to do your job? Has anybody harassed, assaulted, or touched you in a way you didn't consent to?"

"Well, no..." she cut me off.

"Tyler is a senior staff member, and I can't control what people talk about. I really am sorry you're having a hard time. Come back if anything I mentioned starts happening." She pushed her glasses up her nose and started rifling through the papers on her desk.

"But..."

"We're done here, Claire. You can go." I nodded my head and walked out without another word. People didn't even bother to pretend they weren't watching me as I went back to my desk. I kept my gaze focused on the floor, but I saw plenty of smiles as they took in my hot red face and the tears filling my eyes.

That night I went through my closet, pulling out anything that once made me feel desirable. I put them all in a giant plastic tub, slammed the lid and sent them to the back of the closet, where they couldn't taunt me. The remaining clothes were old, drab, comfortable, and bordering on inappropriate for work. I was toeing the line between business casual and casual a little too closely. All I wanted was to fade quietly into the background.

Who would they call a slut if they couldn't see me? All the while, Tyler went about his life, the hero amongst the guys. He was the one who banged the new girl. He was such a gentleman to the women. I begged him to split me in two on my couch before we shared a drink, and he insisted on taking me to a nice dinner first. He had the gall to smile and wave at me each day. My blood boiled at the injustice of it all.

I called in sick at least once, often twice a week, as July faded into August. One morning, I sat on the benches set between the library and City Hall, torn in two by the place I couldn't go because of protocol, and the place I wouldn't go for fear of seeing *him*, the only man I wanted.

The expressions I had seen artfully painted on his face played through my mind, shocked, annoyed, amused, and all the other ways he gifted me with his beauty. The mixture of desire and pain was so strong and strange I didn't have words to describe it.

I pulled my phone out of my pocket, pressing one of the few contacts I had, though I rarely used it. It rang for so long, I thought she would ignore it.

"Hello," my mother's groggy voice chilled me.

"Hi, mom," I whispered out of habit. It was too easy for her to misconstrue my tone.

"What's wrong now?" There was no motherly concern, only irritation that I was bothering her.

"Mom, do you remember what I wanted to be when I was a kid?" I had other things I wanted to say, but I started off small to gauge her reaction.

She scoffed like she couldn't understand why anyone would want to know, "All you ever did was read, Claire. You were a weird kid. I don't know what you want from me." She was right. Reading was all I ever wanted to do.

"Mom... How have you been? Have you seen your doctor recently?" I twisted my fingers through my hair, nervous to hear her answer.

"Don't pretend you care." She hung up the phone.

"Love you too," I told the dead receiver. I wondered if I should go over there and make sure she was taking care of herself. *No, she doesn't want my help.*

The next morning, I finally had enough. I knew it before I even woke up. The tenor of my dreams was hopeful instead of defeated. There was fire inside of me, and a desperate—needy, even—hope. I got ready for work the way I did after the night of my naughty email exchange.

I pulled the tub out from the back of my closet and wore the same outfit. Things were coming full circle for me. I did my hair and makeup a little nicer than necessary; I looked sexy and professional, and from the light in my eyes, ready to fuck shit up.

When I walked in, everyone stared at me. That was a usual occurrence. Instead of it hurting me, I accepted it. This time, I wanted an audience. I looked around, wondering if everyone in the world had abandoned tact where it concerned me. I shrugged my shoulders because I would be rid of them soon enough. The buzz of something juicy to gossip about was thick in the air.

Tyler stood in the corner chatting with a group of guys. He didn't see me as he regaled them, clearly in his element. "... plain horny, that girl, a genuine freak. I bet she'd let you all do her at once, and she's flexible enough to fit you too." He waved his arms to demonstrate the angles they could bend me into.

I strode over to him with supreme confidence, "You know as well as I do, *I* never fucked *you*, Tyler." I said at the same time I gave his shoulder a pat.

He looked back expectantly, like seeing me there didn't surprise him in the least. His face was clear of the barest hint of remorse, but something I didn't recognize hid in the back of his brown eyes. I continued despite the trickle of fear it caused, "*You* invited yourself in, if you remember, and I told you

I wanted to go to dinner. I was nauseous halfway through the date. What kind of man needs to lie about a woman sleeping with him when she's sick? Are you *that* pathetic?"

He faced me then, his face burned red with outrage and embarrassment. The surrounding audience was almost entirely women, their faces ranged from shock and disgust to excitement. "You are an insufferable, lying, conceited twat. I pity any woman stupid enough to sleep with you."

My voice rang out steadily. "I hope your dick falls off." I faced the room, gesturing around myself. "And the rest of you? You're terrible people. You can all go fuck yourselves along with that guy." I hiked my thumb over my shoulder, indicating the guy.

I turned and walked straight out. As the door swung shut, people talked, but I couldn't care less what they said. Gasps and laughs echoed behind me. I don't think a single one was on my side, but that was okay. I was on my side. Sometimes, that's what doing the right thing for yourself means.

Summer was in full swing. The hot air swelled around me as I walked toward the bus stop. I didn't get far before I realized someone followed me. I turned to see Sandy looking flustered. "You know you're fired, right?"

"Yeah." I laughed a little. "I got that before I opened my mouth. He's going to get you sued one of these days." Her face dropped. She understood I was right, and likely hoped that I wouldn't be the one that did it. I left her there, standing stunned on the sidewalk. I didn't know what I would do, but this didn't feel like a mistake, at least not yet.

Chapter Seven

My fingers twitched above the keyboard. The box for the new message stood empty, staring at me with nothing but the proxy email generated by the website that hosted my ad. I picked at my lip nervously. I didn't know his name, or anything about him other than what he told me, and the fact he liked to go to the library. The nerves rolled inside me as I considered how little I knew about this man and how much I needed him back in my life.

I plucked out a few words and quickly erased them. I had already gotten the sentiment wrong a multitude of times, each apology more anticlimactic than the last. He deserved so much better than the nothing I gave him, and if he already moved on, that would be more than fair. I hoped he was angry with me. There was still a chance for us if he was angry, but if I simply killed his interest in me, that was another story. I couldn't fault him for it, but God, would the rejection hurt. I pressed my face into my hands, exhaling hard, then blew a raspberry against my palms. This was the only chance I had to get him back.

Hey Stranger,

I'm sorry I've been a ghost lately. I would have started out with a picture of my titties to soften you up, but I feared you'd find it patronizing. In all seriousness, things have not been easy for me. I lost my job through some elaborate ridiculousness. Now, I'm unemployed and too pitiful to be dejected further. I don't blame you if you moved on. Please let me down gently.

-Very Sorry

He didn't answer me at all that first day. An overwhelming part of me feared he never would, and I prepared myself for the pain of his rejection. The other part—much smaller, and unfamiliarly optimistic—sensed he wasn't far away. In the nearly two months since I first spoke to him, I felt oddly aligned with him. It could be the fact that he kept writing to me when I said nothing in response. Somehow, that alone didn't seem like enough of an explanation. My life seemed tied to his in a way I didn't understand. I couldn't let him go without trying.

The following day, I stayed dressed in my pajamas, eating junk food and staring listlessly at the TV. The shampoo commercial and the sexy sudsy actor I loved so much were both replaced by a bouncy, beachy blonde. "Nothing good ever lasts," I told the gorgeous supermodel as she washed her hair and skipped down a city street.

Each time the ding sounded, my heart jumped into my throat, and then the disappointment crushed me. I unsubscribed to every mailing list I could find and still more arrived. I was so angry with them for playing with my emotions that I made a note of companies I would never buy from again. Heaving myself off the couch, I went for a walk around the block to breathe some fresh air and sense into my brain. None of these massive corporations gave a crap if I bought from them or not, and I was a sucker for coupons.

That night I lay in my bed, not tired enough to sleep, and lacking the energy to get up and do something productive. The email notification went off, and I ignored it. I received so many that were not from him, and the cycle of excitement and disappointment exhausted me emotionally. I stared at the ceiling, trying to distract myself by counting the peaks of the hideous water-stained stucco. When I got to two hundred and the thrumming in my heart still didn't ease, I opened my phone to check who it was. The subject line read "I thought about it."

This was it, he was telling me no. He was finished with me and I couldn't blame him for his choice. I gripped helplessly at my chest, trying to coax my lungs into drawing steady breaths. Passing out would not be the worst thing in the world considering I was already laying down in my soft bed. I fought against the spots of light blooming in my vision, even if unconsciousness was more appealing than reading the words that would sever us and our budding connection. I fumbled with the phone, getting the email open.

Titties are never patronizing.

I laughed out loud. The sound came out more like a shout as the intense relief surged through me. Hopping out of my bed as if sleep was never a consideration, I pulled off my shirt and made my way over to my full-length mirror. A frenzied light shined in the back of my eyes, making me appear wild, but he didn't need to see my face. My hands adjusted my breasts, ensuring they looked round and pert. I pinched my nipples to make sure they puckered for him, but they were already hard from the excitement. I glared at the random crap caked on the glass and decided against taking a mirror selfie.

I flipped my phone's camera to front-facing as I admired the pinkish-brown cast to my nipples. My breasts were always one of my favorite assets, and I was particularly fond of them now as I thought of my friend's cock hardening while looking at them. I took a few pictures of myself, including nothing but my inviting lips pushed into an exaggerated pout and my breasts, which I surreptitiously squished between my arms. I sorted through the pictures, choosing the softest and poutiest, and then sent it to him.

I went back to laying in my bed, not bothering with the shirt. Talking to him always made me feel sexy and uninhibited. I stroked my nipples gently with one hand and ran the other along the lacy tops of my panties, imagining his hands on me. My eyes fell shut as I imagined his flawless face the moment he opened the pictures, his lush tongue darting out to wet his lips. My fingers drifted closer to their destination, but the ping of my email interrupted the movement.

Before I become too enthralled with the most perfect breasts I have ever seen, I need some answers. First, why were you fired? I'm sorry that happened, unless you burned the place down or something, in which case, you deserved it. Though, I have a penchant for destructive behavior and debauchery. So, it's possible I could be okay with it.

Second, what does being let go have to do with the last month or so? Why haven't you answered any of my emails, especially the one where I wanted to know if you were okay? Third, you are too tempting and I forgot my final point.

-Tossed Out and Turned On

The emotions surging through me were more complex than I was used to dealing with. My body pleasing him satisfied me in a way I couldn't justify to myself. His praise lit me up as if he was the only person whose opinion mattered. The intensity of it frightened me. Anger followed right behind it as I reread the words suggesting me losing the job was my fault.

He didn't understand the circumstances, and his assumption stung. Most of the time people get fired because they did something wrong, but in this situation, I was the one who'd been wronged. It hurt me that he didn't assume this was the case. What I really wanted was for him to respond with anger on my behalf, to defend me against the baseless accusations hurled at me. Truthfully, it was my outburst that got me fired, but the rest of the situation was not my fault. He should know me better than that, even if I didn't give him a fair opportunity to. I breathed out a sigh as my anger faded. *Now, how am I going to explain to him the reason he doesn't know me better?*

I went for a meal with a male coworker, stupid—I know. He was horrible. I faked having a stomach bug if that gives you any idea how awful it was. The perfect gentleman lied to the entire office and told them all I fucked him on my couch before he could take me out. In his version of events, he begged to at least buy me dinner first, but my raging, slutty lust for him would not be denied.

To put it mildly, people were mistreating me. I asked my boss for help and she informed me she couldn't do anything. I snapped and screamed at all of them, then walked out. Going back was the last of my plans, but my boss followed me out to fire me anyway. It might not sound very important, but it was hard on me. I miss you, and I'm sorry for not answering you.

-Tits Out and Turned On

I flopped on my pillows, letting my limbs sprawl out. I was truly tired. The anxiety burned itself out and the rest of my energy went along with it. Why did he answer me only now when I waited for him all day? Leave it to him to disturb my patterns and turn my life upside down. I prepared myself for the possibility that he wouldn't believe me, just like my coworkers.

Hell, the way we started speaking to one another said little in my defense. I had asked the dregs of the internet for a random hook-up. He likely assumed he was one of many. He probably thought I was a slut too. The way I built him up in my mind could surely backfire on me, or outright bite me in the ass. *Ping.*

That is terrible. I am so sorry that happened to you. As for not answering me, forget about it, I have. I missed you too. I think you are the only person I've ever met who hasn't bored me for a single second. The scene you described sounds true to form. I would pay good money to watch you in all your glory, defending yourself against people who would treat you less than you deserve. You really are something special, aren't you?

Part of me is ready to demand we end this now. I want to look into your beautiful brown eyes and see that sweet bewilderment as I stand above you. I could make your perfect cheeks flame hotter than they did when I helped you with your dick pics. Talking to you in person without you running from me is too delicious to resist. Though I must admit, running from me may be in your best interest.

Your mind and body serve as a constant temptation, teasing me when you're not even near. I can do things to you that no other man ever could, and I would never talk about them to another soul. The very least you deserve is respect and discretion, but I'd be happy to give you so much more.

The other part of me craves the mystery of it all. I want you in a way I've never wanted another person, but this thing between us feels supernatural. You tell me, where do we go from here?

-Twisted Up and Turned On

I briefly wondered what he meant by suggesting it might be in my best interest to run from him, but I didn't dwell on it for long. He was a fire burning bright and hot beneath my skin. Of course that was dangerous. The thought of his gorgeous cock hard for me made my insides clench.

I glanced over my shoulder at my ass, lush and round in my light blue panties. They were nothing fancy, a little cotton with a lace band, but my ass had a great shape in them. I smacked it a bit, appreciating the jiggle and imagining his face if he was the one doing the smacking. I never felt like this about my body. He made me crazy.

Draping my white duvet over my legs, I posed as if someone was pulling it off me. I took a few pictures from different angles, finding one that framed the swell of my hips and ass in an alluring shape. Attaching the picture to an email, I typed out a message.

I'm not sure I'm ready to end this myself. All of this mutual desire has me feeling incredible. And there is another problem... If I wanted to meet soon, it wouldn't be for what I originally asked for. I would like to date you. I hope you realize your wit and cock won me over and tied me in knots. Tell me now if that doesn't work for you. I will understand.

-Tied Up and Tantalized

I stood up from my bed, going to my window to look at the view of the darkened block. Street lights dotted the sidewalk, and some windows were lit, but most weren't. This wasn't NY, and people actually slept here. I pressed my head against the cool glass, waiting for his response to come. I thought over the interactions we had. The tingling need he sparked within me pulsed between my thighs. The embarrassment I brought on myself made my cheeks hot and my panties wet.

I hoped desperately he'd be interested in more than fucking me once. I wasn't looking for commitment necessarily, and I still didn't think poorly of casual sex, though I learned a lot from my experience with Tyler. Even if there was no genuine connection, I required a base level of trust for anyone I slept with. I had to be more careful about who I gave my unguarded self to.

I didn't need lasting love, and I wouldn't know what to do with it anyway. My father was a mystery to me, and my mother and I were far from close. I did not know what it meant to have someone close to me, to care about me that way, but I had to know him.

A man walked down the street, and I observed him intently. When he stopped and glanced up, I hoped for a moment it was my mystery man. Of course it wasn't and the man most likely wasn't looking at me, only at the building. I was letting the intrigue get inside my head, and was far too worked up and deprived to be deciding anything. I glimpsed the time on my phone. His response still hadn't come and the fear that he was cleverly wording his rejection gripped my throat. I metaphorically slammed my cards on the table, ready to do whatever I needed to.

My name is Claire, by the way.

The notification came a moment later.

Claire,
The thought of you in knots is incredibly sexy. I'd be happy to tie you in some or bend you into them, whichever you prefer. As for not wanting only casual sex anymore, I'm not sure what to say. I don't know what I want, and I don't know you well enough to say for certain.

From your emails and what I've seen in person, it would thrill me to take you on a date. It's always your choice if you want to sleep with someone or not. I would never force you into anything that made you uncomfortable, in or out of the bedroom. Though I would love to force you to behave while I fucked you.

Give me a chance and I'll offer you one too. Let me take you to dinner and we'll see how things go. I'm not ruling anything out, and neither should you.

-Mason

My stomach tightened in such a delicious excruciating way, my toes curled with the intensity. There was nothing that I had to do this week, except get a new job and figure out my life's purpose. I could possibly find a new position tomorrow and be on to better things.

I'm free tomorrow. Meet me for dinner at 7?

-Claire (555)-964-8989

A text came in a few minutes later.

Mason: Alessandro's on 3rd, 7pm, I can't wait.

I wasn't sure exactly how we went from holding off on meeting to meeting tomorrow, but the prospect thrilled me. He was so bossy and sometimes it irritated me, but mostly it made me want to obey. I squirmed thinking of all the ways I'd let him take control. A weight lifted off my chest, and the very real worries of my life melted away. I was going on a date with Mason. I said it out loud, tasting his name on my tongue. My life was still a disaster, but things were looking up. I texted him back with a stupid smile on my face.

Claire: I can't wait either. I hope you sleep well and dream of me.

I sent a picture of my hand inside my panties.

Mason: Good night, tease.

I climbed back into my bed, exhausted in a way I'd never been. And of course, I dreamt of him.

Chapter Eight

Exhaustion turned my body to lead, sticking my eyelids together and weighing my limbs into my worn-out mattress. Surviving on only a couple of hours of sleep was never my thing. With nowhere to go, I tried to stay in bed and drift off into another filthy dream, but the excitement thrumming through me demanded I stand up and face the day. I peeled my heavy lids back and checked my phone to see if Mason texted me. *Mason*, a shiver went through me as I thought his name. *Nothing yet*, I groaned to myself.

I showered slowly, taking more time with my sensitive areas than expressly necessary. The business casual attire I decided on was silly, considering I had nowhere in particular to go, but I hoped that if I acted as I did, my motivation would catch up to my ensemble. I needed to update my resume, but the thought of admitting to that total disaster didn't appeal to me. *Ugh, why can't I just magically have another job?* My downstairs neighbor smacked a broom into his ceiling, irritated with my stomping around.

I brokered a deal with myself; update the resume and print a few copies to bring to potential interviews and consider the day productive. I forced myself to sit down and type in the information from my last employer. Each letter I struck on my keyboard stung a little, but I pushed the rage and shame out of my mind. These feelings wouldn't help me, just hurt me and embarrass me when I should move on.

I saved the document and sent it to myself. Printer ink never made it on my shopping list, so a trip to the library was in order. My neck got all hot and uncomfortable at the slim possibility of finding Mason there again, but I doubted it; he had to work, and I couldn't be that lucky three times. At least I could visit the basement books. With all the tumult and upheaval, I needed something that felt safe.

The summer burned out faster than usual. July had been boiling, but August was cool by comparison. The air swelled hot and thick, like the season sensed its numbered days and hoped to take full advantage of the time remaining.

The air clung to my skin, mixing with my sweat, and I truly regretted my choice of outfit. A sundress would be much more comfortable than a sensible skirt and button-down blouse. My hair expanded with the charge of faint electricity promising a thunderstorm.

A few black clouds gathered tightly overhead as I arrived. I stepped through the door in time to catch the first few drops hitting the pavement. The smell of the wet concrete and the books mixed, triggering a memory I didn't know I had. An image of a field trip to a museum I took in elementary school filled my mind and senses. The vividness surprised me.

Pulling myself out of my daze, I headed for the basement stairs. There was no rush to print my resume, and I couldn't just pass by without saying hello to my old friends. Right as my foot landed on the first step, a commotion at the circulation desk stopped me. The skylights in the ceiling revealed a black rolling sky, the rain unleashed from the clouds, pounding mercilessly against the glass. The fluorescent lights cast an odd, contrasting glow while a man and a woman stood there shouting at one another.

Watching was rude, but I couldn't help myself. The library was usually such a quiet place. I tucked myself into a corner and realized I recognized her as the librarian. My envy for her cropped up more than once over the years, but the emotion seemed silly now. The man she argued with was in his mid-fifties with dark, graying hair and small, somber eyes. She looked a little older than him—if I had to guess—with fluffy blonde hair and winged glasses.

Her hands waved violently in the air. "I'm sick of this shit, Gavin. I won't involve myself in it any longer."

He glanced around, making sure no one watched them. I couldn't hear his next remarks, but his gestures begged her to calm down and speak more quietly. "Eileen, listen, we can make some adjustments," his soft voice echoed down the hall.

He wasn't done speaking, but she cut him off. "I quit, Gavin." He said something else to her in a hushed tone. They were not the words she wanted to hear. Her hands flew up in frustration and smacked against her thighs as she turned around and stormed out of the library. Her kitten heels made a clomping noise that echoed behind her. She didn't even pause when confronted with the torrential downpour, which revealed something about the gravity of their argument. Gavin lifted a hand like he might try to stop her, but dropped it when he thought better.

I stood stock-still, shaking with anticipation. This was the opportunity I scarcely hoped to dream of. The pouring rain threatened to sweep the library away, taking my ambitions along with it. I could turn around now, go to the basement, even run home and forget this all happened. Avoidance would be true to form, typical to keep my mouth shut, lay in my bed miserable, order Indian food, and masturbate to the pictures of Mason. Letting this opportunity slide by would be all too simple.

I didn't want to be that person anymore. I wasn't naïve, and I knew changing my life wouldn't be so easy as one good decision. He might laugh me out of this library, but I had to try. This was the only chance like this I would ever have. I walked up to Gavin, thanking divine providence that I showered and dressed up today. I took a deep breath as I waited for him to notice me standing in front of him. He dropped his face into his hands and I cleared my throat.

He jumped despite the gentle sound. The stress of the situation crumpled his lined face. "Oh, I'm sorry. I didn't see you there. How can I help you this morning?"

Pushing my hair back, I squared my shoulders. "I hate to intrude, but I noticed you have an opening for a librarian. I would like to apply for the position."

Confusion and annoyance flashed in his tired eyes, but I held my ground. "I'm sorry, miss, but in order to be a librarian you need-"

"A master's in library science." I interrupted him with a smile. People rarely knew about the degree it required. "I have one. I'm also timely, a hard worker, and well acquainted with your institution."

He blinked at me, surprised; the wheels turned as he appraised me. This wasn't the best time to get an answer from him, but if I waited to apply in the usual fashion, I would be up against more qualified candidates. I needed to take advantage of the situation. "Do you have any experience beyond your schooling?" My age influenced the question.

"Not in a library, specifically, no." I said the words like they mattered little. "But I have experience with database development for the city." It was a bit of a stretch, but I compiled and structured the entire city records prior to them going digital. The task was extensive, which is why the temporary position lasted eight months.

"Do you have a resume?"

I almost laughed, thanking the fates I finished it before I came. "I can print my resume for you."

He nodded. "I'll give it a look and if I like what I see, I'll give you an interview."

"Thank you, sir." I stuck out my hand, and he shook it. The gesture surprised him, or perhaps it was the entire situation. I moved quickly, trying to capitalize on this rare opportunity. I read my latest addition once again to ensure I left no glaring error that would make me seem incompetent. The paper rested in his hands in less than five minutes, and I went to sit in a plush armchair near the circulation desk.

The nonfiction section surrounded me, and I eyed the books skeptically. I preferred fiction. He walked to the back, not even glancing at it. My teeth tore into my nails, biting them down to stubs. After I waited for forty-five minutes, I started looking through books, reading blurbs and making a mental list of all the ones I could read before I got evicted.

The image of him sitting in the office waiting me out left a bitter taste in my mouth, and I snapped a book back into place with more force than necessary. I couldn't blame him for not hiring me, but politeness demanded he told me that himself instead of expecting me to scurry away with my tail tucked between my legs. I wasn't giving up though, and I would wait here all day if I had to.

Another twenty minutes passed. I found a book I liked and started the third chapter when the clearing of a throat made me jump. Gavin stood in front of me with a skeptical expression on his pinched face. "I've looked over your resume and called your references and past employers. I worry that your lack of experience will be a hindrance, but you came highly recommended."

My boss at City Hall giving me a rave review came as no surprise. He always liked me and thought I did my job well. I tried hard to stay in the moment and not drift back to the day he took it all away. *It wasn't his fault*, I gently reminded myself.

I couldn't say the same for Sandra. Her giving me a good reference more than shocked me. I only included the position because the gap in employment was too wide to explain without some questions. Perhaps the potential for a lawsuit really frightened her. A tiny part of me hoped that she actually meant the things she told him.

"Ms. Green, you need to understand this job is more than a degree. The position is administrative, creative, and interpersonal. The work involved is not only tantamount to the success of the library, but our community. Are you prepared for the responsibility? The board is strict about maintaining the integrity of our institution, and as chairman, I take my position seriously."

I stood then, realizing I should have when he first approached me. "I have dreamed of this and worked for it my entire life. Let me assure you, I will meet the responsibility and challenges head-on with professionalism and passion." I allowed my emotions to seep into my voice. He seemed to care about this place and I wanted him to know that I did too.

"I'm going to give you a chance, even if this is unorthodox. I'm offering you a two-week trial period. If you do alright during that time, I'll give you a month. Do well, and I will extend it to a standard six-month probation period with a contract." The little pinch between his brow never eased, his doubt evident, but that wouldn't deter me.

A smile curved my lips. "Thank you, sir. You won't regret your decision."

"I hope not." He pulled a pair of glasses out of his breast pocket and put them on. The glasses made his eyes larger and his face more handsome. He shuffled through a thick stack of papers he carried, peeling off the top twenty pages. He handed them to me. "Fill these out now and give them back to me.

This one is the acknowledgment of the trial basis of your employment. Beneath it is your tax information and the code of conduct. This information is for the day-to-day needs of the position. Well, some, anyway. I'm sorry to say that these lists are dated. It's important that you hit the ground running. Read this all over tonight and be back here tomorrow at eight sharp."

I took the papers. "Thank you so much."

He put a little folded piece of paper on top of them. "This is your salary. The pay is nonnegotiable and decided by the board. You can call me Gavin." He gave me the first genuine smile of our entire interaction and the joy of what happened exploded inside of me: I was a librarian.

I walked over to one of the tables set out for studying and got to work filling out the mundane questions. When they were all filled in, and my hand ached from the effort, I took them back to the office and handed them off to Gavin.

The décor was not his own, which made me wonder if this would become my office. A little tingle zipped through me at the thought. I went back to the same table and read through the materials. When I came to the point of keeping up to date with new releases and sourcing them, I cringed at how outdated the information was. The previous librarian had been here a long time.

I shook the worry off. This was the part of the job I was most excited about and nothing would stop me from flourishing here. The pay wouldn't provide an early retirement, but the benefits were good. I could support myself and allow some extra things here and there. I needed to prove myself, and for once in my life, that sensation wasn't based on fear. There was no doubt I could do this. The hard bit was over, I got the position. Now I just needed to work harder than I ever had and prove I deserved it.

A couple of hours later, I still worked through the piles of information Gavin gave me, making my own notes and compiling lists. Out of nowhere, I remembered my date with Mason. My stomach sank as I realized there was no way I could meet him tonight and prepare for my first day tomorrow. I left the library without saying goodbye to Gavin as he was busy in the back and likely thought I was gone hours ago.

The gray sky and dreary atmosphere sunk into me. Drops of rain fell, stealing the joy of the new job. Fear set in, and the potential to be disappointed worse than I'd ever been before. Failure would be soul-crushing. I needed to lay my eyes—and other parts—on Mason, but I couldn't have everything I wanted, at least not exactly when I wanted. Raindrops hit the pages I carried, and I hoped the ink wouldn't run. My soaking wet hair stuck to my face and shoulders by the time I made it home.

I opened the door clumsily, nearly dropping the pile of papers, but I caught myself at the last moment. I put the papers down on my coffee table. It was about three. He must be at work, but he would have his phone on him. I pulled off my soaked shirt and wrapped my hair in a towel, then took out my phone and started typing.

Claire: I have good news, bad news, and I'm willing to send nudes.

I followed it up with a long text explaining the amazing circumstances of my new employment. If I didn't cram, and cram hard, I wouldn't be able to hack it. The thought of cramming with Mason nearly broke my resolve. Twenty minutes later, his answer arrived. In that time, I concocted a million reasons why this was the last straw. My text notification went off, and I breathed a sigh of relief.

Mason: Congratulations, that's wonderful. If you don't mind me asking, who hired you? I know a few people on the library's board of directors. Don't apologize. Let's reschedule, but make it soon. Text me tomorrow if you have time for dinner, and in the meantime, I will happily accept your offer of nudes.

I stripped off my clothes and sprawled out naked on my bed, snapping a few artful nudes, showing my breasts, waist, hips, and a tiny peek at what rested between my thighs. My face stayed out of the images just like the others, but my brown curls fell around my breasts, adding a little something to the picture. I sent it to him, hoping he'd love it, then got dressed and started working through the piles of information. I couldn't stop smiling. Could it be possible to have everything I wanted?

Chapter Nine

My first day as a librarian was a lot like my first day of high school. I slept little the night before which was becoming routine for me; the nerves battering my stomach were too intense. Before the sun rose, I was out of bed, doing my hair and my makeup. I picked out a pantsuit that made me appear professional and a bit sexy. I wished I wore glasses; they would complete the look perfectly.

I studied over the notes I'd written for myself, trying to force the knowledge Gavin provided into my head, but I didn't have enough space for it all. To make matters worse, much of the information was missing. The previous librarian clearly didn't plan on being replaced soon and if she did, she wanted to make things as hard as possible for whoever took over.

The thing I worried most about was scheduling the library's employees and volunteers. From the paperwork I had, the library had six paid part-time employees and a massive roster of volunteers. Some of them worked as little as two hours a month and managing proper staffing seemed like a job on its own. Included in my many papers were the schedules for the last several months. Each one was so different from the next I couldn't find any valuable information in them.

I put my lipstick on, smacking my lips in appreciation. "At least you don't need to take the bus," I told the confident-looking girl in the mirror. I strolled out of my apartment, and despite the doubt swirling in my stomach, I held my head high as I walked to my new career. *Career, not job*, I repeated to myself, trying to muster up the right attitude.

Gavin stood on the steps, waiting to open the doors. The time was ten minutes to eight, and he smiled when he saw me. "You're early."

I returned the gesture as I climbed up to stand beside him. "I am."

"Here is your set of keys. The lock is a little finicky, so let me show you how to do it, and then you try to make sure you've got it."

"Sounds great!" He chuckled at my enthusiasm and showed me how one had to hold and jiggle everything the right way. I succeeded on my first attempt and I liked to think the reason was the library wanted me as much as I wanted it.

He walked me around, showing me all the nooks, crannies, closets, and storerooms. He pointed to a little dimly lit alcove, "That is where you'll find the teenagers making out. It's good practice to pop back here occasionally and make sure no one is naked."

I let out a nervous laugh. "You can't be serious."

"Entirely," he disagreed, "several young people wound up with public indecency charges from growing too comfortable."

I shook my head, a bit mystified. Hopefully, nobody would get naked back here, but I couldn't imagine calling the cops on a couple of teens for getting a little carried away. I remembered being hormonal and sex-obsessed all too well, and I wasn't far from that now. "I'll keep an eye out, Gavin."

We passed only one door that he didn't open. "What's in there?"

"The basement, but you don't need anything from down there. We contract the space out for storage." He picked up his pace.

"Oh, really? I thought the basement was right near the entrance."

"The public side, yes." He didn't sound like he would elaborate.

"You're sure I won't need anything from down there?" I didn't want to bug him, but I feared the previous librarian might have stored things down there he wasn't aware of.

"I'm certain. The space is rented privately. The door is locked and they keep the spare key elsewhere."

"Oh, okay." I agreed, trying to let my curiosity go, but a flicker of doubt niggled in the back of my mind.

We ended the tour at the office he'd set up shop in yesterday, which as I hoped, was destined to be mine. He left me a few empty boxes and told me the old librarian would be back to pick up her stuff in the afternoon. He gave me the choice on whether I packed for her or let her do it herself. I chose to allow her simply because I wouldn't want someone rifling through my things. I would settle in tomorrow. "Well, Claire, I'll leave you to it." He placed his hands on his hips and looked around awkwardly.

I picked up the scheduling folder and the book of employees and volunteers the old librarian kept on hard copy. "Let me walk you out, Gavin. I'm going to get started with circulation so I can monitor things."

"Oh, good idea." I waved goodbye to him and set up shop at the circulation desk. It was Tuesday morning and Gavin promised me things would be quiet. The library was open from nine to six, though I would need to be there at least an hour before opening. I only had nine public hours to not screw everything up.

A pretty girl with short strawberry blonde hair and blue eyes walked up to me with a territorial look on her face. "Excuse me, miss, this is the circulation desk. You can't sit back there." I glanced at my list for the morning. This must be Emma, my volunteer.

I straightened up, squaring my shoulders with my new authority. "Actually, my name is Claire. I'm the new librarian here." I gave her a warm smile and held out my hand.

She looked at it for a moment, then shook it limply. "Where's Eileen?" Her words were soft, but the touch of antagonism lurking beneath was obvious. Suspicion flickered in her eyes, and I could tell she hoped I was lying.

"She quit, and I replaced her." I told her matter-of-factly. I wanted everyone to like me but being subtle had only ever caused me problems.

The distrust faded, ousted by open distaste. A barb rolled around on her tongue before she thought better of it and settled on the more appropriate response, "What do you want me to start with?"

"What do you usually begin with on Tuesdays?" I had plenty of ideas about how things should go, but it was probably best to let her stick to her routine. Unless she came up with something obviously fake to mess with me. Emma was one of the volunteers who put in a few days a week. I hoped we would get off to a good start, but that didn't seem promising.

"Returns." She fidgeted with a strand of her silky hair.

"Then get started on them." I smiled brightly. She ignored the gesture and went to wheel the massive bin out from under the slot. That would take her a while. I hoped she would be over the shock by the time she finished, and on to trying to achieve a positive working relationship with me.

The next volunteer, Sean, came in an hour later. He was an attractive guy with dirty blonde hair and light blue eyes. He walked up to the desk with a flirtatious smile on his face. "Hey, are you new here? I'll show you around."

I laughed internally at his flirting. "I am new, but I'm already well acquainted. My name is Claire and I'm the new librarian."

"What happened to Eileen?" He gave me the same dubious expression Emma did, and it took every bit of my strength not to sigh in annoyance.

"She quit." I didn't bother with the full explanation, and from the look he gave me I was certain he didn't want to hear it. He went to the back of the library where Gavin said the teens like to have sex, and I got started on my first project of the day, calling all employees and volunteers and verifying their available days. Caring about people, even if none of them liked me, came naturally to me. I wanted them to each have a schedule that worked. It didn't help them or the library to force people into hours they didn't want.

None of the conversations I had were pleasant. Several people I called stopped volunteering for the library months ago and were still on the list. It surprised me to find that even those who didn't work here anymore were standoffish about me replacing Eileen. They loved her.

I learned to expect distrustful and irritated responses, but the outright anger I encountered shocked me. Two volunteers told me to go fuck myself. They wouldn't work with anyone but Eileen. As I picked up the phone to call another, I wished I could grant their wish and fuck myself, instead of calling the next member of the Eileen fan club. At least that would be enjoyable for me.

The morning went quickly despite the drama, and at lunch, I texted Mason that I could meet him after all. He responded with the name of an expensive French restaurant downtown and the number seven. That jolt of anticipation and lust was enough to get me through the day. The cheerful smile remained on my face, much to the annoyance of the people pointing glares in my direction.

Eileen arrived around three. Emma and Sean both ran to her, meeting her in the wide atrium. I couldn't hear what they said but saw them wrap her in tight hugs and shoot me withering stares. She waved her hands, a smile on her face like the whole thing was no big deal and sent them back to work. She came up to the circulation desk, and the pitying look she gave me surprised me. "Are you the new librarian?"

"Hi, Eileen? I'm Claire." I held my hand out to her, and she shook it. We walked to the office in silence. "I have a few boxes for you. I didn't want to pack your stuff up for you in case I missed anything. So, I'll leave you to it." I shifted toward the exit.

"Claire, wait a moment." Her voice was soft and sweet with a warm, motherly note, when she wasn't yelling at Gavin. I stopped with my hand on the doorknob. "My staff loved me, and I'm sure they will not give you an easy time, but I wanted you to know I hold no ill will about being replaced. I quit, and this place cannot run itself."

I smiled at her, uncertain what to say, but grateful for the words anyway. "Thanks, Eileen. I have big shoes to fill and I hope I can do the library justice."

She nodded her head as she placed her possessions into the boxes. "I do too, but you seem like a nice person, and a lot of this job is dealing with people." She rifled through the drawers, taking her belongings and placing some papers on the desk. "These should help you." I wasn't sure what they said, but I assumed it was more specific details about how she ran things. "One more thing." She met my eyes with fear in her own. "Be careful, Claire, there's more to Gavin Wolfe than there seems."

"What do you mean?" I hoped I hadn't gotten myself into another situation like the one with Tyler.

Her gaze flicked around the room like she thought someone might be listening. "Take the warning for what it is. You're young, be careful."

"I will." I assured her and then left her to pack. *What on earth was that about?* The rest of the day passed in a blur, and by the time six o'clock came, I was all too ready to leave and finally see Mason. I set the alarm, turned the key in the lock and walked home, shocked I had that much power. My first day going well overall filled me with pride, but the warning Eileen gave and Gavin's odd reaction to the basement spun in the back of my mind, tainting my joy.

I went inside, took a quick shower, and blow-dried my hair. Every inch of my body was impeccably shaved and smooth as silk. I pulled on a tight, black dress that hugged my curves and slipped on a matching pair of pumps, the color setting off my olive skin. I did my makeup and piled my hair on top of my head with artful tendrils decorating my face and neck.

I ran to the bus, and when I got on, the driver looked at me with blatant appreciation; I hoped Mason would share the sentiment. Ignoring all the eyes on me, I found a seat. I enjoyed looking good, but only one man's attention mattered to me. I slid my hands over my arms. A light unseasonal chill hung in the air. It was too cool for the AC, but the driver had a sweaty look to him and the rest of us had to suffer.

The bus stopped a few blocks from the restaurant. The walk was short, and I took the time to settle the riotous anticipation coursing through me. Fresh air would do me some good before I came face to face with the object of my obsession.

He stood outside, waiting for me. The red awning hung above him, casting him in shadows. The sight of him stopped me in my tracks. His tall form leaned against the brick wall, his foot propped up behind him. Even without me sitting on my ass beneath him, he would tower over me. The image of me on my knees in front of him popped into my head.

His well-fitted suit accented his broad shoulders, strong but not bulky, agile, and delicious. I couldn't see his soft green eyes from here, but I imagined I could. He checked his watch. He was so perfect, something painful twisted in my chest. His sculpted features appeared smoky and mysterious, lit up by the street lamps and the failing sun. His beauty was too much, leaving me with the distinct impression I could touch it for some time but never keep it.

I forced myself to walk toward him. The last thing I wanted to do was keep him waiting. I wanted to serve him. The thought frightened me, but I couldn't deny the truth. I stood thirty feet away when he noticed me. First, surprise lit his features, but as he gazed at me, low burning heat took its place. A touch of mischief flirted with me, and I hoped more than anything he would reveal the naughty mysteries he kept. My neck and cheeks flooded with color.

I stopped in front of him, and his face settled into a polite expression. "Claire." My name on his lips did something to my blood, electrified my pulse in a way that couldn't be compatible with life. That's why I couldn't breathe. I would die right here at his feet.

He grabbed my hand before my body swayed and his touch anchored me. "You look amazing." The words sounded polite, but beneath them lay a deep dark well of promise. I wanted to splash around, become trapped where only he could pull me back up. He kissed the hand he held, and my skin sizzled like a sunburn without pain.

"Thank you." I leaned in to him as his lips brushed my cheek in greeting. The smell of him overwhelmed me, a subtle hint of expensive cologne and clean masculine divinity. I put my arms around him, completely senseless from the effect he had on me.

At the last possible second, I regained my composure and pretended I was giving him a friendly hug. He hugged me back, the tip of his nose skimmed my neck, and a low chuckle vibrated within his chest. He must have recognized the wild lust raging in my eyes. His arms held me for a long moment, before stepping back and taking my hand in his.

Chapter Ten

He opened the door, revealing a warm, intimate dining room. The whole place glowed dimly in the candlelight. The ones on the wall were electric, but each table held a real dancing flame. Soft music tinkled in the background as a throaty female voice sang about love. The beautiful blonde hostess recognized him immediately, "Mr. Harris, right this way." A warm smile spread across her face, and a pang of jealousy twisted in my gut. How well did she know him?

She showed us to the back of the restaurant, swaying her full hips a little more than was strictly necessary. The round booth sat in a private corner, intimate and romantic. Smooth and supple leather covered the bench, and I appreciated the texture of it as I sat down. The hostess handed us menus constructed of similar material.

I read over the descriptions of the classic French cuisine. They boasted farm-fresh, local ingredients. Before any words were exchanged, a bottle of red wine arrived at the table with two glasses. The young man who brought them over had a baby face and a nervous air. I got the distinct impression he was not our server. He poured the wine and waited for

Mason to take a sip. "It's fine, thank you." He told him without tasting it. The boy nodded and walked away.

My brow arched. "Come here often?"

"I do, I'm fond of the atmosphere." A husky note thickened his voice and made me inch closer to him.

The walls were a deep rusty color, with large photographs of food and French landscapes. The dim light made the table more private, and I thought of all the stolen kisses and touches that must have happened here. "The atmosphere is rather romantic. I can see why you come here often." The suggestion sounded obvious, and he arched his own brow in response.

"I don't come here on dates if that's what you're implying." His long fingers wrapped around the stem of his wine glass, and a brief brush of jealousy went through me as he tipped it to his full lips. What I would give to be that glass.

My lips parted as I took in shallow breaths. "Who would you bring here if not dates?" I forced myself to smile, trying to hide the blatant lust lighting me up. His soft green eyes met mine and my thighs pressed together to quell the heat rising between them. All the naughty things he said to me and the pictures we exchanged charged our surroundings.

"No one." His words hung in the air, clinging to the static sparking between us.

I looked down at my hands, trying to gather my thoughts. It was too easy to become befuddled staring into his eyes, watching the way he scratched his thumb against the five o'clock shadow on his jaw. I liked how he was confident enough to sit and eat alone in a place he enjoyed. Him sharing this with me made me feel special. "You really come here to eat alone?" I wanted to be someone he shared things with.

"I do." He sipped his wine, and my mouth went dry as I stared at his lips. I took a long sip from my glass, hoping to douse the flames, but didn't I know alcohol was flammable? The fire within me didn't need any help to rage out of control.

"Do you try to be mysterious or does it come naturally to you?" I pulled my bottom lip between my teeth.

His lips quirked up in a small smile as his gaze rested on the movement. "A little of both. Does it bother you?"

"I'm not sure yet." I took a long sip of wine.

His brow furrowed as he thought of something unpleasant. "Do you have a car?"

"No."

"Why didn't you ask me to pick you up?" His voice was too smooth, but a threat simmered beneath it.

I didn't answer him immediately, toying with the cloth napkin I'd placed in my lap, trying to think of an adequate response. The truth was, I was wary after my date with Tyler, and I wanted a bit more time to feel him out before giving him my address. It felt silly sitting beneath his heavy gaze. "Maybe, I'll let you drive me home." The suggestive smile I gave him didn't distract him like I'd hoped.

"Maybe I'll drive you home," he teased lightly, not fooled by my attempt at deflection for a second.

There wasn't much I could get past him. He was so meticulously put together, so button-down, and gorgeous. His shirt was crisp and white, the red tie at his neck held a touch of gruesome suggestion. He controlled everything around him, and I could easily imagine how I would become one of those things.

I saw it in the annoyance on his face when we first met, and the enjoyment he'd gotten out of my embarrassment the time after that. The way he stared me down as he played with his wine glass like he knew I was the next fragile thing he'd hold in his hands further evidenced that belief.

"Have a look at your menu." The command gave further credence to everything I was thinking.

I giggled softly to myself. He arched his brow and I shook my head gently. His bossing me around amused me, infuriated me, and made me wet. I picked up the menu and started reading, unable to help the grin on my face. The heat of his eyes touched my skin, but I ignored him. He wanted me to read, and that's what I'd do.

The food sounded lovely, but there were no prices listed. Nervousness replaced the hunger in my stomach as I thought of how to handle this tactfully. Pasta was likely the cheapest option, but they didn't have any. I didn't want to spend his money, not because I feared I'd owe him, but because I could sense how freely he would give it. "Order whatever you'd like." The absent-minded tone was put on. He still scrutinized my expressions intently enough to know exactly what I was worrying about.

Our waitress appeared, all gorgeous and leggy. She had a delicate French accent and warm hazel eyes. Her golden blonde hair tumbled down her back, the ponytail barely able to control the silken tresses. The lust in her eyes as she regarded Mason was obvious, but she was perfectly polite other than the blush on her cheeks.

I couldn't help but think of how attractive they would look together, and I pushed down the jealousy twisting in my stomach. He hardly glanced at her more than politeness demanded, and I knew it wasn't either of them that made me feel that way. It was my sense of inadequacy. What could a man like Mason see in someone like me?

"Would you like an appetizer?" His warm voice left the tiny thong I wore drenched.

I swallowed before I told him, "No, thank you."

"A baked brie to start, Adelie, and I'll have the steak frites, medium rare." He gave her a friendly smile and her blush spread to her neck and collarbones.

"I'll have the same." He smiled like he was pleased with me for following his example. Adelie left us alone again; the approval in his gaze did something to me that I'd rather she didn't see. I slid closer to him, needing to be near him. His strong thigh touched my own, and the warmth threatened to burn me alive. The confident shine in his eye told me he understood my actions better than I did.

My eyes locked on his lips, and his firm hand lifted to stroke my cheek with his rough fingertips. Faint scars decorated the back of his knuckles as if he'd been in a few fights, and it only made him more dangerous, more desirable. A thin scar split his perfect eyebrow, and I wondered how he acquired it.

My head tilted to the side, relishing his skin on mine. His full lips were so close now I only needed to lean forward an inch and they would touch my own. Adelie came back with our salads. I jumped away from him like I'd been under some powerful spell and broken loose.

He laughed softly at my reaction and thanked her. I muttered a thank you a moment too late. My cheeks flamed with embarrassment. The appreciative way he eyed me made my insides molten and once again I thought something had to be seriously wrong with me. Being embarrassed in front of him burned in my stomach and drenched my thighs. "Where were we?" He teased as he patted the bench beside him.

"I'll stay over here." I took a sip of my wine to emphasize my point. Drinking more was a mistake. My hammering pulse and absent inhibitions should have stopped me, but they only egged me on. I laid my hands on the table. This was too intense, too fast. We should be having light first-date conversations. Instead, every word, each action, felt like blood magic. That had to be why he floated through my veins.

He flipped my hand over, holding it in his and tracing patterns in my wrist with the other. A shiver ran up my spine. "Why won't you sit by me?"

Goosebumps broke out on my skin. "I lack control when I'm near you."

"Is that something important to you? Being in control." His fingers moved to the crease in my elbow and back down.

"Sometimes."

"But not always?" A hint of mischief played in his voice, suggesting he was eager to test the limits of my control.

"No, not always." I laid my hand against the one moving over my skin, stopping his progress. "Sometimes the moment can be deliciously out of my control."

He pulled his hands back and sipped his wine, then tilted it toward me. "Steak was an excellent choice for this."

"I should hope so, Mr. Harris," I answered him dryly.

"Mason will do for you." He swirled his wine in his glass with an enigmatic expression. "How was your first day? I was thinking of you rifling through the books, eager to please."

Adelie dropped off our brie, and we ate it off little crostini—it was delicious. "It was great, actually. I was busy all day, and a bit terrified, but I think I did well. There's a lot more to learn, but I do love being around books and I'm quite eager to please." I batted my lashes at him innocently. My nose scrunched up when I remembered the conversation I had with Eileen. "I had an odd interaction with the old librarian, and my staff hate me, but I'll live. There might be something a little weird about my boss too."

"Don't poke your adorable nose into places it doesn't belong." The gravity in his voice surprised me.

"What do you mean by that?" The normal conversation broke some of the spell I was under. I was growing accustomed to him trying to tell me what to do, but this seemed pointed.

"I mean, do your job, and if something strikes you as odd, avoid it rather than trying to turn over stones until you stumble into more trouble than you're prepared for." My eyes traced his full lips, and I had to remind myself to not get distracted by his over-the-top sex appeal.

"Why would you assume that's what I'd do?"

He scratched his thumb along the five o'clock shadow beneath his lip. "You're a thrill-seeker, and you love learning new things. A mystery, real or imagined, would certainly get you into trouble."

"Uh, I am the opposite of a thrill-seeker." I argued. "I'm nervous and awkward, and I rarely move outside my comfort zone."

He laughed, a deep rumbling sound. "But when you do, you leap out of it and straight into the unknown." I considered what he said. He could be right. I stayed in my box until the moment I decided not to.

"How would you know what I would do, or even if there is trouble for me to uncover?"

"You've shown me. I pay attention. And, as far as the library goes, they deal directly with the City Council and everyone knows politicians are usually corrupt. Just mind your business and keep yourself safe."

"Okay." I popped another brie-covered crostini into my mouth.

"Okay?" He lifted his eyebrow at me, torn between distrusting my quick acquiescence and enjoying my compliance.

"Mm," I nodded into my glass of wine.

"You're quite an unusual creature, aren't you?" I tried, but couldn't guess at his meaning.

"So I've heard." Our food arrived and interrupted my train of thought.

"You'll be careful." There was no question, only a command.

"Hm?" I asked through a delicious bite of steak.

"At work, and anywhere you go, be careful." The intensity in his gaze surprised me, as if for the first time I got a peek beneath his carefully cultivated exterior.

"I'll be careful." I promised, breaking the intense eye contact and returning to my food. We didn't speak for a while, eating and enjoying each other's company. The silence between us was comfortable, companionable, like two people who knew each other well enough not to need to fill every moment with inane chatter. Images of what he might do to me filled my mind and the space between us.

"What are you thinking about, Claire?" His words interrupted my fantasy and fueled it.

"The truth?" My teeth sank into my bottom lip.

"Always." The intensity of that single word was too much to bear.

"I was thinking about your hands on my body and your lips..." I trailed off, unable to finish.

"Your pretty cheeks are so red. Is it that embarrassing to want me?" The false innocence in his tone made me smile.

"It's only embarrassing because of how desperate it makes me, Mason." His fist tightened on the tablecloth and his eyes closed for the briefest moment. I'd bet my next paycheck his pants were unbearably tight. I took a bite of my steak, toying with my fork against my lips. That tiny reaction made me feel like a goddess.

We spent the rest of our dinner talking about nothing particularly important, but in a way that felt like we were cracking the secrets of the universe. He told me so little about himself, though I could figure a few things out for myself. For one, he had a dry sense of humor that tickled me. He came from money, and he had a white-collar career.

He wouldn't talk about his work, but I was sure that he was in charge there too. Although I wanted him to tell me more about himself, the fact he didn't left me feeling like he was a ball of yarn I needed to unravel. If I was a twisted, knotted mess, he was a carefully tightened reel of secrets and control.

I told him about my job at City Hall and the way it built me up and crushed me back down. He laughed often but assured me it wasn't at me. "You just have a way of saying things; you make not particularly funny things sound hilarious." He explained between chortles.

"I know you're full of crap." I quipped back.

We shared a molten lava cake for dessert. Consuming the hot and sweet confection with him felt like something sinful passed between us. He stared into my eyes as I fiddled with my tongue and the spoon. It left my insides as liquid as the cake.

He paid the check and led me out of the restaurant with his hand on the small of my back. "Would you like a ride home?" His voice coming from behind me made my pussy clench. I stopped mid-step. He bumped into me and his cock pressed against my ass. Without thinking, I ground myself into him, enjoying the erection already forming.

"Let's go." His harshly spoken words only made me softer for him. He walked me straight to a sleek black BMW and opened the door. I gave him my address, and he pulled out smoothly into traffic. He didn't turn the radio on, but the silence was far more interesting.

"You don't like music?"

He kept his eyes on the road but flashed me a smile. "It's distracting." Controlled—the word didn't do him justice. We pulled up outside my place moments later. If you had a car, it wasn't far. He walked around to my side, opening the door, and taking my hand to pull me out. I knew that perfect gentleman thing had to be an act. Something dark and dangerous hid beneath that suit and mannered upbringing.

My feet landed on the sidewalk, but somehow, I didn't quite have my footing. I drank more wine than I realized and lightheadedness swam behind my eyes. I leaned against his shiny car and stared up at him. My bottom lip popped out in a little pout, and I wrapped my arms around his neck.

A sexy sound ripped from his throat as he tangled his fists in my hair and pulled my mouth to his. He stepped off the sidewalk, pushing me back harder against his car, and pinned me with his hips. His erection pressed into my soft stomach as his tongue slid between my lips, tasting me briefly before conquering my mouth. Lightning shot through me and I moaned into his mouth. He used the leverage on my hair to tip my head back and invade me deeper.

He calmed as he kissed me. The violence fell out of his movements. His hands drifted from my hair, down my body, over the swells of my hips, and skated against my hard nipples. I whimpered as his kiss went soft and gentle, but still deep and possessive. He lost control for a moment, but he took it back quickly enough. His hands gripped my ass, appreciating the feel. "Harder." I whimpered. He obliged me, and his lips fell to my neck, kissing and sucking the sensitive skin. "Please."

"Please, what?" he asked against my skin.

"Fuck me." I whispered.

His teeth pressed into my soft flesh, and I gasped. "Not tonight, baby." His voice left no room for argument. The look on my face must have been something because he laughed outright. "Don't be upset, sexy. What can I say? The idea of you squirming and desperate for me is too delicious to pass up." His lips found my ear, his teeth grazed the lobe. "I want you crazy, wishing I was fucking you." He pressed his lips softly to mine, once, twice, a third time.

He walked me to my door. I twisted the key in the lock, but before I could open it, he spun me around and pressed me against the door. His hands fisted in my hair so tightly I couldn't move. He was inescapable and I was more than happy to be trapped. "Next time I see you, I'll make you forget everyone who's touched you before me." He kissed me roughly, his tongue sweeping every thought out of my head. "I want to see you soon. I'll text you."

He released me and walked down the hall. "Thanks, Mason, I had a wonderful time." I called after him. I stayed in the hallway for a few minutes trying to figure out how to operate my body after he performed a factory reset on it. The haze cleared and my skin itched and pricked nervously, like someone was watching me. I looked around, not finding anyone.

I double checked that Mason shut the front door. He did. I let myself into my apartment, locking the knob, the deadbolt, and the chain. *You're being silly.* I went to my bed and climbed in, quickly forgetting the feeling of watching eyes touching my skin.

Chapter Eleven

The first two weeks at the library were so hectic, I hardly remembered them. Even with the exhaustion, I was happy. Successfully handling my duties gave me a sense of competence and being needed did wonders for my self-esteem. Gavin was pleased enough with me to extend the trial to the full month we discussed, and I had high hopes for the following six months after that.

I didn't have a single moment to spend with Mason those first two weeks. My work started when I woke and didn't end until I slept. Even then, thoughts of the library slipped into my dreams, leaving no room for anything else but the burning desire simmering in the back of my mind. He texted me a few times to check in on me, and each time my heart raced in my chest.

The first day of my one-month trial, Emma was my volunteer. Most of the staff still wouldn't meet my eye, but Emma was slowly coming around. I wondered if Eileen said something to her about me when she picked up her belongings. Emma walked through the door, smiled at me, and went to work putting away the returns. "Emma?" I called her over, sounding unsure.

"Yeah, Claire?" She pulled her head out of the deep return bin.

"You're a journalism major, right?" I tried to shove the nervousness out of my voice. I was her boss and offering her an olive branch shouldn't intimidate me.

Her eyebrow popped up in question, "Yeah, how did you know that?"

"Eileen left me some notes and things when she came by."

"Oh." She looked around, searching for a way out of the conversation.

"I'm working on some acquisitions, and we're lacking in journalistic photo books, world news kind of stuff." Her face lit up like she finally found some interest in what I said to her.

"I know some great ones,"

I gave her a warm smile, "I hoped you'd say that because I could use some help."

"Now?" Genuine enthusiasm replaced the hesitancy she usually had with me.

"After you finish the returns, meet me at the circulation desk."

"Awesome, I would love to!" I smiled to myself, satisfied with my deft handling. I went back to circulation and worked on acquisitions for other genres. My favorite part of this job was choosing new books to stock, and I quickly lost track of time as I perused all the stories I wanted to share with the community. A text came across my phone. I was too distracted reading the synopsis of a contemporary novel, and I waited a few minutes to open it.

Look up.

My brow furrowed, but I did as he said, and my eyes caught his green ones sitting directly ahead of me, watching from a wingback chair near the magazine racks. I smiled at him, as a familiar warmth settled between my thighs. He lifted an imperious finger and gestured for me to come to him, and like the slave my body was, I got up and made my way across the room.

He watched me, a predator observing his prey, a king lording over me from his throne in *my* library. We still did nothing more than kiss and yet I responded to him as if he ravaged every inch of me. I stood in front of him, staring. "Hi,"

"Hi, Claire. You look lovely today." His fingers absently tapped against his strong thighs.

Heat crept up my neck and into my cheeks. "What are you doing here?"

"Aren't you pleased to see me?" He feigned hurt, knowing full well how happy he made me.

I pulled my bottom lip between my teeth to quell the sensations bubbling within me. "I'm thrilled you're here. Can I give you a tour?" I didn't understand the amusement on his face, but he stood and took my hand. I showed him around and that entertainment never left his expression. "Would you like to see my office?"

"Sure,"

I opened the door and led him inside, "What's so funny? That little smirk has been on your face the entire time."

"I know the library well, Claire. We met here if you remember."

The painful blush I wasn't accustomed to until I met Mason, flooded me. "Oh, yeah, you haven't seen my office though, right?" His smile grew wider. "You've seen my office too? Great." I slapped my hands against my thighs and his eyes followed the movement.

"Never with you in it." He walked toward me until he had me backed up against my desk. The heat from his body seeped through the thin fabric of my top. His nearness intoxicated me. He leaned in close enough to whisper in my ear, but still didn't touch me, "It's a much more interesting place with you here." I let out a whimper as he pressed his lips to the hollow beneath my ear. "It's been quite a while since our date. Are you trying to get rid of me?" The confidence in his voice told me he knew better.

I shook my head and made a little moan of disagreement. "That's good because I have thought of nothing but you." His strong, scarred hands lifted, caressing my face. He hovered his lips over mine for a moment before he pressed the lightest kiss on my open mouth. "Let me take you to lunch."

"Fuck me, right here." I countered, not believing the words that left my lips. He was correct about me and my thrill-seeking. The longer I mulled it over, the more sense he made. Him knowing me so well turned me into a puddle, and the way he looked at me didn't hurt.

Heat flared in his green eyes, and a small spasm crossed his features. I would bet anything he was hard, and I wanted to reach out and find out so badly I thought the unrequited urge might kill me. His lips returned to my ear, "Once I've had my way with you, I'll be more than happy to fuck you here whenever you want, but I have a lot of ideas for our first time together, and they don't involve a quickie bent over your desk." His teeth nipped the tender skin beneath my ear in admonishment.

Before I realized what he was doing, he turned me around and pressed his front to my back. His erection pushed up against me and his hands ran over my stomach, one down toward the hem of my skirt and the other up to my breasts. He stopped right before he reached either, his fingers skimming back and forth. "Touch me," I begged.

His teeth and tongue set to work on my ear as he growled, "With pleasure." With easy dexterity, he slid one hand up my skirt while opening the buttons on my blouse with the other, popping my breast out of the cup and into his rough hand. He massaged the swell before pulling my nipple between his fingers. The hand skating against my thighs moved my panties aside, spreading me open and finding my clit effortlessly. His lips travelled down to my neck, leaving wet kisses and bites. "You're so fucking wet." His cock grew painfully hard against my ass.

"Please, fuck me!" My voice sounded unrecognizable.

"No, baby." He worked my clit and my nipple in rhythm with one another. He dipped his finger down and slipped it inside of me. "You're so tight, shit," he hissed. I couldn't respond as he pumped his finger into me with practiced strokes, hitting my G-spot with every move. His palm rubbed against my clit. I was an inch from orgasming and making a sloppy mess all over his hand, but right as I reached that precipice, Mason stopped.

I whimpered wordlessly, begging him to continue, but he turned me around and did up my buttons. He pressed one more kiss to my lips. "Come on, Claire, we have a reservation." I followed him, too stunned to do anything else. I stared at his well-tailored suit and broad shoulders. He lifted his hand to his mouth and a crazy part of me thought he tasted my juices off his fingers. I was losing my mind. He couldn't want me that much.

He took me to a sweet little café with outdoor seating at the park a few blocks from the library.

The metal chairs were the type to leave lattice marks on bare skin. The day was warm, but comfortable, and we sat outside enjoying the scenery and the people passing by.

Couples strolled hand in hand, people walked their dogs; all very calm and picturesque, especially compared to the need burning in every part of me. The playground sat on the other side of the soccer field, but we still heard the yelling and laughter of the playing children.

He left me to my thoughts as he picked our food. It was a mistake to let him take control that way, but I was not inclined to stop him. My soaked underwear stuck to my skin, and I had no time to run home. I would need to keep an extra pair in my purse if we were going to keep seeing each other. He interrupted my musing with a coffee and croissants, "These are wonderful. I hope you like them."

"How Parisian," I pulled the latte to my lips, savoring the nutty flavor.

"Have you ever been?"

The wind kicked up, blowing my hair around my face, "No, I've never been anywhere."

He silently appraised me, "We can change that."

I choked on a sip of my coffee, "You're not serious."

He just smiled at me with clear amusement, hinting he would show me anything he wanted. "Why do you know the library so well?" I managed to ask once the hot liquid cleared from my airways.

"I've had some business there in the past, and I'm fond of the place." He dipped his finger into his mouth, using his teeth to scrape some crumbs off his fingertip. My tongue darted out, wishing to taste him.

A little bird hopped across the ground in front of us. "You never told me why you were looking for that old bird book or what you do for a living."

"No, I didn't." His green eyes held me, waiting for me to back down. I wondered how often this man got exactly what he wanted out of people.

I waited a moment, letting the silence settle between us, "Are you going to tell me?"

He stared into my eyes, calculating. "I'm a lawyer."

I choked on my latte again, "So, that's why you're so proficient at getting what you want,"

He rolled his eyes at me in an agreeable manner before continuing, "When I was a kid, my mom used to teach me about birds," he shrugged his shoulders like the admission wasn't a big deal, but his expression told a different story, "She whistled a lot when she was happy. She'd sing their songs, and they even sang back."

"Your mom sounds like Snow White," I teased, as I reached out and touched the back of his hand.

"I saw her that way," his gaze travelled off, maybe after the birds that took flight, "She had this scientific reference about birds. She would show me their pictures and whistle their songs for me..."

"Why can't you get it from her?" My voice was soft and careful; I sensed the answer wasn't a happy one.

"My mom's dead, Claire, and her things... Well, I can't get them." A faint touch of anger brushed his features, but more than anything, he looked vulnerable.

"How old were you?"

"Fourteen."

"How did she die?" I gulped down the nerves in my throat.

"A car accident..."

I thought about it for a moment. The way he said it, was like he wasn't sure. I wanted to push him further, but I held back, knowing he wouldn't give me any more right now. Even like this, he exercised control. He showed no signs of open sadness. Even the timbre of his voice remained perfectly level, but something deep in those green eyes revealed his pain.

"I'm sorry." I lightly dragged my fingers over the back of his hand.

"Don't be. Never apologize for things that aren't your fault." The command in his tone annoyed me and warmed me at the same time. I wanted to ask him for more specifics about what happened, to hold him even, but I did neither. The steady discipline in his eyes when he chastised me about my unnecessary apology made heat flame through me followed by a trickle of guilt over my ridiculous reaction. *Jesus, Claire. He just told you his mom died*.

"You must have parents,"

I nearly chuckled at the obvious attempt at deflection. "I didn't hatch out of an egg, no." A touch of humor replaced the pain hiding in his eyes. He just stared, waiting for me to go on, "There isn't much to tell. I never met my dad. Well, not since I was a baby, and I don't remember him. My mom and I aren't close, and I have no siblings as far as I can tell. Although, my father may have had more children but I wouldn't know."

"Why aren't you and your mom close?" he cupped my hands in his.

"We're very different people." The practiced line fell easily from my lips, but he clearly didn't buy it. He didn't ask me anymore, and neither did I ask him. We both needed our secrets. He took me back to the library, walked me to the door, and gifted me one brief kiss. He asked if he could see me that night, and when he saw the stress on my face, he told me later in the week would be fine.

I spent the entire next day distracted by the idea he might show up again and have his wicked way with me in my office, or take me to lunch and tell me more about himself while I got to drink him in and grow more enchanted. When the day ended and I walked back to my apartment, the sadness plaguing me made no sense. I was into him. I wanted him in inexplicable ways, but the aching in my chest seemed like an inappropriate response.

I sat down at my desk and dove into the massive amount of work that still needed doing. My hand sat cramped and useless at my side as I took in the darkened sky outside of my apartment. I didn't even notice the sun setting. My phone buzzed with an incoming text, and my heart leaped into my throat.

Mason: Boss Lady, do you think you'll have any time for this, this week?

The picture of his erection attached to the message had my pussy quaking in hollow misery. I closed my eyes and bit my lip as the delicious tightening pulsed through me. I didn't have time. The pile of paperwork I took home would take up most of my nights this week, but the ache in my chest told me my priorities were completely screwed up, and I needed to make space for him too.

I stared at the picture for far too long. His hand was wrapped firmly around his impressive cock. The scars that marred his knuckles added depth that made me wonder how a lawyer scarred his fists. Imagining him stroking himself left me desperate and needy. The board could double my salary and it wouldn't be enough to make me focus on the work I needed to do. I was just a woman, and he was the pinnacle of everything I desired. I wrenched myself out of my daydream, needing to answer him and work out some of this tension or I really might lose my job.

Claire: Things are going well at work. This Friday night would be perfect for me.

I laughed at my too casual response to his picture.

Mason: Friday works for me, don't tease me.

I imagined what his face looked like. I doubted he sent pictures of his dick often, but certainly women didn't ignore them when he did. The thought that he waited for my response, my judgment, made me feel powerful. Part of me wanted to chase the sensation, the other decided it was time to put him out of his misery. I pulled up my skirt and shifted my panties to the side. I took a picture of my pussy spread open with a suggestive finger pressed to my clit.

Claire: Only with this, on Friday night.

His response came instantaneously.

Mason: You're too sexy for your own good. Now, tell me if you liked the picture.

The bubbling warmth in my chest burst out in a fit of giggles, but absolutely nothing was funny.

Claire: Correction, I'm too sexy for your good. You first.

Mason: It would be impossible for you to be too sexy for my good. Of course I like the hottest pussy I've ever seen, and don't get me started on the memory of you wrapped around my fingers.

I couldn't help the stupid smile spreading across my cheeks, or the wayward fingers playing with the hottest pussy he'd ever seen. He probably lied to me, but the flattery lifted my spirits anyway.

Claire: Thank you, Mason. I can't lie, that cock is incredible, and don't get me started on the feel of you pressed against my ass.

Mason: I'm glad you like it. Sleep tight, Claire.

My fingers kept up their steady rhythm on my clit, but it was so much more satisfying when he knew.

Claire: Good Night, Mason. I'm making myself cum thinking of you.

I slipped two of my fingers into myself and worked my G-spot and clit. The way he pressed me against my door and kissed me that first night, the way he held me against my desk and brought me to the peak of pleasure, danced behind my eyelids. It was too easy to imagine him fucking me in various positions, holding me down, tying me up. My need for him and my desperation to please him were more animal than human.

I imagined him holding me against a wall. His muscles rippled as his cock slammed relentlessly into me. His teeth bit into the soft skin of my neck, possessive and rough. I tried to keep quiet while I masturbated, but this time I had no chance. I cried out as my orgasm racked me. God, if the simple thought of him gave me this much pleasure, I wasn't sure I could take it when I got to have him. *Thud,*

Thud, Thud. My downstairs neighbor whacked a broom into his ceiling letting me know how unimpressed he was with my theatrics. I giggled to myself, feeling only a little embarrassed.

After the chemicals from the orgasm wore off, an empty sense of doubt filled me. It wasn't entirely unusual for me to feel low after reaching an incredible high. Sam used to tell me how disappointing it was for him that I would get sad after sex like he let me down and I blamed him for it. It aggravated the situation that I didn't always have that reaction. So, when I did it was especially damaging to his ego. *How could it not be about me, Claire?* his angry words echoed through my mind.

Affection usually made me feel better, but I learned to hide those feelings when they struck, and never asked to be comforted. *If you enjoyed having sex with me, why would I need to comfort you?* The doubts Sam planted in me were deeply rooted. I wanted to talk to Mason, and I knew he would take my call, but we were not established. I couldn't put all this baggage on him. It wasn't his job to care for me.

I typed Mason Harris into a search engine, just needing to see his face. None of the pictures he sent me had the part I needed most. Tons of results came up. None of them were my Mason, and I scoffed at myself for thinking of him as mine. I included our city in the parameters, and still, he didn't appear. *Did he give me a fake name?*

Alarm bells rang loudly against my skull. What if he was married or in a committed relationship? There weren't many good reasons I could think of to give someone a fake name. I flipped through about fifty results, realizing the name was more popular than I thought. I gave up and went to bed, trying to convince myself it would be easier to find him in the morning. The sense of dread settled into my stomach, finding an easy, comfortable home.

Chapter Twelve

The next morning, I sat at the circulation desk, going through my tasks for the day. I picked at a bagel, forcing myself to eat since my stomach was already full of knots. I tried to fill in some forms, but thoughts of Mason had me so distracted I pushed straight through the paper I was writing on and into the page below, soaking the bundle of papers and my desk in blue ink.

I groaned in irritation as I tossed the broken pen and sheets into the trash and plucked some wet wipes out of the drawer. I used a wad of them and still wound up with bright blue hands. *Fuck's sake*, I muttered to myself as I pulled out fresh copies of the needed forms and started scribbling on them.

"Hey, Claire. Are you okay?" Emma's quiet voice made me jump.

My heart pounded deafening blood through my ears as I tried to catch my breath. "Yeah, I'm okay," I surreptitiously clicked out of the browser, hoping she wasn't looking over my shoulder.

Emma and I were getting along much better since she helped me with the photobooks two days earlier. After Mason dropped me off, we spent the rest of the afternoon chatting, and we had more than a few things in common. She apologized for her standoffish behavior, and I was all too happy to accept. We shared a sense of humor, and she was nice in a way that didn't feel phony. Dare I say I liked her, but the sleuthing I planned to do was not something I wanted to share with her.

My search for Mason yielded few results thus far, and the mystery had me so thoroughly distracted I never would have noticed her if she didn't get my attention first. "Why do you ask?"

I twisted a wipe around each of my fingers, trying to clean away the rest of the vibrant blue. She gave me an incredulous look and gestured toward my hands, "Is this about the guy who visited you the other day?" she smiled at me knowingly, as she fanned herself with a stack of flyers sitting askew on the counter.

She straightened them and placed them back down, waiting for me to answer. I learned that Emma was a very straightforward person, able to say whatever she thought with ease. The only time I shared this ability was with Mason, but I quite enjoyed her directness when it didn't make me uncomfortable.

My cheeks grew hotter at her suggestion. "No, why would it be?" I never was a great liar, and the innocent act didn't suit me.

She tapped her fingers rhythmically against the desk, doing a much better job of looking innocent. "Oh, I don't know. You seem so *distracted*, and he seems awfully distracting."

I laughed a bit, "Yeah, he certainly is." I tossed out the rest of the wipes, realizing I had no chance of wiping all the ink away. "Everything is mostly okay."

"Mostly?" she hedged.

"He's so mysterious, and there is so much I don't know about him. I *should* ask, but when I'm with him, I tend to forget my name," I scratched at my neck, not sure if I should share so much with her.

"Mm, mysterious is *hot*." she shrugged, but the dazed look on her face told me she was remembering her own sexy mystery man.

"Yeah, it is..." My voice trailed off as I looked into the distance.

"But?"

"But there comes a point where the secrecy is too much. I've been talking to him for a while and there are too many things I'm unsure of. There has to be a reason, and the options..."

"The options are whatever he's hiding is bad enough, you'll mind, or he has a reason he doesn't want *you* to know," she finished for me.

"Exactly." I rested my chin between my hands, staring down at the mountains of work I needed to do today.

"Can I do anything to help?" The genuine concern in her voice warmed my heart, but I would not be revealing how little I knew about him.

"Thanks, Emma, but I think the only person who can help is Mr. Mysterious himself."

"Okay, well, if you want to share anything else about Mr. Mysterious, I'm all ears." I shook my head gently, and she sighed, "Oh, I almost forgot, I found this note in the return bin, stuck in Lolita of all things." She rolled her eyes as she reached into her back pocket, pulling out a crumpled piece of paper. "They probably didn't mean to leave it in there, but it's creepy enough that I figured I should give it to you just in case." She handed the note to me with a slight shiver.

"Thanks, Emma. You can take your ten if you like." I flipped it over, fingering the torn edges left behind from the spiral notebook.

"Sure."

She turned around and headed to the little break room near the children's section. The entire ordeal with Mason left a bitter taste in my mouth, but at least I had a shot at a genuine friendship with Emma. I sighed as I opened the note. Scrawled in angry blue ballpoint pen were the words:

"If a violin string could ache, I would be that string."

How long until I snap?

The quote coming from the book Emma found the note in didn't surprise me, but the angsty, almost violent addition to it unsettled me deeply. Emma was right. This was creepy, but nothing suggested the person meant to leave it tucked in the pages. I thought about the story as I turned the sheet over in my hands; a depraved, tragically misconstrued sense of love that started with abuse and ended in death. I shivered as I imagined the individual who committed these words to paper.

I scanned the barcode to check the book back in, surprised to find it was returned months ago, and not checked out since. Before that, there was a steady stream of borrowings and returns. The person who'd taken it must have stolen it and kept it for a while. I walked to the section where we stored classic fiction, cursing the dim lighting and the possibility of anyone standing behind the shelves to watch you. I shivered at the thought, why did it feel like someone was?

The rest of the morning went by quickly. I had a lot of calls to make and a few new volunteers to interview. One of them was a library science major named Kiana. She was smart and sweet, and while I happily offered her the position, I hoped she had better luck in her career path than I did. Her availability met the openings I had; where I assumed I needed several people, I only needed her.

At lunch, I spent some time flipping through listings for local Masons which came up blank again. I picked up the library phone and called information, asking for Mason Harris locally.

"Are you looking for a professional listing or personal?" The woman on the other end asked.

"Either," I answered, wondering what business I missed in my search.

"I have one of each. Would you like me to connect you with a specific one?"

"Professional, please."

The phone rang twice before someone picked up, "Harris Florals"

"Can I speak with Mason Harris?"

"Sorry, Ma'am, he's retired."

I called information again, cursing myself for not writing down the other number.

An old man answered expectantly, "Jim, is that you?"

"No, sir. My name is Claire. Do you have a son named Mason?"

I spoke sweetly, repeating myself when he barked, "Can't hear you, girly," I was unsurprised when he continued, "Ain't got no kids, and don't be calling here, I don't have a call waiting and I need to talk to Jim." I hung the phone up, shaking my head at myself for even thinking a landline could be the right person.

When Emma came back from her break, I set her up with a few tasks I would normally be responsible for and hit the computer hard. She raised an eyebrow at me but didn't complain. I stayed at circulation, knowing if I went to my office I would wind up so engrossed in the task I wouldn't do anything else I needed to.

I opened my favorite search engine and widened the parameters to all local Masons; the fact it was also a profession complicated matters further. Far too many existed to make any progress like this, so I narrowed them to any Mason between the ages of twenty-five and thirty-five. Mercifully, that eliminated the tradespeople.

I answered the phone every time it rang as well as a few emails, but I kept flipping through the results, planning to keep my search going as long as I needed to. Emma brought me a turkey sandwich when she went out for lunch, and I shoved the last bite into my mouth when I, finally, found what I searched for. I almost missed him at first. The grainy flip phone quality was the opposite of what I expected, the same with the floppy-haired, sullen teen scowling at the camera.

Excitement rippled through me as I clicked the link to an old social media profile. Sure enough, Mason stared back at me in all of his angsty teenage glory. The name was Mason Mason. I rolled my eyes at his lack of helpfulness both then and now. The page was private except for his pictures.

I clicked through them, marveling at how gorgeous he was. One picture featured him on the lawn of a manicured mansion with spires climbing into the sky like a castle. The iron gate out front didn't show a number or any identifying feature, but the building looked like other mansions I saw in the suburbs surrounding our city. Another was set in the cafeteria of a private school, with a lunch rivaling a five-star restaurant rather than a typical high school slop line. Most of the pictures featured him looking angry and a little stoned.

The phone rang and I let it go longer than I should have, "Circulation, how can I help you?" I spoke into the receiver as I stared into the green eyes I'd become obsessed with. I answered whatever question the person on the other end asked and forgot as soon as I hung up. My mouth fell open as I came across an image of teenage Mason, shirtless and cut, with defined abs and dirty blonde hair hanging in his eyes. I would guess he was eighteen, but his beauty wasn't why I stopped.

The perfect blonde girl wrapped around him like a designer scarf caught my eye, with straight silvery blonde hair spilling down her back. Her legs enveloped him, and he gripped her thighs as they passionately kissed. I couldn't stop staring. They were so pretty together. I needed a few moments to understand the twisting in my gut was jealousy. It was stupid to envy a girl he'd *loved* years ago yet here I was: twenty-six and jealous of an eighteen-year-old.

"You're pathetic," I muttered to myself.

"Oh my god! That's what he looks like under the suit? Fuck me..." Emma's voice behind me made me jump.

"Oh, Emma, um, what do you need?" I blushed furiously as I minimized the browser, but I wouldn't dare close it after all the work I did to locate the info I had yet to read.

She cleared her throat, preoccupied with what she saw, "I wondered why you weren't answering the phones when you told me you'd handle them, but clearly you're *distracted*. Did you find what you're looking for?"

"Not yet." I sighed.

"You have him on the ropes, there's nothing like a research expert to uncover someone's dirty secrets," she winked at me and answered the phone ringing in front of my dazed face. She was correct about one thing: librarians are excellent at research. I did a little more of the work the city paid me for, and Emma moved on to finish another task.

I pulled the browser back up and read the tag on the photo and the caption "When you've got the right girl..." I rolled my eyes as I went to the profile of Rebecca LaMontagne and stopped dead when I realized it was a memorial page.

People still left messages talking about how much they missed her, though they were much less frequent than they once were. Her mother commented regularly saying she still had hope she would come home. My heart ached for her, but after twelve years and an investigation, that didn't seem likely.

Her father left comments talking about how much he missed her, though he didn't harbor any hopes she would return, accepting her death. I wondered if Mason was involved in the search. Had they been together when she went missing? He clearly cared for her, and my heart ached for him as well.

Rebecca's exclusive high school was proudly listed on the top of her page, along with her graduation year. She disappeared shortly after she graduated. I shuddered at the thought. I continued onto their website, shoving aside the borrowed sadness. I still had a mission. Rutherford Preparatory Academy's website was filled with information I didn't need, including the exorbitant cost of attending.

It made sense that Mason went to school at a place like that, but I still couldn't imagine it. The boy in those photos differed greatly from the man I met, but did I truly know anything about him? I found it hard to believe I did, especially considering the lengths I'd gone to uncover his real name. I couldn't deny that what we shared felt authentic. No one could fake chemistry like ours. I moved to their alumni page and easily spotted the class photo for the year she graduated. Sitting in a uniform, looking better than any eighteen-year-old had the right to look, was Mason—Mason Sharp.

Emma came up behind me again, "Boo," but I didn't jump this time.

"You're funny."

She shrugged at the dry tone in my voice, "I like to think so. Mm, I see, you got somewhere finally," she leaned forward and gazed at the picture, "Mason Sharp—why does that name sound familiar?"

"It does, doesn't it?"

"Mm," she nodded, "I wish I could see his expression when he realizes you learned all his dirty secrets. You are seeing him again, aren't you?"

Butterflies filled my stomach at the thought, "Yeah, I'm seeing him again," she squealed as she walked away. I shut the computer down and went to do some actual library work. I was desperate to learn more about him, but I spent enough of the library's time on this and if I didn't get my ass into gear, I would need to stay late to make up for the time lost.

I recruited Emma to help me with a few more of my duties, and once the day ended, I only needed to put in an extra half hour. She stayed with me, chatting happily about the date she was going on that evening.

"Thanks for covering for me today," I told her as we were locking up.

"Nothing like a mystery to keep you awake at night. I didn't mind, but you owe me a favor." She winked as she climbed into her little Honda and drove off. I walked home, turning the name over and over in my head, and still not coming up with anything. The answer floated right on the edge of my mind.

When I sat down at my computer and typed in Mason Sharp, I slapped my palm against my forehead. David Sharp, *of course*. He was a City Council member and investment banker who embezzled an incredible amount of money, most stolen from his clients though they never proved how much nor recovered it.

He was mega rich to start out with, so the theft made no sense, and the entire case was a media sensation. Someone being evil enough to steal millions when they were already incredibly wealthy offended even my mom, and she never cared about anything.

I opened an article titled "No One too Big or too Small to Lose it all." They had a picture of Mason. He looked to be about twenty, standing outside of the courthouse. Controlled anger marred his expression. He cropped his hair short like the day I met him, and he wore an impeccably tailored suit. The hulking men flanking his sides emanated danger.

I flipped through a few more articles, reacquainting myself with the details. I was a teenager when his father went to jail, too distracted by my own problems to pay much attention. It struck me as supremely odd that there were no professional listings for Mason Sharp mixed in with the news stories.

There was another layer to this, and I didn't think I would figure it out without his help. Anger at being lied to filled me, but also shame. I never asked the man's name. Did I have any right to be angry at what I
overheard and assumed? Could I be mad about an arrangement I helped form?

I didn't have an answer, and the potent combination of emotions left me aching and my insides clenching with need. Something was seriously wrong with me, but the uncertainty had me twisted up and breathless, desperate for him. I prayed he had no wife or girlfriend. Despite my moral objections screaming within me, I had no control when it concerned him. I pulled my hands through my hair, untangling the knots, considering the fact my heart wouldn't let him go easily.

I opened my phone and typed out a message.

Claire: Hey, I need some legal advice. Where do you practice?

Mason: What legal advice do you need, Claire? Personal law isn't my specialty, though I could refer you to a colleague. Only you could get into trouble at the library.

Claire: Whoever said I'm in trouble? There are plenty of reasons people need lawyers. What is your specialty?

Mason: I know that, but this is fairly out of the blue, and knowing your tendency to defend yourself ruthlessly, I assumed. Corporate law, but if you're not in trouble, why do you ask?

Claire: I can't find a professional listing for you online, and I wondered why that might be?

Mason: So, you don't need legal advice... Can we talk about it tomorrow?

Claire: Okay...

Mason: I promise I'll explain tomorrow, don't be angry.

Claire: I'm not.

Mason: Oh, no?

Claire: Good night, Mason. I'll see you tomorrow.

Mason: Sleep tight, beautiful girl.

I violently shoved the charger into my phone, wincing when I realized I probably broke another one. The lightning bolt over the battery made me breathe a sigh of relief but the gesture stopped short of easing the tension in my chest. As I closed my eyes, I tried to put myself in Mason's shoes.

He couldn't operate professionally with his father's name after everything the man did. Changing it was sensible, but where did the name Harris come from? *He should have told me.* I insisted to myself, but this entire relationship so far was about mystery and lack of expectation. If he wasn't willing to be honest with me about things, I couldn't fault him.

I thought of the scars on his knuckles, and the one splitting his eyebrow, and I had to wonder, who was Mason really, and did I even care?

Chapter Thirteen

My dreams that night were tumultuous, filled with creeping shadows, green eyes, full lips, secrets, lies, and pain. But when I woke to a bright fresh day, I couldn't deny my newfound optimism; Mason and I would be together tonight and sort this out. It was the only option that made sense, the only possibility that didn't leave me hollow and aching.

I dressed up nicer than necessary, even though I would go home and change before the date. The whole day felt like an event. I waited so long for this, and I'd never been with someone I wanted more than my next breath. Perhaps I should mind that there was so much unknown between us, or that I sat a hair's breadth from falling in love with the man. With everything else I had to consider, I couldn't force myself to care.

I left my apartment early, too energized to sit around. I went to a newly opened coffee shop a block over from the library to kill time. The sleek and modern storefront had glass windows set in a historic red brick building. The cool decor accented the stylish vibe with leather couches and subway-tile lining the walls. Fresh pastries overflowed the case and thousands of dollars' worth of shining espresso machines sat in rows.

The place stood empty except for the barista, who happily designed latte art behind the counter. Her name tag read *Leyla*. She tied her long, sleek, chocolate hair back in a ponytail. Her blue eyes dove deep like the ocean. Her loveliness stunned me, and I needed a minute to remember English.

"Good morning," Her voice sounded patient and sweet, and I finally remembered I should act human.

"Good morning, can I have a cappuccino, please, and what's your favorite pastry?" my gaze flicked down the rows of options. I would be here all day if I had to choose it myself.

Excitement crossed her face as she thought, "Well, if you enjoy sweet, you can't go wrong with the pain au chocolat, but if savory is your thing, the chef is British, and he makes these sausage rolls. Oh my God, they are amazing," her eyes rolled back, and she made a little sound of enjoyment.

"Sounds lovely," I smiled, unable to help myself. Her happiness was contagious.

"Sit, I'll bring everything out to you when it's re-" she stopped speaking, her gaze trained somewhere far off.

"Are you okay?" she didn't answer me right away, and I waved my hand to draw her attention. "Hey, what's going on? You look... scared."

She shook her head, clearing her thoughts, "Yeah, I'm fine. There was a guy staring in the window and he was... intense. I don't know, he was probably looking at the pastries, but it seemed like..."

"Like what?" I coaxed her as I turned to see if I could catch a glimpse of him, but the street was empty except for a couple walking with their young child.

"Like he was watching you," I turned back to Leyla, hoping she was joking even if it would be totally odd and inappropriate. She fiddled with the ends of her ponytail, "Be careful, okay?" her eyes widened with genuine concern, and an uncomfortable feeling curled in my stomach.

"I will," I forced a smile and went to find a seat facing out. The city milled by, and no one stopped to stare at me. After a while, I defrosted. She was overreacting. No one would watch me. I walked to the library even though it was still quite early. I left the lights off as I walked around, not wanting people knocking, hoping I would let them in.

Closing the door to my office, I sat at my desk and opened up my email program. There was one from Gavin telling me that a paid employee gave their notice, with the letter of resignation attached. I rolled my eyes at the fact she went over my head. Most of the employees remained Eileen loyalists, but the trial basis of my employment was not common knowledge. Going to Gavin was a slap on the face, and she knew it.

I groaned as I started working through the schedule, seeing how I could fill this new opening. The days weren't far off from what Emma worked now, and according to the lists Eileen left me, she had more availability. She did a good job, knew the library well, and even though she needed the volunteer work for her degree requirement, she never treated it like a chore.

No one else came to mind for the position. A few of the volunteers would be up for consideration, but they were all retired, and being paid could mess up their retirement. I glanced over my desk, thinking of how to solve my staffing problem, but instead remembered the way Mason pushed me against it and the things his hands did to me.

My nipples hardened in excitement and pressed against the lacy material of my bra. I walked to the door and turned the lock. The place was empty, but I wanted to be sure I wouldn't be interrupted. I undid the buttons on my shirt and pulled my breasts up and over the cups. I clicked a few pictures of myself, showing the desk in front of me, hoping the reminder would make him as hard as it made me wet.

Claire: I can't wait to see you tonight.

His response came quickly. He still lay in bed, wrapped in nothing but a white sheet. I noted he slept with a top sheet and laughed to myself. He was one of those types. Why didn't that surprise me? His perfect pecs and abs glowed in the morning sun, making him appear more god than man. His powerful fist grabbed a shapely bulge covered only by the thin fabric. The impressive outline made me shiver, the suggestion of his cock enough to soak my panties.

Mason: I was already thinking of you. Glad to see you're still looking forward to our date. I wasn't sure after our conversation last night. Let's have dinner at 7. I'll pick you up at your apartment at 6:45, sharp.

I rolled my eyes at the irony, *oh really Mr. Sharp.* That stupid smile he always inspired spread across my face. Once I put myself together again, I checked the time and walked through the library, flipping on lights and starting up the computers.

Claire: Where are we going?

I texted him as I stood beneath the skylight.

Mason: Wouldn't you like to know?

Claire: You get off on surprising me and telling me what to do, don't you?

The image of him getting off popped into my mind, and I bit my lip hard to temper the aching response within me.

Mason: Be patient, Claire. I'll show you how I get off tonight.

My thighs pressed together, trying to bring some friction to my desperate pussy. I looked around the empty library, glad there was no one here to witness my pitiful reaction to him. I needed to remember he still had secrets left to discover. *Stay vigilant, Claire,* I tried to remind myself. His secrecy should break the spell he cast on me, but it only increased his power.

I ran back to my office, smiling like a devious fool at the plan I concocted despite the warning I gave myself. I shoved my panties aside and dipped a finger inside myself, relishing the tiny bit of relief it brought me. With the other hand, I took a picture and sent it to him.

Claire: You can't say things like that and expect me to work. I can't control myself.

Mason: Don't play with me, Claire. Tonight, that's mine.

I went to the bathroom and washed my hands. As much as I wanted to finish the job, I had actual work to do. The hallway to the bathroom connected directly with the atrium and as I stepped out of the bathroom, I could have sworn I saw a shadow moving across the floor beneath the skylight.

Very slowly, I crept toward the open space, looking around for what might have caused it. I didn't see or hear anything out of the ordinary. While my skin prickled uncomfortably, I assumed it must have been something passing overhead, a large bird perhaps.

I finished the opening tasks with a hint of wariness and unlocked the door to find Emma waiting on the steps. "Morning, Claire."

"Morning, Emma. Let's get to work," she bopped in with an extra spring in her step. Her cheeks were rosy like she got an exceptional night's sleep, and a thorough fucking beforehand. I considered telling her about the shadow and the unsettled feeling I had, but I decided not to dampen her good mood. It was probably nothing.

"Did you get what you were looking for last night?" she asked me with a tilt of her brow.

"Close enough, but I'm sure our date tonight will fill in the blanks."

"So, you found out enough to tell if he's bullshitting you?" she put her hand on her hip, to show me she meant business.

"I did." I couldn't help the pleased smile on my face. I didn't discover all of his secrets, but certainly more than he would be expecting. If he planned to continue the ruse about his name he would be in for a rude awakening. "Did you get what you were looking for last night?"

She pulled her fingers through her silky strawberry blonde locks, "Am I that obvious?"

"You are." I teased as I pushed a piece of brown hair out of my face and went to work on the bulletin board. It took up nearly an entire wall. All the postings had dates for when they should come down and I had an enormous stack of new things going up, stamped and approved for posting.

She followed closely behind me, on silent feet—she had an uncanny way of sneaking up on a person.

"I understand why you're still seeing him, you know. I was here when he visited you, remember? He's not just hot, Claire. He's magnetic..." she trailed off with something like stars in her eyes, "I wanted you to know, I'm not judging you."

"I appreciate that." I started pulling down flyers, wondering if I made a mistake in opening up to her. Mixing business and my personal life never worked out well for me before.

She sensed my hesitance and immediately tried to smooth things over. "Anyway, the guy I saw last night is named Steven, and he is scrumptious. He's a linebacker, and I met him at the game last week. We only have one thing in common, but we sure *get along*, if you catch my drift," she wiggled her eyebrows at me, and I gave her an indulgent smile before rolling my eyes. Yeah, I liked her too much to regret my actions.

"I'm glad you're having fun with Mr. Right Now."

"I am, but *you're* in pretty deep," she leaned against the wall with cool confidence, like she held the secrets of the universe.

"Am not,"

"Do you think he's *the one?*"

I scoffed at the ridiculous question. "How would I know?"

"That's the thing about love: it's irrational, and the people in it are often the last to realize," I was close to it, sure, but not there yet, and the certainty in her voice grated on me.

"I am not in love."

"You're proving my point," she blew out a dramatic sigh.

"How convenient, a point that is proven no matter what I say," I pulled down a flyer with a bit more force than necessary.

"Convenience is important." She tried hard to stifle a laugh.

"Get working, Emma," I snapped, but my voice lacked any anger, coming out more like an admission of guilt.

"Of course, boss. I'll start on the returns," she giggled as she walked away and left me to my task. I wished I could say things were peaceful without her pestering me, but her words stuck in my head. Falling for Mason would be all too simple. I clung to the edge with sweaty fingers that ached to touch him. Once I slipped, he could break me with ease. More doubt replaced the calm acceptance I felt earlier.

I pushed Mason out of my thoughts. If I didn't obsess over him, Emma wouldn't have more ammunition to tease me with. I focused on all the old fliers as I took them down. They reminded me of my time in City Hall. All the irrelevant bits of information lacked a purpose, but they were meaningful in their own way. Although I no longer considered those eight months the best of my life, I still cared for them deeply.

Some notices advertised gigs bands played weeks ago, poetry slams, and job offerings. It represented an amazing cross-section of the community. I came across a few papers that had no official library seal and wondered about the different types of people, the rule followers, and the rule-breakers. I always thought of myself as the former, but now I was uncertain.

My hands stilled and my heart sank as I read a small piece of paper pinned on top of an advertisement for speed dating. *You can't ignore me, bitch*, was scrawled in angry red letters. I wanted to dust it off as a prank, but I realized the writing was familiar.

I went to my office and pulled out the note that Emma found tucked inside Lolita. I was no professional, but the handwriting matched. A chill ran down my spine. I knew the library had security cameras in the common areas, but I didn't have access to the footage. I would talk to Gavin and see if we couldn't figure out what was going on.

The shadow I saw took on a more sinister meaning, but it wasn't possible. All the doors and windows were locked. No one could have gotten in without my knowledge. I took a steadying breath. *Whoever left that note, left it during business hours.* I soothed myself.

Emma appeared in the doorway, and I jumped halfway across the room. "Damn you're quiet."

"I'm sorry, Claire. You're so jumpy today. Is everything okay?" She looked like she was about to start in on Mason again.

I picked up the paper and handed it to her, "I found this pinned to the bulletin board, and I suspect the same person who left the note inside Lolita wrote it."

Concern twisted her brow, "What do you think we should do?"

"I'm going to talk to Gavin. For now, be careful, and tell me if anything or anyone acts suspiciously." She nodded and walked out.

"Oh, Emma, what did you want to ask me?" I called her back before she got too far away.

"It's nothing. You have enough on your plate." She waved a dismissive hand like whatever she wanted was unimportant, but that only made me more curious.

"Please, tell me," I encouraged her, pulling out a chair for her to sit in.

She sat down and glanced around the office nervously. She was usually so calm and confident. "Well, I know that there's an opening for a paid position, and I hoped you would consider me. I can give you my updated resume if you need it. I've done quite a lot since I started here."

"How do you know about that? Tammy only tendered her resignation this morning,"

She fidgeted with her hands. "Well, she talked about it for weeks and she sent out a mass text telling us all goodbye. I'm sorry I didn't tell you, but-"

"But, nothing." I cut her off, holding up my hands. "People threaten to quit all the time and don't follow through. I do not expect you to come tattling to me every time someone complains."

"I'm so glad you're not upset, and earlier, I probably overstepped..."

"Emma, I am already considering you. Final selection will be made next week and I'll keep you posted." I smiled warmly at her, happy she wanted the job I planned to give to her. If it were solely up to me, she would be hired, but as long as I remained on probation, Gavin had to okay those decisions. I didn't see any reason he wouldn't. Doubt niggled in the back of my mind, and I hoped she wasn't trying to get close to me so I would give her the job.

She left the office, and I sat there mulling over what Eileen, the old librarian, had told me about being careful with Gavin. I surely didn't think he left the creepy notes around the library, but the entire place had a sense of foreboding. I loved being here, but every change in my life pivoted on this institution, from meeting Mason, to this career, to the threatening notes popping up. "What secrets do you hide?" I asked the walls of my office.

The rest of the day passed uneventfully. The worry about the notes, the shadow, and Emma's intentions faded into the background, eclipsed by the still pressing concern of what was going on with Mason. I wished those doubts occupied most of my thoughts. That would be the sensible thing, anyway. Instead, I obsessed over his body, and what he could do to me with it.

I headed home from work just after six. Emma was a dream to close up with and I hoped Gavin would give her the position, even if I doubted her intentions. She seemed authentic, but maybe I sucked at judging character. I called Gavin on the short walk, telling him I wanted to talk to him about a few things. He agreed to meet me at the library on Monday morning. At least I dealt with one thing. The only issue left in my mind was the painful anticipation snaking its way through my system.

I walked into my apartment, pleased with how neatly I kept the place lately. Part of the secret was rarely being home. The outfit I picked earlier laid on the bed. I slipped on the skimpy lingerie I bought *especially* for this occasion. I admired my reflection for a minute before pulling on a silver dress that was a little over the top. It had barely any more fabric than the lingerie, but I felt desirable. I slid my hands over my body, practically panting, thinking about masculine ones replacing my own.

A knock sounded on the door while I finished applying my makeup. *A lady doesn't run.* I reminded myself, but who was I kidding? I wasn't a lady. I pulled back the door, and the breath caught in my throat at the sight of his gorgeous face. He let his hair grow out, and while it was still a bit too short, I greatly preferred this style over his buzz cut. His green eyes sparkled as a breathtaking smile spread across his face.

His tailored navy suit fit his body immaculately. His broad shoulders begged my hands to run over them. "Hello, Mason. Won't you come in a moment?" I asked in my most seductive voice, then turned, swaying my hips, and hoping to catch his eye, "I'm almost ready."

He followed me in with a touch of displeasure on his face, "We have a reservation," he chided. "The front door was propped open, do your neighbors make a habit of risking your safety?"

"They do." I agreed with a roll of my eyes he didn't see and mischievous lilt to my voice. His imperious tone irritated me and amused me in equal measure. I couldn't help but tease him. Fire exploded within me as I turned, launching myself at him, taking his plump, delicious lips with my own. I wrapped my hands around his neck, securing him to me.

The kiss started off soft enough but was rough and passionate by the time I bumped him against the door. He groaned deep within his throat as he swept his tongue through my mouth. His cock hardened between us and I greedily reached for him through the expensive fabric of his pants. I stroked him, thinking I won, when he pulled back and said, "Mm, Claire, let's not miss our reservation."

I didn't listen. I gripped his erection more tightly and pressed my hips into him. He grabbed my shoulders and pushed me back but kept his hands on me to soften the rejection, "Food now, fucking later," I let out a windy sigh and he laughed as he took my hand in his.

"Are you sure I can't convince you?" I asked as he held the door for me to the street.

The sun had set and the light from the streetlamps glowed soft and romantic. He ran his thumb over my bottom lip, "You are incredibly appealing, but no," he placed his knuckle beneath that lip and pinched hard enough to sting, "behave," he cautioned. He pushed my hair back off my shoulder and pressed his lips to the hollow beneath my ear. I gasped at the contact. "Be patient. Let's eat dinner, and then we have all the time in the world."

Chapter Fourteen

He led me to his passenger seat with his hand on the small of my back. He opened the door for me, and I melted into the sumptuous leather. The car purred to life, and he drove us through the city. I scarcely paid attention to where he took me. His features lit by the dashboard display were far more interesting.

"Do you like Italian?" We pulled up alongside "Il Bacio," a restaurant I never would have gone to without him.

"How nice of you to ask after we already arrived."

He smiled at my chastisement, "I guess I'm used to having my way."

"I can't imagine why." He flashed me a perfect smile as he came around to open my door for me. I didn't understand why I waited and didn't hop out of the car myself. He held my hand as he led me up the sidewalk, and to the restaurant with fairy lights in the bushes and modern angular lamps on either side of the door.

"They do an excellent risotto here."

When we walked in, the maître d' ran over to us with comical exuberance, "Mr. Harris, we have your table ready for you. Right this way, please."

We trailed behind him as I eyed Mason with disbelief— and he stoically ignored me. As we took our seats, he slipped a bill into the man's hand. I did my best not to laugh or make a comment as he poured the wine already set on the table.

He pulled out my chair for me. "Thank you, *Mr. Harris*. What a gentleman,"

He raised his brow at me as he sat, "You look like the cat who swallowed the canary, Claire. Care to share your secrets?"

"I don't know what you mean," I couldn't deny how false my innocence sounded.

"Well, we had a rather unusual conversation last night. I expected you to be angry, and instead, you look... satisfied," he tested the word as his eyes bored into mine.

"Oh no, I'm not satisfied, *not yet*, anyway." I chuckled as I inspected the wine.

His hand came down, squeezing my thigh above my knee. I gasped despite the lack of pain. "Out with it, Claire."

"You have a lot of nerve to handle a lady like that, Mr. Sharp." His palm jerked away. He stared at me with such genuine bewilderment, I nearly laughed. He swallowed hard before his mask slipped into place. "You wanted to know," I prompted him.

He glanced around the room, making sure no one heard me. "Don't say that name."

"Why not?" I pressed, thoroughly enjoying the upset to his perfect control.

"It doesn't gain me any popularity if you can believe it." The hard angles of his face intensified in the dancing candlelight, and a frisson of excitement ran through me at the danger implicit in his tone.

"Because of your father..." I could not stop myself from poking at the first chink I found in his armor.

'My father isn't the only one with an unpleasant reputation, Claire. Let's leave it at that." His hand returned to my knee. His thumb rubbed circles on my sensitive skin and I pressed my thighs together to temper the response my body had to him. He smiled at me knowingly.

"But I have so many questions and you promised me answers." The breathy cadence in my voice should have embarrassed me, but there was no shortage of embarrassing things I did in front of this man and wanting him was *not* one of them.

His teeth dragged across the stubble beneath his lip. "Why doesn't that surprise me? Since you uncovered many of the answers in your sleuthing, can they wait until later? When we're alone..."

I picked up my glass and took a sip, *delightful*. Damn, he was great at picking wine. "Most of them, sure, but why does the staff recognize you everywhere you go?"

He laughed with a throaty sound. "I tip well, Claire."

"I can only imagine how motivating your *tips* are. You could solve nearly all of my problems with one of them." I let my gaze drift toward his lap.

His lips quirked up in a little smile, "That's not very polite."

"Maybe you should punish me. I don't plan on becoming more polite as the evening goes on."

"Don't tempt me."

"I wouldn't dare, Mr. Harris." He dug his fingers into my thigh, making me gasp. The server came over, giving me a reprieve from the intensity of his gaze and his grip. I ordered the risotto he suggested, and he requested roasted chicken and a glass of Pinot Grigio.

"Why did you choose red if you wanted white?" I indicated the drink in my hand.

His lips dragged up into an alluring smile, "I hoped you would order the risotto and they pair well." The satisfaction in his voice was as full-bodied as the wine.

"I think you may be too aware of your good looks and charms and the power they give you over mere mortals such as myself. They're a devastating force of nature, and here I am, without my answers, standing in the face of a typhoon," I rolled my eyes, pretending it was only a joke.

"My looks are the least of your concerns, Claire." The flicker of menace dancing in the depths of his eyes heated my blood. The color reflected springtime and new beginnings, except the darkness there, screamed in need of the light those warm days promised. Just like that, he breathed life into the fears I had about him: the power and danger emanating from him.

His lips kicked up, but his expression remained. "Besides, if anyone's beauty is a natural *disaster*, it's yours." I knew without a doubt he was imagining me on my ass in a pile of dick pics.

"Who, me?" I cleared my throat, unperturbed by my thoughts of danger. My insides liquefied at the idea he might be dangerous.

"I think you know exactly how sexy you are, and how much I want you."

I shook my head in disagreement. "I'm sure you find me attractive, but I don't think I'm especially sexy, not that it matters much..."

"Your opinion of yourself is the only one that matters." The way he looked at me, for a moment, I thought he was as close to falling for me as I was for him. He tapped his finger thoughtfully against the lips I needed to sample. "But it's important to remember that a man like me wanting you so badly may *not* be in your best interest."

"Why?" I slid my foot forward and hooked it around his ankle, moving up his leg toward his groin. To my utter shock, he gripped my ankle hard and pulled it up to rest on his thigh. My legs spread, my pussy exposed, covered only by the thin, lacy fabric.

"Because I'm dangerous."

The server returned, leaving our dinners on the table between us. Mason dismissed him with a polite nod and 'thanks'. His hands rolled over my flesh with practiced strokes, not breaking for a moment. I kept my expression as even as possible.

I wondered if he ever did this professionally, and I wasn't sure if I meant massage or seducing women. *Dangerous*, the word battered around inside my head until it was meaningless, just a combination of letters and sounds with no purpose. His hands dancing on my skin dazed me. It was all I could do to keep my gaze on his face instead of letting them roll toward the ceiling.

"Would you like me to go further?"

I gave the briefest moment of consideration to our lovely dinner going cold. My eyes flicked around the restaurant, debating on whether anyone paid us strict attention. I couldn't remember when the place got busy. The tension blurred the rest of the world from existence.

The atmosphere was intimate. The space between the tables without candlelight was dim, and our tablecloth ended on the floor. If I was careful with my expression, I didn't think anyone would notice. "Yes, please," the words were barely more than a breath.

He slid his chair closer to mine and moved his place setting with him until he pressed against my side and we simply looked like a couple who couldn't stand to be apart from one another. His left hand held his wine glass. He took lazy sips while his fingers skated closer to where I wanted them most. He traced the lacy fabric of my panties. I dropped my head into my hands and moaned softly. He chuckled at my response.

The warmth of his touch soaked through the lace, and I couldn't find it in me to care that the slick wetness was ruining the fine fabric. He placed his thumb on my clit over my underwear and pressed down hard enough to send a little jolt of pleasure through me, but didn't move a centimeter. He waited for my rapid breathing to slow. My dress was bunched up around my thighs, my fists clenched the material trying to brace some of the impact his touch had on me.

No one ever found my clit with such ease, and if I thought for a moment, it was dumb luck. He erased that insulting assumption as he rolled his thumb against it. "Ah," I couldn't help the moan escaping me.

"Eat your dinner, Claire." He kept dipping and swirling, eliciting soft groans. The material between us irritated me and egged me on. I needed him against me with nothing between us.

"What?"

"You heard me." I stifled a moan as I leaned forward to grab my fork and have a taste. "How is it?" The bastard had a cocky grin on his face and we both knew he wasn't talking about my dinner.

"Amazing, but I need something more filling,"

"Is that so?" he taunted as he pushed my panties aside and touched my skin.

"Oh, God..."

"I know," —he took a sip of his wine— "I told you, they make excellent risotto." He slid his fingers from my clit to my entrance and pressed his finger slightly into me, "Would you like some more?"

"God, yes, please..."

"Have another bite then." I looked at him like I might try to take his head off, but I obeyed. "Good girl," he praised me as the fork left my lips, and he pushed two of his fingers deep inside me.

"Uh, oh, Mason,"

He leaned into my hair, pressing a kiss to my ear. "I know, baby, you're incredibly tight." He pumped against my G-spot while he kept up a constant stream of praise, "This pussy is so wet. I love having you wrapped around my fingers. I can't wait to have you on my cock."

"Mason, please stop," my voice didn't sound like my own.

"Why, baby? Don't you like it?" he teased but immediately stilled.

"You're going to make me come," I whimpered.

"That's the idea." He went back to stroking my G-spot.

"Mason, please..."

"Why, Claire?"

"I'm going to squirt, and I can't bear the embarrassment of walking out of this restaurant drenched in my cum and needing to pay for a chair," I was so close to the release I begged him not to give me, tears pricked my eyes.

He pulled out of me gently, covered my pussy with my panties, and slid his fingers into his mouth. He fisted the same hand in my hair and dragged me to him so his mouth was tight against my ear, "Are you telling me if I make you come hard enough, I get to drink your pussy as well as eat it?"

"Yes," I whimpered, scarcely able to believe his dirty words.

"God, Claire, I have got so many plans for you." He used my hair to turn my face to his, crushing his lips to mine in a brief but consuming kiss. He tasted like wine and sin. "Feel me."

I reached toward him with timid, appreciative fingers. My confidence disappeared about the time he told me all the ways he hoped to consume me. I gasped softly at how hard his dick was. Inspiring that reaction in him had me writhing in my seat.

"That is for you," he promised as I pulled his zipper down and slid the impressive length of him out of his silk boxers and slacks. The tablecloth covered him perfectly. No one could see anything.

My fist gripped him tightly as I worked his shaft up and down. His face remained so impassive it insulted me. I squeezed him hard, and a little grunt slipped between his perfect lips. "That's what I'm talking about," I whispered to him, running my thumb over the head of his cock spreading his pre-cum.

"As good as that feels, Claire, I'm not planning to fuck your fist tonight." He pulled my hand away, tucked his erection into his pants. He lifted my thumb and pressed it against my lips. I relented, tasting his cum with a smile. "Mm," I ground my pussy against my chair, desperate for friction. He slid his place setting back and returned to the opposite side of the table.

"Where are you going?" I couldn't help pouting.

He reached out and pinched my lip between his thumb and his forefinger in the same fashion he had earlier. "Far enough from you that I don't put your ass over this table and fuck you for everyone to see. Now, eat your dinner."

I obeyed, ignoring the way I ached for him, and we ate in loaded silence. The tension hung so thick it nearly solidified between us, trapping me there permanently. Nothing interrupted us but flirtatious smiles. He ordered tiramisu to share. It was one of my favorites. He already knew how to read me so well, "How did you know?" I asked as the server set the dessert down.

"Lucky guess," The green dancing in his eyes shined more vibrantly than normal—summer instead of spring. The mascarpone was light and delicious and the ladyfingers were fresh. I was so pleased I couldn't help the little smile on my lips.

I thought back to the words he said before he picked up my leg and turned me into a puddle. "What did you mean when you said you're dangerous, Mason?" His eyebrows lifted in surprise, but he quickly settled them into an expectant expression.

The muscle in his jaw ticked. "There are a lot of things I have done that I'm not proud of." He hesitated, guilt marred his features, "Let's talk about it later."

He waved our server down and paid the bill with a sleek black credit card. He ran his fingers mindlessly over the back of my hand as we waited for the waiter to return. "I'll answer your questions, Claire, but you may not like all the answers,"

"How bad could they be?" The words were teasing, but the look he gave me was anything but.

"I try to be a good man, but I have not always succeeded at it."

"Are you a good man now?" I whispered, not sure why I trusted him so much despite his words and my better judgment.

"I like to think so,"

"Then that is enough for me." The server returned with the check. Mason signed the paper and tucked a crisp hundred into the folder.

"Let's go."

He grabbed my hand and led me to my feet. I trailed slightly behind him, staring at the way his suit held onto his shoulders. The night was chilly, and the breeze raised goosebumps on my legs and arms. When we reached the car, he opened the door for me, but before I could slip inside, he caught me around my hips and pulled me tightly against him. His hands slid to my thighs pulling me up and wrapping them around him. My dress rode up and his erection pressed into my pussy.

His hands slid up my legs to grip my ass. He kept one hand there, helping to support my weight, then moved the other tightly into my hair. I wanted to kiss him so badly. I hovered an inch above him but his unrelenting grip stopped me from descending on him, "Kiss me." I demanded as I ground my hips against him. He laughed softly, tightening his hold on my hair. "Ah," my mouth fell open as some strands ripped straight from the root.

He used my moment of weakness to pull me down, capturing my mouth with his, and forced his tongue inside. His strength and dexterity melted me until I slumped against him. I moaned outright as his hand slid out of my hair, down my shoulder, and over my breast. My nipples pressed against the fabric of my dress. His thumbs met the peaks reverentially.

His lips ran over the shell of my ear. "Your nipples have been hard all night, Claire," he pinched them lightly for emphasis, "You have no idea how badly I wanted to suck on them in the restaurant, how badly I wanted to lay you out on the table and make a meal of you!"

"No," I gasped as he sucked the sensitive skin beneath my ear.

His teeth followed his tongue, scraping my sensitive nerve endings. One hand remained on my breast and the other slid forward, away from my ass and to the dampness between my thighs. He pulled the hem of my dress back until the cold air kissed my pussy. He slid his fingers past my panties, spreading me open, and shoving two fingers deep inside me. I screamed, unable to help the pleasure clawing its way out of my throat. He withdrew his fingers, and gently placed me back on the ground, "Get in the car before I fuck you in the street."

I tore my gaze away from him and gasped as I noticed a couple across the road looking pointedly away from us. It was clear from their body language they'd been watching. Embarrassment flooded me. Why the hell couldn't I keep the slightest bit of sense around him? "Don't worry, baby, they loved it," he smacked my ass, then grabbed my hand and helped me into the car.

"Can we go to your place tonight?" He smoothly pulled out into traffic and I made a little noise of assent. Butterflies flipped in my stomach. I was finally going to slake the raging desire within me and despite the doubts I had about his past, I knew tonight would be unforgettable.

He parked down the block, and we walked the path together. The silence between us pulsed with the tension of what was to come. When we reached my apartment, I unlocked the door, and pushed it open, satisfied that the cooling temperature made it work better.

My hips swayed in an exaggerated dance, begging his eyes to follow. "Make yourself comfo—" the words never finished leaving my lips. His mouth collided with mine, smothering me in an intense kiss. His fingers tangled in my hair, pulling tight enough to secure me at the edge of pain. My hands instinctively went to his chest to support me and feel the defined muscles under the fine fabric. *God, this man is just too sexy.*

He inspected my tongue with his own, before tipping my head to the side and tasting the tender skin beneath my ear, down my neck, and across my shoulder. I gasped wildly, my skin raising in pleasurable goosebumps. My arms wrapped around his neck, trying desperately to twist into his hair, but it was still too short to grip.

He untwined my fingers and returned them to my sides, and slid the straps of my dress over my shoulders and out of his way. The fabric rubbing against me added to the lushness of the sensation. He bit down on my shoulder, making me cry out in surprise, and planted little nibbles along my jaw. My greedy fingers moved to his waistband, undoing his belt as quickly as I could. He made a low noise of admonishment in his throat and tugged my hands away.

I wasn't having that. Dropping to my knees in front of him, his look of shock was almost as delicious as his body. My intrepid fingers finished the belt and popped open the button on his slacks. He grabbed me under my arms to pull me back up and continue things at his pace. "Please?" I pouted at him, and to my surprise, he relented.

With a triumphant grin, I dove into his underwear and lifted his hard cock into my hands. I pumped the length of his shaft a few times, watching his perfect face for a reaction. When he gave me none beyond the heated look in his eyes as he stared me down, I took it as a challenge. I pushed his pants and boxers down his legs, touching his muscular thighs. His cock sprang free. The pictures didn't do him justice. My hand in his trousers wrapped around him didn't do him justice. Mason's cock was huge, thick, and downright magnificent.

My pussy twitched in fear and desire as I mentally calculated how I would fit it all inside of me. I leaned forward, placing soft kisses and licks on his thighs. He tasted like salt and sin. I sunk my teeth into his delicious skin, overwhelmed by an urge to consume him. He groaned, the sound coming from deep in his chest. Mason's bites did something unspeakable to me, and it seemed mine had a similar effect on him. He liked it rough too.

My hands wrapped around his achingly heavy cock, stroking him a few times before my lips enveloped the tip. *Mm, God, he's delicious.* I moaned outright, swept up in the indulgent feel of him on my tongue. I was right about just one of his tips solving nearly all of my problems. Mason grunted as I sucked hard, and hungrily licked away each drop of pre-cum bubbling out of him. Control is great, but a willing mouth sucking the life out of you is better.

I stared him down as I relaxed my esophagus to the best of my abilities and hollowed my cheeks, pulling him to the depths of my throat. I gagged around him and tears pricked in my eyes, but the satisfaction in his green ones as he met mine was too good to pass up. My muscles spasmed as I tried to pull him in deeper, revolting against the intrusion. Tears rolled down my cheeks and spit dripped down my chin.

Indecision warred in his gaze as I felt his cock swell impossibly harder and pulse with his impending orgasm. His hand brushed gently against my cheek, sweeping away the tears. "You want to swallow my cum, baby?" I nodded frantically, my jaw and throat aching from the intrusion. He gripped his fists in my hair, pulling just the way he already knew I liked, fucking my eager mouth, groaning, rough and loud. He didn't break eye contact for even a moment as he spilled his hot load and I swallowed every drop.

He stepped back, kicking off his shoes and the clothes still bunched around his ankles. "Fuck, Claire. That was unexpected." He pulled me up and onto my feet, kissing me forcefully. The juices streaming down my thighs only picked up pace as he tasted himself on me.

"Haven't you figured it out by now, Mason? I'm entirely unexpected." The words were meant to be teasing, but the depth of feeling in his eyes surprised me.

"Truer words..." he murmured as he turned me around, pulling the length of my body against his. I was pleasantly surprised to find his erection pressed into my ass, not as hard as when we began, but he would be there soon. *Fuck me, he reloads quickly.*

His hands gripped my hips, and he bit a line from the nape of my neck down my back. I whimpered as I pushed into him with violent need, grinding into his cock that hardened further by the second, practically begging to take him inside me. He pulled me against him harder, helping me gyrate on his exposed cock. "Do you know how tempting you are?" His teeth closed around my earlobe.

"No clue." I meant to sound cheeky and teasing, but the breathy desperation in my voice ruined the effect. Little puffs of air tingled my skin as he laughed.

He slid his hands up my stomach and gripped my breasts. "Do you know how many times I fucked my fist to the pictures you sent me of these?" He dipped his fingers into the dress, tracing the lacy lingerie before pulling each of my breasts up and out of the cups. He pinched my nipples and gently rolled them between his fingers.

"No," the word escaped me with a garbled cry.

"And this..." he left one hand on my nipple and moved the other beneath the hem of my dress, cupping my pussy, "Claire, do you have any idea how crazy the thought of this has made me?"

"I know how many times I came thinking about you." The surprised gasp he let out was like gasoline on my libido. I ground myself into his grip, silently begging him to push my panties aside and finish the job he started months ago. He rubbed my clit through the fabric. "Please, Mason,"

"Please, what, Claire?"

"Fuck me."

"Right here? With nothing supporting you and nothing to hold on to? Or should I bend you over the back of the couch and slip your sweet pussy over my cock? Should we take our clothes off or would that take too long, dirty girl?" I moaned in response as the tension in my body and the rhythm set by his fingers took over.

He led me over to the back of the couch. His powerful hands unzipped my dress, letting it pool at my feet, before gently pushing me against it until my ass rested on the hard ridge supporting the cushions. He slid his palms over my body, admiring my skin. My breasts still sat propped on top of my bra, and my juices dripped past my panties. The hungry look in his eyes burned away any touch of self-consciousness.

He trailed his fingers along my hips, then slipped them into my underwear and pulled them down my legs. My heels stayed on my feet as he used his knee to spread my thighs. I held onto the couch for dear life as he dropped in front of me and inhaled. "Do you like her?"

"I'm not sure yet. Let's see if this pussy tastes as good as she looks. Spread her open for me." he commanded, holding my thighs to keep me from tipping backward. I did as he asked, heat rising in my cheeks at how exposed I was. With one feral grunt, his mouth was on me. His tongue worked against my clit, followed by a little bite.

"Oh fuck," I shouted, as he swept figure eights over it, soothing the touch of pain into pure ecstasy.

"Shit, Claire," he grunted, around my pussy, "You're a goddess!"

His words fueled the pleasure building within me, and when he slipped two fingers inside my tight hole and started pumping them, I was a lost cause. "Mason, I'm going to come," I whimpered, fear filled me. My orgasms had always been messy, and not everyone appreciated it.

"Are you going to squirt for me?" he mumbled into pussy.

"Yes," I mewled, trying to hold back in case he didn't want it. I remembered what he said in the restaurant, but maybe it was all talk. He wrapped his lips around my clit and sucked hard, and like the slave I was to him, I came, drenching him in my juices. The world disappeared and reformed as I fell back to earth from the incredible height he raised me to. My legs shook weakly as he licked my thighs.

"I need to fuck you." He told me as he swept me up into his arms and carried me through the apartment, "Bedroom?"

"That one." I pointed, and he pushed the door open with his foot.

He dropped me on the bed. "Take your bra off, but leave the pumps." He stepped back and slid out of his jacket. I licked my lips, taking in the wet spot on his chest. He unbuttoned his shirt and peeled it off. He stood before me, gloriously naked, his cock jutting out as hard as steel, with eyes so hungry I thought he might consume my soul.

"I never waited so long to fuck a woman in my life!" It felt like a threat and a promise.

"I can imagine you're used to getting your way quickly."

He gave me a satisfied smirk as he spread my legs and climbed up on the bed between them. "Are you on birth control?" I nodded. "Have you been tested recently?"

"I haven't been with anyone in two years, and I've been tested since."

"Are you seriously telling me I'll be the first man inside you in two years?" he stared into my eyes, desperate for my answer.

"Yes,"

"God, baby, are you sure you can take me?" the length of his impressive cock rested against my thigh.

"It'll be tight, but I will fit you." I promised as I kissed his jaw. "Have you been tested?"

"Yes, I'm clean. Can I fuck you bare?" His lips trailed down my neck. "I'm dying to see you full of my cum. You looked so pretty swallowing it."

"Please," without a moment to spare, he pressed the head of his thick cock to my entrance and pushed inside, stretching me further than I'd ever been stretched. I shouted his name as he bottomed out, hitting my cervix and nearly pushing me over the edge into another orgasm just by entering me. The delicious fullness was hard to adjust to, and he hovered over me, perfectly still as I acclimated.

"You are so fucking tight." I relaxed as much as possible, and he started pumping his hips into me. His cock was too perfect, and the sensation of him inside me would ruin me for the rest of my life. I was sure of it as I wrapped my legs around his ass and tilted my pelvis up to meet his strokes. My heels dug into him, leaving marks.

Moving in tandem with him completed me. His forearms supported his weight on either side of my head, and I kissed the musculature as he pumped into me. He dipped down to suck my nipple into his mouth. "Oh fuck, Mason, I'm going to come."

"Already, baby?" His cock throbbed, driving home the point.

"Yes!" I screamed as I pulsed on him, a shaking orgasm that wrung me out and left me forever changed. My pussy drew his release with lightning efficiency. He grunted in my ear as his cum spilled inside of me, continuing to fuck me all the way throughout our orgasms.

He slid out, taking a moment to appreciate how my pussy looked full of his cum and starting to spill down my thighs. His finger trailed along his release and carefully pushed it back in. He closed my legs, wiped his fingers against his chest, and fell on the bed beside me. Strong arms wrapped around me as he pulled me into him and nuzzled his face in my hair. I stopped panting and my breathing settled to a steady rhythm. I slipped easily into happy dreams, safe in the embrace of the only man I would ever love.

her. I never thought she would actually kill me, but I can't say the same about herself." A huge weight fell off my shoulders as I voiced my fears to another person for the first time. "She wasn't always angry. She was empty, unable to care for either of us."

"That's exactly what I meant; you protected her. You are still doing it, even without speaking to her much."

"How do you figure?"

"You worry about her, and your guilt over pushing her away is a lot more intense than you'd like to admit. It eats at you." There was no question, and once again I wondered how he knew me so well in such a short space of time. I showed him more of myself than I ever offered another person, but the way he got me was deeper than that.

"Yeah, I do."

"You're not wrong for protecting yourself, Claire. You're worth it, and you deserve to be happy." I had nothing to say to that, in part because it was sappier than I expected, and because I didn't believe it was true.

We laid together in silence for a while. "Mason," I broke the sweet calm surrounding us, "I'm not afraid of you. I feel very safe with you but, but... you said you were dangerous." I bared my soul to him and revealed parts of me no one else had seen. Getting to know the man holding me, the man who peeled away my layers and left me exposed, was all I needed.

"I did." The tension replaced the comfortable silence between us.

I waited a couple of minutes for him to gather his thoughts and speak, but he didn't. "What did you mean by that?" His rigid body had my heart battering against my ribs. I could barely breathe through the ball of anxiety swelling in my throat. The rise and fall of his chest were the only things interrupting the stillness, and the longer he went without calming my worries, the worse they became.

"Why don't you have any business records under Mason Sharp?" It wasn't the question I needed answered most, but I hoped it would be easier to get him talking from there.

"I legally changed my name after my father's arrest, and that's the name I practice under. I went to college and law school under that name as well."

"Which is?"

"Dubois," I turned the name over in my head, trying to place it. It sounded familiar. *Mason Dubois*. No, just Dubois sounded familiar.

"And what about Harris?" I hedged, trying to make sense of the many layers of all of this.

He sighed, "Mr. Harris started as a joke when I went through the process of changing my name. I considered taking an entirely new name, as my mother's family has a bit of a reputation of their own. A few of my friends would make our reservations under the name, and it just kind of stuck. It would be embarrassing to tell my favorite places the name they served me under is fake. So, I went with it." Mason letting anyone control any aspect of his life was beyond bizarre, but also hilarious.

I would have giggled at the absurdity of him being pressured into an embarrassing situation by his buddies, but the click in my brain when the pieces finally fit was nearly audible. "Your mother's family owns Dubois, the multibillion-dollar corporation that is regularly in the news for hostile takeovers and stepping on the little guy." I tried to keep my tone level.

"You could put it that way, yes." *Holy shit. He's rich, rich.*

"I read an article about their use of slave labor overseas and the extensive tactics they've gone to cover it up." Fury coursed through me. They literally *enslave* people.

"That's among the reasons I considered choosing something else entirely, but I wanted the connection to my mom. She was nothing like her brothers or my grandfather." Anger sparked in his tone, and I realized I stepped too close to insulting her.

"Do you work for them?" The hand that played with his chest hair slapped against my thigh and I pulled my head away from him, looking off into the darkness. I always assumed that corporate law was a shady business. Lawyers didn't have the best reputation for honesty and fairness, but I hated the idea that he helped them conquer the world and exploit the masses.

He rolled toward me, gripping my hair and forcing me to face him. In the muted light, I could just discern the cold steel beneath the green in his eyes. "No, I don't. I like to keep companies honest and legitimate, and I only take positions that allow me to do my job correctly. Supporting slavery is not acceptable, and I don't accept their money. I have what my mother left me and what I make on my own." The fight went out of me, but his hold stoked a fire of its own.

He chuckled darkly at my apparent relief, "But none of that is why I'm dangerous, Claire." His lips hovered an inch from mine, close enough that I could dart my tongue out and taste him.

"Then, why?"

"You know about my father's imprisonment, *obviously*." I would have laughed at the accusation in his tone if the tension in my body and his hands in my hair didn't wind me so tightly. "The things they convicted him of were the least of his crimes."

The heat between us melted my brain, and my impulse control went with it. "What could be worse than stealing the livelihoods of thousands of people, decimating their lives and futures?" I didn't mean to say the words out loud, and I regretted them all the more when pain flickered in his eyes. He pulled away from me, dropping his hands from my hair, and left me lying naked on top of the sheets. I shivered at the abrupt chill from his hot skin parting with mine. He sat on the edge of the bed, poised like he might leave the room.

"A lot of fucking things, Claire." He nearly shouted, and the intensity of his anger shocked me. I curled my knees into my chest, becoming smaller to avoid the potential effects. He gripped my mattress, controlling the emotions raging inside of him.

The dim light of the streetlamps mixed with the moon to illuminate him, showing off the breadth of his shoulders and the perfect musculature lining him. His tendons stood out from his hands and the urge to have them on me overcame my fears. I needed nothing more than to comfort him. The truth of his past and his anger were secondary.

I crawled toward him, emboldened by him staying put and not trying to escape me. I wrapped my legs around his waist and my arms around his chest. His heartbeat steadily beneath my hands as I laid my head on his strong back. "Was he mafia or something?" I couldn't believe how silly the question sounded, but to be worse than his known crimes, he had to be truly dark.

He laughed with no amusement, "The mafia prioritize their family above all else. Their business is secondary to their sense of honor and duty. They may kill, corrupt, and destroy, but they obey a code, and that makes them predictable. If you behave within their rules, you can assume a certain level of safety. Nothing holds my father other than money and power. There is no respectable code or rulebook to keep a gun out of your mouth if he considers you a threat, if he considers you a bother."

Fear shimmied down my spine, but I hugged him more tightly. I kissed across his shoulders, hoping my affection would lighten the weight of the world burdening them. He was under a different type of pressure than me, but the burden of responsibility for our parents crushed us both. That's how he recognized how I felt about my mother so easily. He held himself responsible for the sins of his father.

"You're not like him, Mason. You're a good person."

"You hardly know me, Claire, and you're wrong." His chastisement stung, but I wouldn't back down.

"I know enough, and the rest I can learn if you let me."

"You don't understand what he did, what he made *me* do. You have no idea what I'm capable of." His hands moved onto my thighs, digging into my skin thoughtlessly.

I kissed his shoulder blade once again. "I don't need to. You created a good life for yourself despite the sins of your past, and who your father is doesn't change how I feel about you. I don't need to know what things you did when you didn't have another choice. Clearly, you regret them."

"I always had a choice." He didn't sound like he was speaking to me anymore.

"Not if your father is half the man you described. Is he as bad as you said?" I demanded, shaking him gently, bringing him back to the present.

"Yes."

"You were practically a kid when they put your father away. You don't do those things anymore, do you?"

"I don't, but you can't excuse my actions with childish ignorance, Claire. At eighteen, I was a man, and one I'm not proud of. I knew what I was doing and plenty of people suffered because of my actions." The image of his hands covered in blood popped into my head and I tried to cover the shiver that raced through me. A thought occurred to me, and if it weren't for the safe darkness blanketing us, and the fact I bared my soul to him, I never would have asked.

"Mason, was one of those people Rebecca LaMontagne?" The stillness around us was a separate entity, forcefully making its presence known. Tension bristled through his body and for a moment I feared he would push me away. I watched in the moonlight as his fists clenched and unclenched.

"How do you know about Rebecca?" His voice was deathly quiet.

I shrugged, feigning nonchalance. "I had to dig pretty deep to find your real name."

He nodded, "I don't know what happened to Rebecca, but I've always worried it had something to do with me."

"Were you together when she disappeared?" I ran my hands over his chest.

"No, we broke up just before graduation. I was getting in deep with my father, and we were going to separate colleges. It seemed like an opportune time to end things." His soft voice sounded sad like there was more to it than he was letting on.

The next words burned like acid, and I couldn't fathom why I felt so strongly about them. "Did you love her?" I whispered, feeling bereft and empty at the possibility he did.

"Maybe I did at one time..." His voice drifted off. "I don't really know, but I didn't love her when we broke up, and I wasn't crushed when she went missing." He drew in a ragged breath. "I've never forgiven myself... for not caring more. I was sad for her and her family, worried it had something to do with me, and that guilt ate at me, but I never missed her presence in my life." The muscles in his neck tightened as he clenched his jaw. "What kind of sick bastard feels that way?"

I kissed his back and squeezed him more tightly. "You had already broken up, Mason. It's not as if you didn't care. She just wasn't a part of your life anymore. If my ex died, I would feel sad too, but I wouldn't miss him anymore because he was truly out of my reach."

He let out a long sigh, "I've never told anyone about that..."

"You can tell me anything, Mason. I don't ever talk about my mom, but with you..."

"It's different," he filled in for me.

"Exactly... Mason, would you ever do those things again? The things you did when you worked for your father..." The silence between us was impossibly heavy as I waited for him to respond.

"No, not unless I had no other choice." The vow in his voice sewed up any doubt I had left.

"That's good enough for me." There was no way I could turn him away now. I was in far too deep. I had been trying to fight off my feelings for him since the first time I laid eyes on him. It may already have been too late when he searched for that bird book.

"I'm still dangerous, Claire."

"And why is that?" I pressed kisses along his shoulder blade.

"Because the sins of our past catch up to us, regardless of how hard we work to right them. And..."

"And what?"

He turned toward me, wrapping his arms around my waist and swinging me until I straddled him, "When darkness burrows deep enough inside of you, all the light in the world isn't enough to drive it out."

"I think I understand exactly what you mean..." There was no amount of goodness that would make my past meaningless. He took my mouth in his, kissing me deeply before placing his already hard cock at my entrance. With one swift move, he slipped inside me. His hands gripped my hips as he worked me up and down. Despite all the parts of me I revealed, I didn't feel exposed. I felt protected.

We fell asleep in each other's arms and didn't wake again until after ten. He drove home to get some clothes that weren't drenched in my cum and then came back to take me out to brunch. Having him in my apartment had me practically bouncing. My place was nothing compared to what he was accustomed to, but he fit comfortably. He sat on my couch with his legs spread, looking supremely at ease. "Is there anywhere you would like to eat?" he asked, as I climbed into his lap, unable to help myself.

"Yeah, there's this cute café a few blocks over. I think you'll like it. Wait, did you ask me where I want to go?" I popped an eyebrow at him in disbelief. I loved him in suits, but he looked scrumptious in a pair of jeans and a long sleeve t. The soft fabric revealed the planes of his chest.

"I can be flexible." He shrugged like it was no big deal. *What a load of crap.* "Though I've discovered you're much more so than I am." I smacked him lightly on the arm, unable to hide the pleasure on my face. "Dirty girl," he whispered in my ear as he fondled my ass.

A few minutes later, we walked to the chic little café where I met Leyla. The day she thought someone watched me from the street flashed in my mind, the same day we found the note inside Lolita, and I saw the shadow beneath the skylight. I shivered like eyes were on me now, but that had to be wrong. There had been many occasions where I felt like someone was watching me, but it was paranoia fed by an overactive imagination and an inflated sense of self-importance.

"This place looks great." He beamed at me as he opened the door. We walked up to the counter, and Leyla smiled at me. "Hey *you*, glad to see you again. Back for another sausage roll?" She was just as dazzling as the last time I saw her, but I was prepared.

"Definitely," I agreed with a smile, flattered she remembered me with all the people she served coffee to daily, "You have a great memory." I glanced over at Mason, wondering what he would think of the supremely beautiful barista, though he wasn't paying her any particular attention.

"I always remember the nice ones, and well..." her eyes drifted off, and at first I thought she was checking out Mason, but her gaze moved past him and to the street.

"Well, what?" I pressed gently.

"That guy on the street, the one I thought was watching you? Well..." she fidgeted nervously with her fingers, not wanting to continue, "He came back a few times, and he waited around for a while. Only ever ordered a coffee, but it seemed like he was looking for someone. It creeped me out." She placed her hands on her hips and ran her eyes over Mason. "I was worried about you, but you have a tough guy to protect you." I laughed at that, but Mason's face was hard and cold as ice.

"What did he look like?" he asked her in an unnaturally calm voice.

"Mm, normal I guess, I think dark hair and dark eyes, thirty tops?"

"You're not sure what he looked like. How is that possible?" I nudged him in the ribs with my elbow, disliking the way he questioned her.

"I'm sorry."

"It's okay, Leyla. I'm sure it's nothing to worry about." I exchanged a few more friendly words with her, hoping to convince her everything was fine. Mason wouldn't look at me.

"And for you?" Leyla kept her voice smooth and friendly despite his attitude.

"Same as her, but we'll take it to go." I shot him an annoyed look but didn't argue. He clearly wasn't in a reasonable state.

I sat down in a leather armchair as we waited for our food and coffee. He stood beside me like a sentinel guarding me against anyone's approach. Leyla smiled at me and gave him a dubious glance when she brought everything over. He grabbed my hand and practically yanked me out of my seat.

"Grab your coffee." He murmured, but the intensity of it felt like he shouted the words at me. I did as he said, and he pulled me out of the restaurant, shoving the door open in front of him like it offended him personally.

"Mason, what is it?" I shouted over the noise of the street and the anger pouring out of him like another entity surrounding us. I yanked my arm back as hard as I could, forcing him to face me.

"Nothing, Claire." He barked, and turned back around, pulling me down the street.

We arrived at my building, and he finally looked me in the eye. "I have some work to do. Can I see you again this week?" He shoved both of our breakfasts into my hands.

"Sure, whenever you want," I muttered, taken aback by his pained expression, and the suddenness of his action.

He smiled at that, but it didn't reach his eyes. He leaned forward and pressed a quick kiss to my lips.

"I'll call you later tonight. Go inside, and lock the door." He pulled out his phone and angrily dialed a number as he walked away. I opened the door to the building, and as I climbed the stairs an empty feeling settled into my chest.

Chapter Sixteen

The next morning, I had a text from Mason waiting for me when I woke up.

Mason: I'm sorry I took off yesterday. I had some things I needed to deal with. I didn't have a chance to call.

I skimmed it and shoved my phone away, still irritated with how he reacted. I got ready for work putting on my clothes a little harsher than necessary. I wouldn't stay mad for long, and that knowledge irritated me as much as he did. He was clearly terrible at handling his emotions, and I couldn't blame him for it. His mom died when he was young, still in need of her guidance desperately, and his father, well, was his father. I slung my bag over my shoulder as I headed out, decided on making him wait a bit longer before I let him off the hook.

Leyla's words from the day before came back to me, and I found myself walking to the café without giving it much thought. I loved the place, the delicious coffee, and the buttery sausage rolls, but more than that my morbid sense of curiosity got the better of me. Would the man be waiting for me, and could I possibly end this all by pointing out to him I was just Claire Green, and not whoever he was actually looking for?

I pushed the door open, and the bell overhead announced my entrance. Some people looked up, and some ignored me entirely, but none matched the description Leyla gave. When I said good morning to Leyla, she didn't mention him again, but she did ask me if everything was okay with my handsome friend. I rolled my eyes as I told her, "Your guess is as good as mine." She smiled at me sympathetically, and I took my latte and sausage roll to go. On my walk to the library, I forgot all about creepy men as I enjoyed my breakfast.

Mason popped into my mind at regular intervals like a sexy, irritating alarm clock that I kept pressing snooze on. I never understood how people enjoyed fifteen-minute intervals of interrupted sleep before getting up for the day, but here I was similarly torturing myself. Despite my irritation, I couldn't fight the desperate clenching in my stomach every time images from the weekend drifted back to me. God, I would never tire of him; the guarded look on his face when he bared his soul to me, the dirty words he grunted in my ear, or the feel of him coming inside me.

Later on, I sat at my desk pushing papers around, wondering if there was a single thing the man could do to push me away. He gave me a lot to consider in our late-night confessional. His family's sordid histories were far from what I expected when he hinted he was dangerous. The scars on his knuckles and the one splitting his brow made me think he was a fighter in his younger days. Maybe he had an explosive temper. That's what I assumed back when I didn't even know his name. I never asked him for specifics, and those thoughts seemed so silly now. When he confessed the ugly truth, I specifically told him I didn't want to know. Partially, because I trust him, but more so because I didn't want to bear the guilt of knowing that he had killed people, and I just didn't care.

If his father was a murderer, a tyrant, then it made sense he would expect the same from his son. If I were smarter, I would cut my losses and find a less satisfying man who offered more stability and fewer demons. A nervous pit formed in my stomach as I considered what all that bad karma meant for us. Had he really killed people? He never said he did, but he never denied it either. More frightening, what did it say about me that I could easily accept a past like that? I sighed as I stamped library approval on time off requests. *There's just as much darkness in you as there is in him.*

Someone knocked on the door, interrupting my musings on morality and love, "Come in." I popped the last bit of breakfast into my mouth and chased it down with a sip of coffee.

Gavin entered dressed in a suave suit, accented by a red tie that reminded me of spilled blood. I was no fashion expert, but I was certain it was designer, and pricey. Compared to Mason, he might as well be wearing rags. I internally rolled my eyes at myself; did everything have to be about that man? "Gavin, you're looking very nice today," I told him honestly, if not a little suspiciously.

"Thank you, board meeting later." He pulled out the chair opposite my desk and sat with a huff, "You needed to speak to me." He ran his hands over his lapels, straightening his suit like my compliment made him self-conscious. He sounded friendly enough, but the stress was poorly hidden beneath his smile.

"Yeah, there are a couple of things I wanted to speak to you about, but before we get down to business, should I be concerned about this board meeting? I'm not entirely sure what responsibilities I may have when it comes to them." I smiled at him confidently, hiding my very real nerves.

"We have some budgetary considerations to make, and I will report on your progress here, but you have done a wonderful job so far, and that's exactly what I plan to tell them. You don't need to have any involvement with the board so long as your job here is handled."

"Thank you, Gavin." His praise surprised me, but I didn't miss the not-so-subtle hint that I should stay out of the board's way. I didn't know much about them, and much like his suit, his words made me suspicious.

"No thanks needed, why don't you explain to me why you called this meeting?" His fingers tapped nervously against the armrest, and he glanced at his watch.

"After a lot of consideration, I'd like to put Emma up for the paid opening we have."

"Do you believe she is the right fit?" He pulled a small notebook out of his pocket and flipped through the pages, barely listening.

"I do. She's a hard worker, and quite dedicated to the library."

"You've given me no reason to mistrust your judgment. Give her the job, and feel free to hire or fire as you see fit. Is that all?" My brow rose in shock but I wasn't about to argue. My official contracts weren't even signed yet. He glanced at his watch again and stood.

"Well, no, actually. I'm sorry to keep you, but there is something else I wanted to mention, though I'm not sure what to make of it..."

"Oh, what did you want to tell me?"

I pulled the notes out of my desk and handed them to him. "Someone left these around the library, one in the returns, and the other on the bulletin board. I hate to make a big deal out of something that is likely a prank, but I thought mentioning it to you couldn't hurt. Maybe we should check the cameras?"

He read them over quickly, the nervousness in his expression switching to concern. "I'm glad you did. I'm not sure if this is anything to worry about or not, but keep an eye open and tell me if anything changes." It was almost verbatim the advice I offered to Emma. "Is that everything?"

"That's everything," I agreed. He handed the notes back and wished me a good day as he left. I sat back down, wondering if he even heard my suggestion that we check the cameras. I considered contacting Eileen to ask her how to do it, but I wasn't sure I wanted to go down that road. The last time I spoke to her was foreboding enough.

I opened up my various email accounts, ready to get to work for the day. One account was dedicated to general library questions, the other went to me personally, though it was still based on the main server. Most of the time I let Emma deal with the general emails, but she had a pile of returns so high it jammed the slot.

An excited giggle burst out of me as I imagined her response when I told her she got the job. She was going to be so excited. I could call her in now and tell her, but I wanted to sit on my secret for a little while longer. It struck me as more than bizarre that I had a job where I could offer jobs to others. *No, not a job, a career,* I reminded myself, and Gavin gave me permission to make these decisions on my own.

I sifted through the mountain of questions in the general library email. I groaned as I repeatedly copied and pasted the link to our FAQ section in response to the same inane questions. "This is a library, some reading is required," I told the computer. I laughed out loud at a kid requesting a graduate-level essay on the Iliad when he was likely still in high school. *Yeah, that's going to fool your teacher.* I nearly finished when I opened one titled "Random Meetups". My breath caught in my throat.

"This fall I think you're riding for--it's a special kind of fall, a horrible kind."

I'll make you scream louder than he ever could, you worthless fucking bitch.

The quote was from Catcher in the Rye. The book meant a lot to me. I defended it when people suggested it was darker than it actually was. At that moment, I was sure I would never pick it up again. There was no signature, and the return address was a collection of jumbled numbers and letters like it came from a proxy server.

A *proxy server, random meetups*. With a resounding click, everything fell into place. My heart dropped as the trickle of fear I nursed for weeks developed into full-blown terror. All of those notes *were* for me because of that stupid ad I placed. All those times I felt eyes creeping over my skin were because *I* put myself out there and asked for something I didn't actually want.

Showing those notes to Gavin was a huge mistake. What if the ad came to light and he decided to get rid of me? It would be all too easy to decide I was more trouble than I was worth, and if he did, who would hire me? There were so many ways this stranger could ruin me.

He was the man at the coffee shop, waiting for *me*, not someone else. My heart pounded recklessly against my ribs. My breath squeezed from my lungs until I saw stars. How did he find me? The whole thing was randomized. The physical description I gave wouldn't be enough to pick me out of a lineup. I went to the website I used, opened the ad, and read it over.

There was plenty that might spark the interest of an unwanted stranger, but as I thought, nothing particularly identifiable. How many sexy brunettes lived in this damn city anyway? I scanned through the multitude of responses. The only ones that threw up alarm bells were the emails calling me a whore and telling me I would burn in hell. Was it one of them?

Somehow, I didn't think that was the case. There was nothing in those self-righteous ravings to make me think their senders wanted me and this new email was rife with jealousy and violent implications. The thought that they listened to me screaming for Mason made my blood run cold. I reread the emails that were overly personal and flowery. None of them triggered anything but sadness and my fear continued to grow.

I thought briefly about calling the police, but I knew there wasn't enough here to do anything about. They might feel bad for me, but they wouldn't waste city resources on this. Plus, that would ensure Gavin finding out and firing me.

I concentrated on the screen in front of me so hard that I didn't hear the door opening. I practically jumped out of my skin and let out a little yelp when Emma popped her head in. "Jesus, Claire, are you okay? I didn't mean to scare you. I knocked, but I don't think you heard me." She nervously toyed with her hair.

"No, I didn't. I'm okay, come on in." She closed the door softly behind her. I had a few volunteers out on the floor today, including Sean who I met on my first day here. I would never be close to him like Emma, but he was more trustworthy than I imagined. The library would be fine without us for a little while.

She sat down in the chair opposite me, looking bright and beautiful compared to its previous occupant. Her sunny disposition was at extreme odds with the storming turmoil in my stomach. "Are you sure you're okay? Did something happen with Gavin?" Her soft voice filled with concern, but her hands twitched in anticipation.

Annoyance trickled through me. Some creep was stalking me, and she was worried about getting a job. I closed my eyes for a moment, beating the ugliness back. She didn't know those notes were aimed at me, or that I was asking his permission to hire her. As far as she knew, I was mulling over the decision.

"No, nothing bad happened with Gavin. We briefly discussed the board meeting and I told him about the notes." I forced a smile onto my face. "He said to keep an eye open, but he's not overly concerned."

She nodded her head, not entirely convinced. "Okay, well, there hasn't been anything since. So, maybe it was just a prank,"

"No, nothing else." I agreed with a sharp twist in my gut. "I do have good news though; I am giving you the paid position."

She jumped out of the chair, hopping up and down in excitement. "Oh my god, Claire. That is amazing! Thank you so much!" She stopped her jumping, realizing I still looked like I saw a ghost. "Do you not want to give me the job?" she hedged, "I mean, I know we talked about it, but I understand if you changed your mind..."

"Not at all," I interrupted her. "I'm more than happy to give it to you. I just have some personal stuff going on."

She walked around the desk and placed her hand gently on my shoulder. "You're my boss, but we're friends too. I want you to know you can talk to me. Actually, I'm going out for drinks tonight to celebrate and you have to come. Drag that stud along, unless he's the reason you're upset. Then we can talk shit about him and dance all night."

I rolled my eyes at that, but it comforted me she would have my back, at least with relationship squabbles. "I'm not sure this is a great time." Rifling through some papers on my desk, I tried to seem busy and disinterested enough to deter her.

"It's the perfect time. I got a new job and you, my friend, work too hard. Please?" She pouted at me with her pretty lips and blue eyes.

"It's Monday, Emma. We both have to work tomorrow."

"Oh, come on, Claire! You're not that old yet. You can handle a late night of drinking and dancing."

"Fine, I'll go." I gave her a tight smile, and she wrapped her arms around my shoulders. I was such a pushover, but the idea of having a little fun appealed to me.

"You're the best, and bring the guy too. He looks like the super-serious type. You could both use some loosening up." She giggled to herself.

"We'll see, Emma. Get back to work."

"Thanks again, Claire," she told me happily as she bounced out of my office and back to the returns.

I texted Mason, ignoring the contents of his earlier message, and invited him to come out with us. To my surprise, he quickly agreed without pressing me to accept his apology or demanding a reason for my silence. The rest of the day passed as normally as possible, given the situation. I jumped every time a person walked near me, or a door closed, but otherwise things were okay.

"I can't wait to take you out tonight. This club is incredible. I can't believe you've never been. It won't be packed either, which will be great for you since you're skittish with crowds."

I shot her a dirty look. "I am *not* skittish with crowds."

"Oh please," she waved a dismissive hand at me, "I see how you get when there are more than twenty people in here. You need to get drunk and chill out."

My eyes shot around the library, in search of possibly dark-haired stalkers. Leyla really didn't offer a good description so there were a lot of potential prowlers. "I'll have a drink, but I make no promises. I'm not the getting drunk type." The empty bottles that often littered my childhood homes, and the screwdrivers my mom drank for breakfast when she couldn't bother to scramble an egg for me, were *my* secret. *It works better than the pills.* I barely spoke to her and yet her voice was clear as day anytime it drifted back to me.

"Which is exactly why we're getting drunk tonight. Stepping out of your comfort zone sometimes is good." She rolled her eyes at me as she walked away, singing a little song about shots. I sighed, wishing I would stop letting those memories affect my life. I was better about it now than I was when I dated Sam. If I drank some wine, I could relax without the world caving in on me.

Back then, I wouldn't drink at all, and Sam's voice came back to me as easily as my mother's. *My friends think you're weird because you won't drink with us.* He was full of shit. His friends never paid enough attention to me to notice. He was the one who thought it was weird. I took a deep breath, cleansing myself of the memories of both of them. If I did a shot or two, it would pacify Emma. Hell, it might even be fun.

Later that evening, I asked her to hang around with me to lock up. She seemed a little surprised but didn't argue. I didn't have it in me to be there by myself after everything. She drove me home, as I requested, and promised she would be happy to do it for me anytime. She made a face when she realized how close I lived. I told her I needed more time to get ready. I'm not sure she believed it but I was extremely grateful to not be on the darkening streets alone.

When I walked into my apartment, something felt wrong. I looked around carefully, noting that everything looked to be in the right place. I wasn't particularly good at remembering where I left things but it seemed okay. Still, I recognize the same creeping sensation I sometimes felt in the hall or on the street. I opened all the doors and checked the closets, but didn't find anything unusual. I let out a windy sigh as I stripped down and picked out a hot dress to wear for my man, feeling the intense need to cover my body, but it was silly. No one was here, I already checked.

Mason knocked on my door at exactly a quarter to ten. I pulled it open, marveling at how his proximity made everything better. "God, Claire, you are the sexiest woman alive." He wrapped me in his powerful arms and kissed me enthusiastically without any other preamble. His hands cupped my ass, and he gave it a hard squeeze. I squeaked and the soft bulge in his pants hardened in response, "I love the noises you make."

"I would tell you what I think of your looks and noises, but your ego doesn't need any help." I teased as I ran my fingers down the lapels of his dark blue suit and drifted my fingers over his erection. "You know we're going to a club, don't you?"

"I came straight from work," he claimed my lips again, "and, I can wear whatever the fuck I want." He growled into my open mouth.

"You sure can." I agreed, as his tongue swept over mine. "Come on, Emma is expecting us." I pushed off his chest, and he wrapped his arm around my shoulder.

"I assume from the greeting everything is alright between us," he commented as he led me out of the building.

I let out a windy sigh. "Everything is fine, Mason."

"I've learned that when women say things are fine, they're anything but."

"I'm not happy with how things happened yesterday, but I promise we are actually fine." I gave him a kiss to prove my point, and he caught me before I tripped down the stairs.

"Since we're going to a club, you should know I don't dance." The effortless grace with which he did everything made it hard to believe it was some lack of ability preventing him. He held the door open for me and the cool night air wrapped around me.

"Neither do I." I agreed. He flashed me a perfect smile at my answer, and the fear gnawing at my gut faded away entirely.

The club wasn't far from my apartment. We walked there, enjoying the last bits of the decent weather. The night was well lit, full of stars and street lamps. His hand constantly skimmed my lower back and the exposed backs of my thighs. "You make me crazy," he commented with a light groan.

Crazy. The word kicked loose all the thoughts and fears I had before his presence erased them entirely. "Mason, I need to talk to you about something."

"Fuck, Claire, did I misread things between us that badly?" He hid his genuine concern behind a joke. "You're still mad."

"No, no, that's not what I mean. I'm crazy about you too, and I'm not angry about yesterday. It's just..." I chewed my nail absently, and he pulled my finger out of my mouth.

"Just what?" He used the hand he held to turn me around and stared into my eyes. My body pressed against his and I laid my hands on his chest.

"Some weird things have been happening lately..." My gaze trained on his shirt buttons.

He tipped my chin up, forcing me to meet his eyes. His face hardened. "Like the guy at the coffee shop. What else happened, Claire?"

"Someone left a few threatening notes at the library. I didn't think they were meant for me at first, even though I've been feeling like someone is watching me lately. I got an email today that made me realize it was all connected and directed at me." He turned on his heel, grabbing my hand and dragging me back the way we came. I nearly toppled off the heels I wasn't entirely used to. "Mason, stop! What are you doing?"

"Someone wants to hurt you, Claire. We're going back to your apartment and I'm going to take care of this." The cold efficiency in his voice frightened me. How did he plan on 'taking care of this'?

I used all of my strength to pull my wrist out of his grip. "Mason, stop, seriously, you're hurting me. I promised Emma I would come out with her tonight. We don't have to stay long, and you'll keep me safe, won't you?" I looked up at him through my lashes, hoping my pleading would have some effect on him.

He spun around to face me with his hands fisting in his hair, "Fuck's sake, Claire. I'm the one putting you in danger!" he was just managing to hold back from yelling.

"How do you figure? I was the one who posted the stupid ad." I pulled his fists out of his hair and held them.

"Why do you think it has something to do with the ad?" He pressed his forehead to mine.

"Because the email today came from a proxy server similar to the one the website uses, and the subject line was the section I posted the ad in." I cupped his face in my hands, determined to calm him down.

He took a few deep breaths, his hands twisted in my hair, holding me tightly to him. "We're staying for one hour, no more."

Chapter Seventeen

The darkened club just started to fill with people. The night was still early, most of the crowd wouldn't be here until closer to eleven. Purple and blue lights flashed over the dance floor and the deep bass beat vibrated through my chest. The thick aroma of sweat and sweet drinks floated through the air, a scent that would never fully fade.

This was impressive for a Monday. Our city was small but thriving, with several colleges and lots of enterprising young people ready to have fun regardless of weekdays. I was never into this scene, but I saw the appeal when I looked hard enough.

Emma shouted to me from the bar, and the fact I heard her was a miracle granted by a dip between the chorus and the verse. Joy broke across her face at the sight of me, although we'd parted only a few hours earlier. I couldn't blame her for her over-the-top enthusiasm. I understood the satisfaction that came with achieving something you wanted so badly. It occurred to me I never properly celebrated getting my dream career, instead opting to launch headfirst into work. I wouldn't take away from her big night, but I decided I was celebrating myself too.

The person following me terrified me, but I couldn't ignore that Mason and Emma made my life a lot less empty than it once was. I had the career I dreamed of, and if not for the horrifying potential waiting around the corner, things would be perfect. We met her at the sleek black bar, with pink lights flashing behind the bottles. "Hi, Mason!" she enthused as she hopped off a stool and wrapped me in a tight hug and turned to him expectantly.

"Congratulations on your new position." His smooth voice lacked all warmth, and the blue light hit his green eyes, bathing him in a cold and dangerous cast. She dropped her arms, abandoning the idea of an affectionate greeting.

"Thanks," she mumbled to him, thrown off balance by his curtness. "Let's do a shot!" She turned back to me, unwilling to let his bad mood dampen the occasion.

"Okay," I agreed, knowing full well two would be my max.

"Glenfiddich, neat, and two shots of Don Julio for the ladies." He slapped some cash on the bar, and I smiled at the reference to the first emails we exchanged. *He remembered.* My heart fluttered.

"Yes, sir." The bartender grabbed the bottles, then poured our drinks with a flourish.

"Keep the change," Mason told him as he rifled through the bills at the register. "Thank you, sir." The man's eyes lit with excitement—even in a shitty mood, Mason tipped well.

"Thank you, Mason." Emma smiled at him, pleased with the top-shelf liquor. He nodded and started sipping his drink. We did the shots, and I relished the fine tequila, loving the ritual of salt and lime.

"Do you want to meet some of my friends?" Emma asked both of us, but Mason leaned back onto a barstool, taking himself out of the equation. Emma grabbed my arm, squealing in excitement, and walked me around like her prized pony. "Michael, this is Claire, my boss. Claire, Michael." Michael looked at me with blatant interest. The dress I wore for Mason was catching more attention than I planned on.

"Wow, boss, huh? You can't be older than twenty-one." He was very cute, with his smooth brown skin and bright white teeth.

I tried my best not to roll my eyes at the flattery. "Twenty-six actually, and yeah, I'm her boss."

"You're fulfilling the fantasies of men the world over." He licked his bottom lip, thinking he was quite smooth.

"Oh, how so?" He smiled at me, and opened his mouth, likely planning to tell me what a sexy librarian I was when something over my head stopped him. His mouth hung open, and I turned to find Mason glaring. The scotch in his hands added to the power emanating from him.

"It was nice to meet you, Claire," he muttered, then hurried off to the dance floor. I offered Mason a smile, and he took a sip of his drink with his eyes boring into mine.

He was angry, but I didn't understand why he was keeping me at a distance. Our relationship had gone from heated tension to serious faster than I could make sense of it. I understood why everything that was happening upset him, but before today I had nothing to tell.

What was I going to say? *Hey, guy I'm seeing, I think someone is following me and leaving me threatening notes? You're not my boyfriend, but take care of me, please.* Yeah, right, because people were clambering to take care of me. "Come on, Claire, dance with me," Emma shouted above the music.

"No, I don't dance." I yelled back.

"Hell, no! We're dancing." She grabbed my hand and yanked me onto the dancefloor with her. The music was louder here, and the bass pounded in my chest like my heartbeat. She gripped my hips and ground on me, laughing like a madwoman the whole time. "Dance with me, or I'm going to keep humping you." She had a few shots before I arrived and they were catching up with her.

"Fine!" I swayed my hips gently, and soon the beat took over and I just moved for the fun of it.

A little while later, Mason came up behind me and placed his hands on my hips. Glancing over my shoulder, I confirmed what I already knew; I would recognize his touch anywhere. "I need to make a call." Nodding, I watched as he stalked out of the club.

Emma and I danced for another song, then another. When the third ended, I tapped her on the shoulder. "I'm going to check on Mason." She nodded, then grabbed the closest hot guy. He was all too happy to dance with her, and he seamlessly replaced me. I walked out and found Mason standing at the edge of the building with his back to the door, holding his phone so tightly to his ear his knuckles whitened.

"I don't give a fuck what your *guy* said. I'm telling you to get this done," he paused, listening to the person on the other end, "If you think I've gone soft, I'd be happy to come down there myself." He was so distracted he didn't notice me standing directly behind him. The voice rose in pitch, "That is exactly what I fucking *thought*."

He shoved the phone into his pocket and put his hands in his hair. "Mason, who were you talking to?"

He turned toward me with the same anger in his expression as he had inside. "Don't worry about it, Claire."

"You just... It sounded..."

"Sounded what, Claire?" He gripped my shoulders hard, giving me a little shake.

"Scary." I choked out. "Like you were talking to someone from-"

He barked out a short angry laugh, interrupting the accusation I was about to hurl at him. "You think that's scary? You haven't seen scary yet!"

"Mason, you need to calm down. I am not Rebecca and this isn't about you!" I regretted the words as soon as they popped out of my mouth, but the enraged, slightly crazy look in his eyes terrified me.

"Come on," he shouted as he grabbed my wrist and dragged me back into the club. Emma stared at us as he pulled me past the dancefloor and down a hallway. I gave her a little wave before we slipped out of sight. A stumbling drunk guy coming out of the men's room bumped into him, and for a moment, I thought Mason was going to hit him.

"Watch where you're going." Mason bit out as he brushed himself off and kept on yanking me. *Is he taking me to the bathroom?* I wondered right before he opened the door across the hall and led us into a storeroom. Slamming it shut, he turned toward me, looking every bit as dangerous as he once warned me. *How did he know this was here?*

He pushed me against the closed door with his body, caging me with his hips and nearness. His hands pressed against the door on either side of my head, demanding my undivided attention. "Don't *fucking* look at me like that!"

"Like what?" my breathless voice escaped in a whisper. The force of him overpowered everything else.

"Like you're afraid of me," he growled as his teeth found my ear, raking over the lobe. My body immediately sparked to life. My head lolled to the side, giving him better access, craving anything this man wanted to offer me.

"I'm not afraid of you." I panted, my lips near enough to his shoulder that I considered biting him. The words were only partly a lie. He was so intimidating when he was angry, and I had no experience dealing with him this way, but my pussy was aching to take him exactly as he was. "Tell me who you were talking to." I couldn't be sure if I was really asking or trying to rile him up.

"I'm going to protect what's mine, *Claire*." He ignored my demand, emphasizing my name in a way that told me he would not easily forget the comment I made about Rebecca nor the danger lurking over my shoulder. One of his hands wrapped around the back of my neck and the other tipped my chin up to him. My hands flew to his chest, holding me steady, and feeling the delicious muscles beneath his shirt.

His fingers pressed into my skin a bit too hard as he stared deeply into my eyes, trying to communicate a message that held the weight of the universe. His unrelenting grasp and the power of his gaze ensnared me too tightly to care about the hint of pain. "You are mine," he vowed, "and I'll tear this world to shreds before I let someone touch you." Desperation for him raced through my veins, weakening my knees and making my grip tighten on his shirt.

He licked the seam of my lips with artless aggression, and they parted on a gasp, yielding to him as he invaded me, still pressing his thumb into my chin and holding tight to the back of my neck as he ravaged my mouth. My hands moved to his hair, tugging on the golden blonde silk that was finally long enough to twist my fingers into. He tasted like home, and sin, and all the good and bad in the world rolled into one decimating package.

"Do you understand?" He broke our kiss, waiting for me to answer.

"Okay," I gasped, senseless, his words making almost no sense in competition with my pulse hammering and the desperate consuming heat snaking through me.

That was the wrong answer. He nipped my neck, hard. I cried out at the punishment. A smirk lifted the corner of his mouth, but there was no levity in his eyes. "Take off your dress," he murmured into my skin as he sucked bruises over my collarbone, teasing the flesh with his teeth, and soothing the aching spots with kisses.

I whimpered at the pain of his bite and the pleasure that chased it. "What?"

"Take off your dress before I rip it off." His big hands slid down the column of my neck and onto the fabric clinging to my breasts. Mason tensed in preparation to tear it off me. He stared me down with a warning in his eyes, telling me just how serious he was about shredding the only respectable means I had for walking out of this club. My nervous fingers flew to the zipper and I let the garment fall to the ground without a care for what sticky substance was covering it. My back rested on the cold door, and my exposed nipples hardened even further at the onslaught of cool air.

He stepped back, looking at me with blatant lust and fury. His shirt was pulled up and mussed, along with his hair. The suit jacket clung to his shoulders, accenting the breadth of him and the power in his stance. His lips parted, and I watched in amazed fascination as he pulled the bottom one between his teeth and bit into it like he wished it were me instead. His cock straining against his pants had me desperate to drop to my knees and take him into my mouth, to taste his skin and swallow his cum. Except the look in his eye told me not to move an inch.

"Did you skip the bra tonight to tease me?" I shook my head rapidly, and the smallest smile flashed across his lips. He pulled open his belt buckle, and my eyes stayed glued to the motion as he tugged it free from the loops. His perfect control was utterly absent from his flushed face. This was raw need.

"Put your hands out." I obeyed him, placing my wrists together and offering them to him in a prayer, but for what, I couldn't be sure. He was like gravity: completely undeniable in his pull. He doubled the belt over, creating some kind of loop, and shoved my wrists inside. Pulling the end, he tightened the restraint a bit too hard.

I wondered which life he learned this in—son of a criminal or wealthy playboy? I moaned as he rolled each of my nipples between his fingers and gave each breast a rough smack. He dipped down, sucking one into his mouth like he couldn't resist having a taste. My wayward fingers reached out, just brushing his achingly hard cock. He smacked my hands, letting me know he was setting the pace, taking his time to explore and suck my nipples until I was a puddle, writhing and begging to be filled.

Finally, he took mercy on me and turned me to face a series of shelving units lining the wall. Thick poles supported the shelves, and he led me to the nearest one with his front pressed to my back. His rigid cock rested against the cleft of my ass and his hands worked my nipples with harsh pinches. He didn't bother to lock the door behind us. "Hold on," he directed as he lifted my hands and wrapped them around the metal.

I did as he said, gripping tightly, but still asked, "Why?"

"I'm going to fuck you senseless, and you'll need the support." His palms ran over my hips, pulling my panties down my thighs. "Step," he commanded as he pulled them off of me and stuck them in his pocket.

He spread my legs, skating his hands over the insides of my thighs as he stood, one hand lightly slapped my clit. I yelped, and he dipped into my opening, shoving two thick fingers inside. The other palm spread my ass cheeks and his fingers playfully tested the resistance. "So wet. So tight." He grunted in my ear as I shivered and quaked on him. He withdrew from me, leaving me aching. The soft ripping sound of his zipper pulling down only added to the slick wetness, but soothed the animal willing to fight to be filled. He positioned the head of his cock at my entrance.

"Mason, what if someone comes in?" I gasped wildly, thinking of all the people in the club and how easy it would be for one of them to stumble in here, or an employee who needed something. The inventory lining the shelf in front of me gave credence to that concern.

"If someone comes in, they're going to see what I already know. You are *mine*." With that, he gripped my hips and shoved into me, nearly taking me off my feet with the force of his thrust. I crumpled, barely able to hold on, but still my hips tried their hardest to grind into him, my need for him was feral. The exquisite fullness was almost more than I could take and only made me want him to wreck me.

I moaned loudly, unable to help myself. "You'll have to keep quiet if you don't want them to hear you, baby." His hips pounding into me elicited another long moan as my pussy gripped him, trying to dislodge both of our orgasms. He laughed as he pulled my hair back from my face and neck, and bit into the spot where my neck met my shoulder blade. I held on tighter as his fingers dug bruises into my hips and his cock pumped into me in the most sublime punishing rhythm.

He reached around, pinching my clit, and I let out another cry. "Tsk tsk," he admonished me, slowing his relentless pounding long enough to pull my panties out of his pocket, "Open your pretty little mouth, Claire." I obeyed, and he shoved the wet fabric in; the sweet, musky taste of my arousal driving me higher.

"If you can't keep quiet, I'll keep you quiet." He slapped a hand over my mouth, keeping the makeshift gag in place. "You're delicious, aren't you, baby? No one tastes as good as you."

He kept up his deluge, fucking me within an inch of my life. "You're mine, Claire. Don't you get that?!" I whimpered wordlessly. "Do you really think this is casual?" His hand went to my throat, holding me tightly like he was a collar around my neck. "Feel me inside of you. There is *nothing* casual about this." His other hand lifted off my hip and landed hard, slapping my thigh. "If you're ever nervous, if you think for half a second you're in danger, you come to me."

His hand came down on me again, and I cried into the gag. "If you ever keep me from protecting what's mine, I will beat this ass until you can't sit for a week." His cock throbbed, nearing his orgasm. "Do you understand me?" I nodded frantically, moaning as he pinched my clit harder this time. He pulled my underwear out of my mouth. "Do you fucking understand me, Claire?"

"Yes, Mason, God, yes, please let me come."

"Who do you belong to?" he grunted.

"Mason!" I whined, so desperate for release I would say anything, but this was the truth.

"Mason, who?"

"Mason Sharp!" I shouted so loudly, someone was certain to come looking.

His lips tenderly kissed the hollow beneath my ear. "You're goddamn right you do."

His hand went back to my clit, pinching and teasing as he relentlessly thrust into me. My pussy spasmed around him, coating him in my juices as I screamed through my orgasm. "That's. My. Good. Girl." he praised me as he fucked me through my release, a thrust punctuating each word, and with a grunt, he spilled inside of me.

He leaned his head against my back as he drew in ragged breaths. His cock slid out of me, dragging our mixed release down my thighs. I listened, stunned, as he lifted his pants, pulled up his zipper, and did his button. I stayed holding on to the pole, not sure why, but I wouldn't move an inch until he permitted me. Our release continued dripping down my thighs. Perhaps the compromising position should have left me feeling exposed or dirty, but all I felt was safe and sated.

He took a roll of paper towels off the shelf and started cleaning the cum off my thighs. His touch was so gentle, it brought tears to my eyes. He kept my panties, but lifted my dress off the floor, helped me step back into it, and zipped it up. He softly rubbed the spots he struck. "Let go, baby," he told me in a controlled voice.

I did as he asked, and he gently turned me around. He undid my bindings and massaged the red marks on my wrists. They weren't deep or painful and would fade soon, but that didn't keep him from making sure I was fine. He looked up, realizing tears streamed down my face, "Claire, are you okay? Did I hurt you?" His full lips thinned, and his eyebrows pushed together in concern. He wiped his hands across my cheeks, but more tears spilled to replace the ones he dried.

"No, I loved everything." I shook my head back and forth to quell any thoughts he might form about how insulting it was to him for me to cry after sex.

"What's wrong?" his tone lacked all judgment, and I cried harder.

"I don't know. You were so mad at me, and I'm scared. So much has happened recently, and so many things have changed. Sometimes, I get like this after sex."

He rubbed an aggressive hand over his brow, "I was mad at you but even more so with myself. I know you think this is about that stupid ad you placed, but Claire, I have a lot of enemies. There are many people who want me to suffer, and hurting you is a damn good way to ensure that."

"Why?" I whispered.

"Because you're mine, and I would never forgive myself if I let something happen to you." He wrapped his arms around me and nuzzled into my hair, "I couldn't live with myself if someone hurt you."

"I still think this is about the ad." I insisted.

"I understand that, but baby, you can't imagine the type of people I'm used to dealing with. They'd torture a child for revenge without batting an eye. A beautiful woman would be a pleasure." Chills raced up and down my spine, but his comforting arms kept me whole.

"How would they know things about the ad, then?"

"There are a lot of ways. A hacker could find every single thing you did online in minutes. You don't have any security measures in place on your computer, do you?"

"No, I don't, but..."

"But nothing, Claire. You need to stop being naïve about this. It doesn't matter where he came from. What matters is someone is trying to hurt you, and I can't let that happen." I pressed my head into his chest, sobbing quietly. "Is this all about me being mad, and the stalker, or is the sex part of it too? I hate to think I did something you didn't want."

"I loved the sex, and I swear this just happens sometimes," I was glad to be tucked away into the comfort of his fine suit and not looking him in the eye.

"This didn't happen last time we had sex," his voice was inquisitive, but not accusatory.

"No, it doesn't happen every time, just once in a while. I guess usually when I'm overwhelmed, and right now I'm terrified by whoever this is. I think all the feel-good chemicals are too much and then after it goes back to normal levels, there's nothing left..." my voice broke on the last word.

His arms tightened around me, "Claire, I see you think I'm going to be mad or disappointed or something, but I'm not. As long as I didn't go too far."

"Definitely not." I'd actually like a lot more of that, but it didn't feel like this was the time to tell him.

He pressed his lips into my hair. "I can't stand the idea of you being in danger, especially not if I'm the one who put you there."

I sniffled a few times, not wanting to argue anymore about the source of the danger.

"I'm yours." I told him, knowing deep in my bones it was true, and we both needed to hear me say it.

"I protect what's mine, Claire. I will do anything to take care of you." The vow in his voice frightened me. I loved him, but I wasn't ready to share that yet. Did he love me back, or did he need to own me?

"No one has ever taken care of me before," I confessed into his delicious-smelling chest.

"I know that, beautiful girl."

"Please take me home."

He wrapped his arm around my shoulder and led me back into the club. Emma was doing an excellent impression of a mating dance with a sexy guy. They seemed like they knew each other and I wondered if he was the linebacker she said she had nothing in common with. He was sleek and dangerous looking, with dark hair and a devilish glint to him.

There was no way it was the same guy, but now I was desperate for whatever story there was between them. I caught her eye as I passed, pointing to the door and waving. She nodded and waved, her usual joking light missing from her eyes, as she turned back to the man. I giggled a little, thinking of how pushy I was going to be when I demanded her to tell me all about him.

The night was chilly, and midnight quickly approached. We stayed longer than he said initially. I wanted to tease Mr. Control Freak about the fact it was his doing, but his serious face was not in the mood for jokes. Mason kept his arm tightly around me as we walked back to my apartment. His eyes darted back and forth, constantly surveying our surroundings. I leaned into him for support, trying my best to not let his vigilance wear off on me. Goosebumps prickled on my skin, and I couldn't tell if they came from the cold or the eerie feeling of unknown eyes tracing over me.

Mason and I climbed the steps up to the building, and I shoved my key into the lock. The tenants kept the door wedged open during the day, but none of us were crazy enough to leave it open at night. Even crappy d-list apartments have things and people worthy of protecting.

I glanced up at Mason, unable to believe a man like him wanted to protect *me*. A little shiver ran through me at the thought, but the sensation morphed into something else as we climbed the stairs up to the second floor. From the hall, everything looked fine, but it felt decidedly off.

Mrs. Jones popped her head out of her apartment, "Listen, girly, if you want to stay up all night fucking that man of yours, I can't stop you, but smashing the place up is too damn much. Your other friend scared my cats and I won't be having that!" she shouted at me with a pointed finger aimed in my direction. Her gray hair hung limply around her angry face.

"What do you mean my other friend? I don't have any other friends." One of her cats darted to freedom, and I bent to scoop him up. I handed him back to her without thanks.

"That's not what he said," she disagreed.

"Someone was here, and you spoke to him?" A sickening chill raced up and down my spine.

"Get inside and when I knock you better answer," Mason seethed. Mrs. Jones opened her mouth to argue but withered beneath his hard stare. She nodded her head as she stepped back and shut the door. His hands gripped my cheeks, his green eyes met my brown ones with a silent plea, "Stay behind me," his rough command didn't match the begging in his gaze. He dropped his hands and turned, pulling a gun out of his waistband. *How the fuck did I miss that?*

He threw the door open without resistance. *I locked that.* The sight of my apartment stopped me dead. I wanted to scream, but nothing came out. All of my things were flipped, broken, or smashed, but most concerning of all were the giant red letters painted angrily across the wall: *Whore.*

Chapter Eighteen

Buzzing, earth-shaking vibrations were all I heard, though Mason was arguing loudly with Mrs. Jones out in the hall. *Brown hair, young, but all you fuckers look young.* That's all he got out of her about the man she'd seen before I tuned them out, and now the shouting was irrelevant noise. Police sirens blared in the distance and I wondered if they were heading toward me, but they faded into silence.

"Does the building have cameras?" he yelled at her, breaking through the feedback in my mind.

"The fuck you think this is, the Ritz?" she shouted back, and if I wasn't so stunned, I would have laughed. No one was watching, except my useless neighbors and an uninvited guest. Mrs. Jones was right, *this certainly was not the Ritz.*

I sat on my slashed-up couch, sticking my fingers into the gaping holes, and toying with the bits of fluff, tugging them out and rolling them into tight balls. Mason placed me here after he cleared the apartment with his back to the wall and his gun trained like on one of those cop shows. The cuts on the couch were long and thick, fueled by rage. The violence in the act would have shocked me if not for the many worse displays surrounding me. I stared blankly at the wall ahead, over my ruined possessions. *Whore.* I imagined the rest of the sentiment painted as well. *Whores burn in hell.*

Tons of people answered my ad. At the time, the angry ones calling me names struck me as ineffectual zealots, shouting into a void, hoping one of their barbs would wound. So many worse postings went up in the casual meetups board regularly, genuine prostitutes, and extreme fetishists. I was surely one of the many. None of those scathing emails felt personal, but this did.

I turned over what Mason told me about the people he dealt with and the lengths they would go to. Was this torture? I didn't think so, but I was too numb to tell. Perhaps, they wanted me to be afraid before they made me pay for *his* crimes. I believed what he said about the people he knew. It was possible this had something to do with him, but part of it still didn't quite fit. I didn't know what to do with the blistering intuition quietly burning me up. *You're missing something, Claire.* It taunted me from the back of my mind.

"I'll make the old bitch let you sit over there," Mason told me for the tenth time.

"No. I want to stay with you..." my voice sounded dead, even to me.

"If her couch wasn't soaked with cat piss, I would force you myself." He shook his head in frustration. His knuckles whitened as he clenched his fists repeatedly. This was a rough night for him. His perfect control was as shredded and tattered as the couch I found at the salvation army two years ago.

"Mason, why do you have a gun?" I knew the answer; of course I did. It was the same reason he was certain someone was trying to hurt me to punish him. His past was creeping up on him. I was naïve enough to think he wouldn't carry a gun everywhere he went, only taking the weapon out for special occasions. I wondered if he had it on him before that day in the café with Leyla, or if the threat to me upset him enough to pick it up again. Mason told me to stop being naïve; he always had it.

"If I needed a reason before tonight, I don't anymore." He confirmed my thoughts. I nodded at him.

A picture of me alone at graduation lay smashed on the floor. I couldn't bear the sight of my sad face or think about the thick ribbons of the pearly substance covering the broken glass. I didn't want to imagine where else I might find bits of the person intent on ruining me. *Coating my pillows, my panties...* I shook myself, dislodging the thought process before it broke me entirely.

Mason barked orders into the phone, but I couldn't make sense of what he was saying through the buzzing.

"Should we call the police?" I pressed as I was sure it wasn't a nine-one-one operator on the other line.

"I'm taking care of it." I didn't have the strength to argue or investigate the extent of the damage. Objects were never an important part of my childhood. I had few toys or clothes, things to call my own. Those particular items I collected for myself meant a lot to me. It took me so long to put this place back in order after the mess I made of it.

A tear slipped down my cheek at the memory of all the days I laid around doing nothing, feeling like no one, surrounded by my mess. I got up, got a job, cleaned the apartment all on my own. The thought of someone coming into my home and destroying the semblance of peace I built for myself cut deeper than the fear, though the fear was certainly present. What did this person want from me? To punish me, rape me, kill me?

More tears followed the first, and I let them fall. Why did someone want to hurt me when things were finally going well for me? No one other than Mason noticed me when my life was hell. I barked a short, crazed laugh. "Claire, come on, let me take you across the hall."

"Mason, I swear to god—" I didn't finish my sentence because of the hard knock on the door.

"Come in," he shouted. Three men in black suits filed in. Their features blurred in my unfocused eyes as they drifted through my peripheral vision. Why did I put this couch here? Something about the view, but now I couldn't see past the paint marring the wall, the liquid I hoped was paint anyway.

They looked through the apartment, picking things up and turning them over. I couldn't help but notice they didn't wear gloves. These were no crime scene investigators, and I shivered at the thought of what these men would do with the information they found. They made comments to each other, but I couldn't make out their words, except them calling Mason *Mr. Sharp* stuck out in my addled mind.

The tallest of the three stooped in front of me, picking up the cum-covered picture of me. He hissed in disgust, and I couldn't blame him, "Mr. Sharp, you should see this." Did he need to? Did he have to show the guy I was seeing the load someone shot all over my picture? I wondered if the intruder jerked himself off before or after he tore my life to shreds.

A shape interrupted my view of the angry red letters. Mason stood in front of me with a pinched expression covering the rage vibrating beneath. "They're not cops, are they, Mason?"

"Come on, I'm taking you home." He reached down, grabbed my hands and pulled me up. He wrapped his arm around my shoulder, knowing if he let go, I would drop back down.

"I am home." Despite the truth in those words, it felt like a lie.

"No, my home. You'll be safe with me." He tried to coax me into walking, noticing I couldn't force my feet to move, he scooped me into his arms and carried me out the door. I burrowed into his chest, smelling the delicious musky scent of his cologne and his body. I closed my eyes, letting the comfort he always brought wash through me.

"I'm so sorry, Claire," he whispered into my hair as he put me down to open the back door to his car. I didn't understand why he chose it over the passenger seat, but he laid me down and wrapped me in his suit jacket in answer to my unspoken question. I sat myself up, leaving my legs sprawled over the seat. My eyes stared blankly at the building as he pulled away. Someone stood on the sidewalk watching me, though before I could make out his features, he disappeared.

The darkened streets rolled past us, every blurred figure morphed into a monster with sharp claws waiting to dig into me and rip me open. When I couldn't stand looking for another moment, I laid down and snuggled into the warmth of Mason's jacket. It seemed like hours later we were passing the city limits and driving through the quiet suburbs.

Mason never struck me as the suburban type, but he had been full of surprises since I met him. We pulled into a horseshoe-shaped driveway and parked in front of a gorgeous stone-sided mansion.

The night was too dark to tell the color for certain, but the shape was a classic colonial. Warm lights lit the walkway, and with the glow from the moon and the lamps, I saw the overwhelming size of the place, and I gasped.

"Are you okay?" He reached back and stroked his thumb across my cheek. I couldn't remember if he tried to speak to me on the way over, but I knew for sure I said nothing.

"Just surprised," I told him honestly.

"About?" He turned my face toward him.

"I never imagined you in a place like this," I envisioned him in a sleek and modern high-rise, with glass windows, and the city beneath his feet.

"Like what?"

"Like a family should live here with their staff, not a solitary bachelor,"

He smiled, but the expression didn't reach his eyes, "I have staff,"

His door opened, and he walked around, opening mine and pulling my limp body out.

"Do you need me to carry you?" The satisfaction in his tone made me think back to the club and the way he'd promised to protect me. He was following through on his promise faster than I could have dreamed possible.

"No, I can walk." He held me tightly as he led me up the path. The door opened for us and I nearly screamed, but Mason stayed steady at my side; the older woman was meant to be there.

"Good evening, Rochelle," his warm voice surprised me, "Rochelle, this is Ms. Green. She will be staying with me for a while. Is dinner ready?"

"Good evening, Ms. Green," she nodded to me with professional grace, "It is, sir. Everything is under the food warmer. Would you like me to set the table for you?"

"Claire, are you hungry?" I shook my head, "Give us an hour."

"Yes, sir." She smiled at him and walked toward the back of the house. She looked tired, and a little rumpled and I would bet my next paycheck she was usually off duty at this point. Mason didn't strike me as the type to call on his housekeeper all night.

He led me up a sweeping staircase and down a pristine white hall. Pictures lined the wall, and I made a mental note to check them another time. The door at the end stood open, and he pulled me inside. The room was vast, with floor-to-ceiling windows overlooking the back of the property. Plots of land were typically small here, but he had a spacious backyard.

Long gray curtains hung, framing the view. A red leather couch sat in front of it, making this a prime spot for him to sit and look over his estate. A king bed rested against the wall to my right. The enormous space dwarfed the wide mattress that overflowed with fluffy pillows and bedding. Mason sat me down on the edge and went to his dresser, rifling through the folded clothes.

He pulled out a white t-shirt and a pair of boxer briefs, reminding me I had no panties on and nothing to change into.

"Did you bring any of my clothes?" What a silly question. I should have brought my own, but I didn't, and was hoping to slip into something familiar.

"Come on, baby, stand up."

I ignored him. Why wasn't he answering my question? I thought of the semen splattered on my picture and a pit formed in my stomach, "He did something to them, didn't he?"

He kept his expression stoically bland as he lifted me to my feet, removing my dress for the second time tonight. I lifted my arms, and he pulled the shirt over my head as if I were a small child. He dropped to his knees, took off my shoes, and coaxed my feet through the leg holes. The clothes were oversized but the elastic on the underwear was tight enough that they wouldn't fall down with regular walking.

"I'll buy you new clothes," he assured me as he ran his hands gently over my thighs, smoothing his underwear into place.

"I don't want you to do that, Mason. It's not your job to take care of me!"

"Like hell it isn't." He pushed me down on his bed.

"I'm not even your girlfriend," I argued as he returned to the dresser and pulled out a few more items.

"Do you want to be my girlfriend, Claire?" he asked over his shoulder with a dismissive air. He picked up the jacket he loaned me and put it on a hanger.

"Yes," I whispered unhappily. He smiled briefly at my tone.

"Then you're my girlfriend, and I will replace the... damaged items." He pulled off his shoes and placed them back in the closet.

"What a nice way to say cum stained."

He flashed me a warning glance as he unbuttoned his shirt and stepped out of his slacks. The lounge pants and band t-shirt ensemble was the last thing I expected of him. A nervous laugh erupted from my throat as he sauntered over to me with a smirk on his face, "Something funny?"

"I've never seen you in anything so casual,"

"You've seen me in jeans and a t-shirt,"

"Yeah, but even your jeans make you look like you're stepping off a runway. You look so homey." He kissed my cheek, flashing me a genuine smile for the first time all night.

"Come on, baby, cuddle with me." He pulled me into his arms and back onto his bed. I snuggled into his chest and let the comforting scent of him fill me, "You're safe here."

"I'm not sure I'm safe anywhere," I disagreed.

"You are! Everything your little apartment lacks in security, this house has in spades." He chaffed his hand against my arm, trying to warm me, but the goosebumps had nothing to do with the temperature.

"This is not a house, Mason. This is an estate."

He made a dismissive noise, "This is only a big house; don't be silly." He reached over, grabbing the duvet and wrapping me up.

"Is Rochelle your housekeeper?"

"Yes, she is. Rochelle has worked for me since I bought the place." He pressed his nose to my hair, and I wondered if he liked the way I smelled.

"Does she live here?"

"Yes, she does. Does that bother you?"

"No, but I don't think big houses usually have live-in staff. That's more of an estate thing."

"Would you know a lot about estates?" He knew as well as I did that I didn't. So, I ignored him.

"How do you afford a place like this?"

"I told you before, I make good money, and my mother left me quite a bit when she died."

"*This* much money?" I couldn't wrap my head around the idea.

He let out an annoyed sigh, "I don't particularly want to talk about money, but I have enough that I never have to work a day in my life if I'd prefer not to."

The same shock that made me deathly quiet now had questions spilling out, unable to stop myself even if I wanted to.

"Do you always carry a gun?"

"Yes. Does it bother you?"

"It would have before tonight, but now it doesn't." He stroked my hair and planted kisses over my face. "Why didn't you call the cops?"

"What do you mean?" The false innocence would have made me laugh any other time.

"Those men you called were not cops, Mason. Why didn't you call the cops to deal with it?"

"You're too important to me to let some beat cop try to blame you for whatever's happening,"

"I thought you left all that behind. Is my apartment worth opening that door again? Am I?" I gestured vaguely, his arms wrapped around me restricted my movement.

He grabbed my chin, turning my face to his. The intensity in his eyes distracted me, and I drew in a ragged breath.

"I left it as far behind me as possible, but like I told you not so long ago, the darkness has a way of clinging to you. There is nothing on this earth worthy of opening that door for, aside from you." If that wasn't an admission of love, I didn't know what was. My mouth fell open as I tried to understand. I wanted to ask him more, get more specific answers about what the favors he was asking would mean from now on, but I was too tired, worn down to my bones, and when his lips crashed into mine all I could do was kiss him back.

Chapter Nineteen

An hour or so later, Mason and I sat in a comfortable breakfast nook. The walls were a warm yellow with little flowers painted around the trim. To say it was the last thing I expected in this pristine, monumental home was an understatement. "This is so pretty," I commented to him as he pulled the lid off a tray of lasagna.

"My mom had a room like this in the house I grew up in. I wanted a place to remind me of her." His face softened the way it always did when he spoke of her.

"I'm surprised there aren't any birds."

He pointed to a clock with birds instead of numbers, "It sings different songs on the hour." I giggled at his sweet, embarrassed expression.

"That smells delicious. Did Rochelle make a lasagna in the middle of the night?" I wanted to distract him from the vulnerability that made him so uncomfortable.

"No, she keeps things in the freezer for me to have on her days off, and she put this in the oven for us when I called her."

"Ah,"

He cut us each a piece and dug into his own. On our trip through the house, we passed the dining room, and I was beyond relieved not to be having this meal in that banquet hall. I took a bite, and while the food was delicious, it flipped miserably in my stomach.

The table sat in front of a window, revealing the well-lit backyard and men in suits pacing the grounds. I nearly screamed, but bit back my terror. I looked to Mason, seeing he watched them too. "They're supposed to be here?"

"Yes," he agreed easily as he put another bite into his mouth. They were either the same guys from the apartment or more of the type he was supposedly done with. Except I was here now, ruining everything he built for himself. The emotions turning inside me were too complicated to make sense of, but anger and pain were winning the battle.

"What are you thinking about?" He grabbed my free hand and clasped it in his.

"Nothing much, just how I'm wrecking both of our lives with such startling efficiency. First thing I have truly excelled at..."

"You're not doing anything to wreck our lives, Claire. You are dealing with a situation outside of your control. If this is about your ad, it is not your fault some *psychopath* took an interest in you,"

I pointed to the men in the yard with my fork, "But you're certain it's your fault," he scooped up another bite, ignoring my words. "You know, your tendency to blame yourself for everything is downright pathological."

He shot me a glare, "Let's not talk about *pathological* behavior over dinner." The implication made me see red.

"This is not dinner, *Mason*. This is a middle-of-the-night 'your stalker destroyed everything you own' consolation lasagna." I pushed my fork into the noodles like they offended me, though they were delicious and considerately prepared for me.

"Do you want to fight, Claire? Would it make you feel better?" The muscle in his jaw ticked as he watched me.

"What I *want* is a quiet life, without all this *bullshit*! I don't want my *boyfriend* calling in armed goons to deal with my stalker in the middle of the night. I *want* you to practice law and *abide* by it!" My hand slapped against my thigh as I panted in utter outrage.

"You want a lot of things," he commented with no emotion. "Eat your consolation lasagna, Claire."

I slammed the fork down on the table, aware I was throwing a tantrum and unable to help myself. "Or what, Mason? What the fuck are you going to do if I don't shut up and eat?"

"I never said you needed to shut up, but so help me god if you don't settle down and eat your *consolation lasagna*..."

"You'll what, Mason? *Beat this ass until I can't sit for a week.*" I mocked the words he spoke to me in the club earlier. It must have been another lifetime and not a few hours ago, but the threat rang loudly in my mind.

He placed his fork down gently and stalked around the table toward me. He tipped my chin up, forcing me to meet his eyes. His fingers grazed the line of my jaw, sparking wild and consuming flames through my body. "Is that what you *really* want, baby?"

I leaned into his touch. My chest heaved and my thighs desperately pressed together. The turmoil raging inside of me was more than I could make sense of. "I don't know..."

He bent down, pressing his lips to the hollow beneath my ear. "I'm not petty enough to fight with you after everything you've been through, Claire, but something tells me arguing is not really what you want..."

"What do I want then?" I gasped.

"If I'm reading you correctly, you want me to spank you and fuck you so thoroughly you won't remember your own name." I moaned softly as he bit into the tender skin above my collarbone, "Is that what you want, baby, for me to make it all go away?"

"Yes, please."

His hand slid down my throat, then fisted in the hair at the nape of my neck, "I'll give you exactly what you want, Claire, but first you're going to finish your *fucking* consolation lasagna." He tightened his fist until I yelped. Satisfied with my response, he straightened my tresses, and returned to his seat.

I did as he commanded, shoving angry bites of noodle into my mouth while my eyes roved hungrily over his body. He stared back at me as he ate, and I couldn't quite discern if I pissed him off, made him laugh internally, or turned him on. Perhaps all three. I ate half of what was on my plate before I pushed it away and went to stack the dishes.

"Leave them," he commanded. I dropped the dish, letting it clatter onto the table. The corner of his mouth kicked up in a little smirk. "Stand up." I obeyed him, rolling my eyes as I did. "You see those men out there?"

"Obviously, I see your goons, Mason."

He shot me a warning glance, and I swallowed hard, my mouth suddenly parched. "They are here to protect you. Shall I spank and fuck you in front of the window for them to see?" I fidgeted nervously as I stared through the glass, not sure if that's what I wanted or not. It sounded incredibly hot, but did I really want to be exposed that way?

Before I could worry too much about my answer, I caught the clear amusement in his expression, "You're interested in people watching us? That's good to know, but don't fret. I'd never let the *goons* watch what I'm about to do to you."

His green eyes held me captive. The glint of possessiveness in them was so hot I was about to melt at his feet. "Are you going to be a good girl for me, Claire? Or do you want to fight?"

My gaze flicked around. "But you said..."

"Not that kind of fight, baby." He swiped his thumb along his bottom lip, scratching at the perfectly cultivated stubble. I imagined licking that spot and how my tongue would tingle as it scraped against his skin. It took a moment before his words clicked. He was offering me an outlet for all the feelings raging within me. Not just a thorough spanking and fucking, but an all-out pursuit, an opportunity to defend myself and take back some of my power. I caught the flash of excitement in his eyes before I turned and ran as fast as I could through the darkened house.

Adrenaline pounded within me as I raced down the hall, clueless about where I was headed. This *mansion* was profoundly large despite what he said, with rows of closed doors, twisting halls, and a *staircase, yes*. I flew down the steps to the lower level.

"I'm going to catch you, baby," his voice lilted in a singsong manner.

I quieted my footfalls as I landed on the bottom floor. I expected a basement with cement floors, beams overhead, a water heater, but I did not expect a fully finished labyrinth of more rooms and corridors. I tried them all, only to find them locked. My breath came harder and faster as I attempted to open another and then another. Finally, one gave way. The room was completely dark except for a blinking red light, part of the security system. Each time it flashed, the beam reflected in a mirror lining the opposite wall.

I tucked back behind the door and instead of paint or drywall, my back was met with cool glass—mirrors lined the entire room. I stood there silently for a while, counting the time with my slowing heart beats. My breaths came evenly, and I wondered how much time passed. I would have given up, gone and sought him out on another day, but not today. Today, I needed this.

With no warning sounds, such as footsteps or breaths, the door flew open. "I found you," he taunted as he stalked toward me. Darkness shrouded his face. I could see only the shape of him in the glow from a far-off hall light and the blip of red flashing. His hands came up to grab me and I dodged him as best as I could, but my foot caught on something hard and heavy, and I went sprawling across the floor. The impact knocked the wind out of me but wasn't especially painful.

I tried to crawl away and get on my feet, but he was too quick. Mason grabbed my ankles, pulling me back and shoving my legs apart. His weight pressed into me, and part of me screamed to give in, but I needed the fight. He grabbed my shoulders and flipped me over, so I was facing him. My hand lashed out, slapping him hard across the face. The room was deathly silent for a moment before his low sensual chuckle disrupted it.

His inescapable hands came down on my wrists, pinning them over my head. I kicked and thrashed and did everything I could to throw his body off mine, but his hold was iron tight.

"Tell me to stop and I will," he murmured in my ear as his tongue trailed over my neck. I grunted, trying harder to shove him off me, but I wouldn't dare tell him to stop.

His fingers tightened around my wrists. I groaned as he pushed them together over my head, holding them as he bit into my skin and ground his erection into me in a silent promise. He leaned up, binding my hands with something soft and silken. His breath came hard as he fought to contain me, and his achingly stiff cock pressed into my stomach. I bucked my hips against him, mindless in my need for him.

He moved to my ankles and I kicked hard as he grappled me to confine them too. Once he trussed me up, I continued my futile attempt at escape. He placed a hard smack on my thigh as he stood up. I rolled onto my stomach, climbing to my knees and elbows to attempt to crawl away again.

The light flicked on, and the brightness nearly burned out my retinas. My eyes blinked furiously, squeezing shut. "I knew you were here the whole time, baby. I just needed to pick out a few things and give you a chance to think you'd escaped me, but you don't actually want to get away, do you?" He walked back over to me, flipping me onto my back with ease.

I said nothing, staring at him when I could open my eyes without pain. He towered over me, dark and glorious, menacing in the best possible way. Glancing around, I realized we were in his home gym. Machines and weights lined the space, and mats covered the floor. That's why it didn't hurt much when I smacked into the ground.

"The mirrors are to check my form, but they'll work perfectly for this too," *God, I'd like to check his form.* The smile on his face told me he knew what I was thinking. He shrugged, beyond pleased with himself, "I've caught you, baby. Are you going to behave?"

"Fuck you," I spat.

"As you wish."

That was all Mason needed to stalk toward me, his smile slipped from his face as he took on a predatory stance. He dropped to his knees above me, straddling me and holding me tight beneath his strong thighs. His fingers gripped my chin, forcing my mouth open, and he shoved a scrap of fabric in.

"These are your panties from earlier. I kept them for a special occasion, and well, you don't disappoint." His gaze was heavy with delighted possessiveness. I bucked my hips hard against him as he removed a thick roll of masking tape from his pocket and ripped off a length of it. "Shake your head once and I'll put it away." I stopped fighting; my sudden stillness confessed my incredible need for him. He gave me a satisfied smirk as he slapped it over my mouth, pressing down on the edges to keep it in place.

"You look so pretty all tied up for me. Did you know I've wanted to see you this way since the first time I saw you at the library?" I shook my head. "It's true, baby," his hand smoothed down my throat, his thumb pushing hard into the flesh beneath my jaw, "You made me wait a long time, don't you think?" I nodded my head, and he drew in a quick breath, way more affected than he seemed.

"What a shame you made me tie your legs..." he patted my cheek, as he regained control, "But, that's okay. I can work something out."

Mason bent down, pulled me into a sitting position, and hefted me over his shoulder like I weighed nothing. His one arm wrapped around my knees, securing me.

I watched in the mirrors as his other hand fondled my ass through the boxer briefs I borrowed from him. His fingers slipped beneath, squeezing my bare skin. He spread my pussy, slipping into the wetness. A strangled cry filled the air as he pumped two of his thick fingers into me, working my G-spot with such expertise I knew he could force me to come draped over him just like this. "You're so wet, baby. You almost make me think you want this." I whimpered as he brought me over to the weight bench and placed me over it with my ass in the air.

He came to stand in front of me, "Look at me, Claire," I lifted my body as best I could to meet his gorgeous eyes, "Clap your hands," my brow furrowed in confusion, but I did as he asked. "If you want me to stop, clap, and I will stop immediately. Do you understand?" I nodded, and he ran an affectionate hand over my cheek.

I observed as he went to the back of me and pulled the boxer briefs down to my knees, leaving me exposed. Both of his hands rubbed my ass as he stared at me reverentially. His fingertips slipped between my labia and spread me out for him. I cried into the gag as he thrust his face roughly into me, fucking me with his tongue. The beautiful stubble on his face scraped against my thighs, burning in the most delicious way. So quickly—I didn't have time to argue— he dragged his tongue up my ass and shoved it in there as well.

He chuckled at the way my body tensed up. Heat flooded my already flaming cheeks at the little vibrations his laughter sent through me. This felt wrong, dirty, or something forbidden, but the sensation was much more pleasurable than I imagined it would be. I nearly died of embarrassment, but my pussy quaked, empty and envious. He pulled back and his big hand came down hard on my ass cheek. I shouted in surprise, expecting more exploration from his tongue and not a smack.

I breathed slowly, closing my eyes, as I managed the pain. His fingers soothed the spot he struck. His other palm fell on the opposite side, "Ungh!" I cried. My heart pounded in my chest, panting as I handled the sensation. Goosebumps prickled over my skin as the pleasurable endorphins rushed through me.

He waited a while, touching me gently. I opened my eyes, checking what he was up to. My face was red and my pupils were blown out with lust. The tape across my mouth aroused me further rather than frightening me. He stared at me, waiting for something. This was safe because I was the one in control. I gave him a brief nod to let him know I was okay, and just like that, his hand came down on me again, harder this time, catching the junction of my thighs and my labia.

Shattering, every bit of pain, worry, fear, and anything else inside of me broke and fell away, leaving only beastly carnality. My heartbeat pounded in my ears. My arousal coated my thighs. He dipped down, running his tongue over the escaping juices, then slid it all the way up my pussy and into my ass, thrusting into the tight hole.

I opened my eyes to watch him, fascinated with the sensation and the fact a man like him would want to taste me there. I whimpered into my own panties as he met my gaze in the mirror and stared me down while his tongue fucked my ass. He pulled out of me with a wicked glint in his eyes and brought both his palms down hard on each of my cheeks.

I shouted strangled cries as he rained them down again, and again. I clapped my hands, and as he promised, he stopped immediately. "Do you want me to stop everything, Claire?" I shook my head, desperate for him to use my body and bring me the release every inch of me ached for. His hands cooled as they rubbed circles into my heated skin. I mewled pathetically, flinching each time he came close to touching the spot I wanted him to stroke most.

The tip of his cock pressed against my ass, testing the resistance, and I let out a frightened squeal.

"Don't worry, baby, I'm not taking that tonight," he soothed me as he slipped his hard length down to my slick center. With one solid thrust, he entered me. I was so full of him I didn't have room for anything else. No pain, no fear, just raw, primal fucking. He grunted above me, absent of all the dirty words he liked to whisper as he plundered my body.

There was nothing but the two of us in all existence as my pussy choked his cock, spasming and gripping him with my orgasm. He responded to me as if we were made to go together this way, spilling his load as my release still wracked me. He leaned over me, pressing his front to my back, catching his breath for a moment. When he lifted his body up, he took me with him. We both watched from our knees as he removed the tape from my mouth and undid my bindings.

He swept my hair off my sweaty neck and planted kisses from my ear to my shoulder, "Look at me, Claire," I met his eyes in the mirror, drinking in the way he looked at me. "Everything is going to be okay."

I didn't believe him, but at that moment, I didn't care.

Chapter Twenty

I woke the next morning tucked safely inside of Mason's enormous bed. Light filtered through the window, warm and inviting, far enough away that it didn't hurt my eyes. Having a large bedroom had more perks than I initially expected. The down comforter wrapped around me like a cocoon of pure warmth and fluffiness. *Why don't I own one of these?* I wondered for a moment, before remembering it likely cost more than I would spend on a car.

Mason was already dressed in a tailored blue suit with a silver tie. His gelled hair and perfect face brought back delicious memories of the previous night. He pulled his bottom lip between his teeth, scratching at the skin beneath it, followed by his tongue. I blushed furiously as I thought of all the things he did to me with it and how thoroughly I enjoyed them. With cataclysmic force, the awful images of the night before also replayed in my head, ripping away thoughts of pleasure and replacing them with fear and pain. It took me a moment to make space for all the mixed emotions raging within me, and I grimaced as I sat up.

"You should call in sick today," he told me while straightening his tie and fiddling with his cufflinks. "Last night was too much. I'm worried about you pushing yourself too hard."

"I'm not doing that. There are too many things to do, and I'm still on my probationary period." I pushed the blanket off of myself, and his gaze flicked over me with intense heat. "You don't need to worry about me. I'm excellent at compartmentalization."

He rolled his eyes as they met my face. "I expected as much, but even you have your limits."

"What do you know about my limits?"

He smiled at me in the mirror's reflection. "Not enough, but I plan to learn more." I giggled as I stretched. "Seriously, Claire, this is all going to come crashing down at some point and it would likely be better for your career to do that here instead of at work."

I ran my hands through my hair. He could be right. I still hadn't lost my shit over what happened, and full-on sobs were close by, but for now, I was in control of myself. "I can leave if I feel it coming on, but I need to at least make an appearance."

He nodded, noncommittally, and pointed to a chair in the corner. "That outfit should fit, and is work appropriate."

I walked over to the clothes he pointed to, my body sore and used, but in the best way. He fucked me within an inch of my life twice the previous night, though so much happened, it felt like a few days rather than a few hours. I stretched and groaned, catching his watchful eyes in the mirror above the dresser as he checked me out. The items were beautiful, the right size, and nicer than anything I owned.

"This is too much, Mason." I picked up the silk blouse, shivering at how wonderfully it brushed against my skin.

He walked toward me with that delicious, predatory gleam in his eyes. "It's not, and they are the least of the things I plan to give you." He placed his hand gently on the small of my back and pressed a kiss beneath my ear. "Shower, get dressed. Breakfast is ready for you downstairs. My driver will take you in, and *no*, he is not involved in any unsavory activities. He just works for me." He winked at me, suggesting that anything to do with him must be untoward. From the residual sting in my ass cheeks, I had to agree.

"Okay," I sighed, feeling a little inadequate in the face of all this largess. We could argue about all this later; the clock above his armoire said I only had time for getting to work or fighting, and I decided on the more responsible of the two choices. "What's your driver's name?"

After I finished taking the best shower of my life, and dressing in the nicest clothes I ever wore, I went down to the nook Mason and I sat in the night before and found Rochelle fussing over an espresso machine.

"Oh, Ms. Green, Mason told me you favor lattes. Your breakfast is on the table and I'll have your coffee for you in a moment."

"Um, thank you," I muttered, feeling awkward, but not wanting to interrupt her doing her job as instructed. I got the distinct impression that arguing with anyone around here about Mason's orders would result in nothing but them being as uncomfortable as I was. She left me alone to drink the best latte I ever had, and to eat a crab meat eggs benedict. I groaned outright as I ate, glad to be alone and not have to worry about how embarrassing my reaction to the food was.

I put the dishes in the sink, hating that I was leaving them for someone else but knowing that's what was expected. Dishes in my sink at home didn't bother me because I was the one coming back to them. I shook my head, forcing myself to get over the remorse of making other people clean up after me. I would be here for at least a few days, and it would make everyone's lives easier if I played along.

I stepped out the front door, finding Lawrence standing outside a black town car waiting for me. The temperature dropped several degrees overnight and the cool breeze nipped at my skin.

"Good morning, Ms. Green. Are you ready to head out?" Lawrence wore a crisp suit, and I nearly rolled my eyes at the ridiculousness of the situation.

"Good morning, Lawrence. Yes, I am." I couldn't blame him for my *boyfriend* having more money than sense and ridiculous ideas about how things should be. As I did with Rochelle, I accepted the service amicably, though I would rather not. He opened the door for me, and I ducked in, settling into the soft leather. Mason was sweet for doing this for me, but I seldom ate in restaurants, and being waited on to this extent made me jumpy. I twitched nervously the entire ride, feeling like I should do something, help in some way.

We pulled up at the library at eight-thirty. Emma stood on the steps, glancing around. I almost laughed at the confusion on her face as I stepped out of the car, and then the smile when she realized it was me.

"You had me worried!" she shouted as I approached. "You are literally never late, and I'm the one who brought you out last night." She shook her head like she regretted the idea. "Mason seemed pissed. Is everything okay with him? What happened after you left, and why exactly did he take you to the *back* of the club?" She jabbered at me relentlessly as I walked up to the door. I rolled my eyes at her. As I put the key in the lock, she placed a hand on my shoulder, trying to look serious. "Claire, were you screwing him at *my* celebration?" She would enjoy nothing more than to hear that I was.

"Emma, aren't you hungover? You talk too much."

She laughed as I pushed the doors open and let us in. "Yes, I am, but I took some aspirin and drank some pickle juice. So, I'm okay."

"Pickle juice?" I gaped at her. "You drank pickle juice? Why the hell would you do *that*?"

"What? It's great for a hangover!"

"If you say so." I shivered at the thought and headed back to my office to do my usual checking in. My breath caught as I opened up my emails. I exhaled, finding only normal library-related questions awaited me. I put my head between my knees, hyperventilating as I tried to calm down, and wondered if the breakdown Mason predicted was on the horizon. *Stay alert.* I reminded myself. *No email doesn't mean no trouble.*

Whoever this person was, they wanted me to suffer, and maybe they thought of a better way to do it than sitting behind a keyboard. *Like destroying everything you own.* My text notification went off, and I checked my phone to find a message from Mason.

Mason: Claire, I hope you are well. Do not leave without Lawrence. He will take you wherever you want to go. He has my credit card in case you need anything. Do not go home. It's not safe. I will have everything you might need delivered here. Be safe.

Claire: Mason, that is ridiculous. The man can't wait here all day while I work to take me out whenever I might like. I need stuff from my apartment. Stop telling me what to do. I know you want me safe, but I'm the boss in this library, not you.

Mason: He can. That's what I'm paying him for. I know you're the boss in the library, but I'm going to keep you safe everywhere. We can replace everything in your apartment. Don't argue with me unless you're looking for more of what happened last night.

I tapped my fingers against my desk, thinking of the best way to handle him. I would talk to him about all this tonight. He could be reasonable sometimes, but we would not agree through text while we were both frightened for my safety. Warmth bubbled through me. All of this madness was because he cared for me. I could forgive a little craziness.

Claire: Fine, I'll let Lawrence take me where I need to go, but this isn't the end of this discussion.

Mason: Thank you.

Someone knocked on the door, making me jump. "Come in."

"Hey, Claire. Just letting you know, Gavin is here. Not sure what he needs, but thought you'd appreciate the heads up."

"I do. I'll be out in a moment. Thanks." She turned and left, but not before I noticed the nervous expression on her face. The people-pleaser in me wanted to rush right out and greet him. I held back my enthusiasm and waited for him to approach me. He knew where I was and may not want my help with whatever he came here for. After about ten minutes, I gave in and meandered out into the library.

Emma sat quietly at the circulation desk, checking in books, and my new volunteer, Kiana, pushed the cart, returning them to their shelves. I shot Emma a questioning look, and she shrugged, understanding I was asking where Gavin went. I walked around and didn't see him anywhere, so I headed to the back storeroom, thinking maybe he was looking for something.

I passed the locked door to the basement. Gavin's voice arguing with someone on the other side stopped me in my tracks. He told me he didn't have a key, that they did not keep it on the premises. Clearly, that was a lie. My heart hammered as I leaned in, pressing my ear against the wood. My curiosity overwhelmed my fear of getting caught. *There's more to Gavin Wolfe than there seems*, Eileen's words ran through my mind.

"That's not what I meant. The task has not been as simple as you suggested." Something thumped against the door, maybe his fist. His tone raised with a pleading note. "You don't need to do that." He paused, listening to the response. "I understand. No, things haven't gone exactly as planned." His hand slapped against the wood. "I understand. I will deal with it." The vibrations were mildly distorted, but I heard him well enough.

He must have stood on the top of the landing, looking down on whatever they stored in the basement below. I pressed myself harder into the door, unable to discern his next words.

"All debts must be settled." He paused as he listened to the response on the other end. "Of course, I don't give a shit about the librarian personally. I gave her the job because you asked me to. I kept an eye on her because you asked me to." *The librarian,* he was talking about me. "I'll get it done, Mr. Sharp." *Holy shit, he's talking to Mason.* I waited a moment longer, but instead of more conversation, the knob turned.

I ran for the storeroom, closing the door behind me just in time. I left it open a crack and watched as Gavin locked the door, tucked a gun into his waistband, and sauntered down the hall. *What the fuck was going on here?*

Mason asked him to keep an eye on me and give me the job? That happened before we went on a single date. Why would he do that? I waited long enough to be certain Gavin was off somewhere else in the library. I didn't want him to find me here. He could suspect I overheard his conversation. Anger and betrayal spilled like black ooze inside of me.

Something weird was going on. Mason knew it all along, and kept it from me, even maneuvered things so I got this position. The warning from Eileen, the way Gavin warned me off the board, that damn locked door. Why was he at this stupid library so much? I choked back a sob; was the bird book even real?

He was a corporate lawyer, and yet I met him here more than once in the middle of the day. None if it made any sense. He didn't lie about his profession at least. After he told me about his name change, I searched Mason Dubois online and found all the things I expected to find the first time I typed in

Mason Harris. That much was true, but what about everything else? Tears spilled from my eyes, but I remained quiet.

I ran over all of our interactions, thinking about the serendipitous way we seemed to fall together. He lied about his name and confessed that he was a criminal. Was I beyond naïve to believe the noble things he told me about wanting to be a better man? *He's the one stalking you.* The thought slithered through my mind, destroying everything else the previous ooze left untouched. Could it have been him the whole time?

Mason insisted he was dangerous, and I ignored him, too wrapped up in what he made me feel to care. He told me this was all his fault. *I'm the one putting you in danger.* He yelled the words at me as he gripped his hair in his fists. I assumed they were nothing more than self-deprecation, but what if it was guilt? The man who waited for me at the café could have been one of his goons, throwing me off the scent.

That night at the club, he was yelling at someone on the phone. Was he sending them to smash up my things then? Did I tell him that I loved Catcher in the Rye? I couldn't remember if I did or not, but the notes were terrifying, poignant, and from books that made me feel deep and unsettling things.

He told me a tech guy could find out everything about me in a matter of minutes, and the fear he knew that from experience dug into my gut. I thought of Mrs. Jones and the utter lack of fear through the whole ordeal of someone smashing up my apartment. I assumed she didn't care, but maybe he paid her off too. He had enough money to never work again, he could surely afford to pay whatever he needed to get her to play along. *Does he know what happened to Rebecca?*

I didn't know what to do, but I needed to escape Mason and this whole library. This entire city was a cesspool of misery and pain, despite the immaculate crime rates. I rolled my eyes, thinking of how high this place ranked on national safety lists. Everything around me was a lie. I lived, worked, and fucked in a hornets' nest, waiting for them to aim their stingers at me. Enough stings and I would be dead.

I walked out into the library, breathing deeply and working on my manufactured, serene expression. "Where's Gavin?" I asked Emma as I passed her.

"He left. Didn't he talk to you?"

"No, he didn't."

"Huh, he's been acting weird lately." *You took the words right out of my mouth.* I sneered internally.

"Well, I'm headed back to my office. I have a pile of things to deal with before I go for lunch."

"Okay, see you later."

I thought about Emma as I went. She had been here a lot longer than me, and suspicion flickered. How much did she know about this place, and how much of our friendship was real? I assumed she used me a bit to further her career goals, but what if the reality was far worse than that? I slipped into deep darkness.

I only had a few personal things here, but I took them all, uncertain if I would ever return. Creeping toward the backdoor, I tried to walk as normally as possible. I glanced over my shoulder repeatedly to make sure no one saw me. I pulled on the hoodie I kept in my office for emergencies and tugged the strings tight to hide my face. Lawrence sat in his car out front waiting for me, though he could have a whole gang back here prepared to snatch me up if I ran. No one grabbed me or called out to me as I slipped through the door and down the street.

I cleared the block, then took off in an all-out sprint. I gasped wildly as my feet pounded against the pavement. Certainly, few salvageable things remained in my apartment. I should collect whatever I could and get the hell out of dodge. I had a little money tucked away in my closet, and I doubted anyone found it. The funds were enough to buy a bus ticket to take me far from here, across the country, and toward a new life.

I thought about the fact that ruining all of my things made me entirely dependent on him and I gagged. *Oh God, what have I done?*

I ran up the stairs to the second floor, casting withering glances at Mrs. Jones' closed door. When I stood in the hall, knowing eyes watched me, did they come from her apartment? Did he stand inside and watch me? The door to my apartment was unlocked. *Why bother locking up?* My venomous thoughts seeped through me, and for once, I didn't need to force the knob. It gave easily under my hand like I was finally on the right track.

I pushed it open, catching the big red letters. *Why would he do this to me?* I stopped in my tracks, stunned to see a familiar face sitting in a chair beneath the word. *Click.* The gun cocked. "I've been waiting for you." I swallowed hard, hating myself for all the wretched things I thought in the last half hour. There was more to the story than I knew, but this part of it had nothing to do with Mason.

Chapter Twenty-One

"Come on in, Claire. Make yourself comfortable." He ran his free hand over the barrel of the gun like he was petting the metal. My stomach contorted, trying to turn itself inside out. It took everything in me not to puke my guts up, let alone force myself to respond.

I cleared my throat a few times before I managed. "What are you doing here, Tyler?"

"I came to see you, of course. You're my favorite whore, my pretty little toy." He sounded pleased as if we were old friends and this was a happy visit filled with tea and cookies.

I stared at him with gaping, open-mouthed confusion. "How am I your toy?" I spluttered.

"Hunting you has been the most fun I've ever had. Watching you, deciding on the right time to strike. Look how scared you are! *Fucking delicious.*" He tapped the gun against his chin, and his lack of respect for the weapon only increased the fear coursing through me. "I would have come for you sooner, but you've been awfully busy spreading your legs for Mason *Fucking Sharp*. So busy, you haven't even thanked me for my notes and *gifts*!" His tone mocked me like I was a naughty child. "That's rude, you know."

Thoughts battered around in my head in a blur of color, none of them making much sense. I wondered how he learned Mason's real name, but that wasn't what was important. *Survival* forced its way to the front. All that mattered was getting out of this alive. I needed to keep him talking until someone noticed me standing here at gunpoint. The door was still open, there was a chance a neighbor could help me.

I thought about Lawrence sitting outside the library and prayed Mason might send him to check on me as lunchtime quickly approached. He would expect me. Thinking back to the conversation with Gavin, I wondered how I'd gotten things so wrong. Was this part of the breakdown Mason predicted?

"I don't think I got your gifts, Tyler." His name burned like acid on the way out, but I laced it with false affection. "What were they? I want to thank you." I needed to keep him talking, do anything that might get me out of the situation alive.

He licked his lips as a savage grin crossed his face. "Well, for one, I redecorated your apartment. Anything is better than this *pathetic* hole, but you would know all about pathetic *holes*, wouldn't you? And having them filled." He tapped a thoughtful finger against his chin. "Has he claimed your ass? I wanted to be the first, but that's unlikely with your *situation*." He laughed as he gestured broadly with the gun lazily clutched in his hands.

I shuddered at his words. Wicked excitement flashed on his sickening face. "He hasn't claimed your ass? Aw, you left something for me, after all..."

"I, it's not..." I tried to argue.

"Shut the fuck up, Claire! I'll take every one of your holes by the time we're done here, and no matter what you say, I can see it on your face, you saved your ass for me." I shook my head frantically, and he aimed the gun in my direction, effectively stilling me. "I'm surprised you didn't notice my gifts all on your own." He gestured to the "whore" painted in rusty red. It was darker than the night before, oxidized. That wasn't paint. *Whose blood covered my wall?*

"You knew I was here with you. I saw the way you looked back and forth over your shoulders when you dressed, making sure I was looking. Don't worry, I was."

I shivered in disgust. He was here? How many times? There were a few instances where I felt eyes watching me but I brushed it off. Before the club, I checked the whole place but didn't find anyone. "You were under my bed." It was the only spot I didn't check.

"I knew you felt me with you." The idea cheered him up, but when I didn't intuit what gifts he left, his pleased expression fell. "That's okay, you're not the brightest bulb, so I'll explain all the generous presents I left you." He shrugged like it was the most obvious answer in the world.

"You're a whore, and whores like cum. So I put mine all over the place. I jerked myself off into your pillow days ago. Did you feel me near you as you slept? Did your cunt tremble when you smelled my cum? Did you notice yourself coming harder when you fucked yourself with that little toy in the drawer of your nightstand? I covered that too." Tears pricked my eyes, acid raised in my throat, burning the sensitive skin, but the pain was hollow.

"Whose blood is that, Tyler?" I hoped it would distract him from the line of questioning. Sickness seeped out from my soul at the thought of him watching, of me touching his toxic sperm, of any part of him inside me.

"That is the least of your concerns, Claire. How about you explain to me why you're happy to take loads from a scumbag such as Mason Sharp, but you won't even thank me for all the loads I left for you?!"

"How do you know his real name?" The question popped out of my mouth, though it likely wouldn't help me stay alive any longer. I should have thanked him as he wanted. Mason's fear that all of this went back to his criminal connections seemed so ridiculous with Tyler standing here, but Tyler knowing his secret, hinted toward Mason being right.

He laughed with a manic, terrifying sound. "We went to school together, Rutherford Prep, a place that wouldn't hire a person like you to scrub the toilets. People thought he was so smart, so attractive, but I'm better than him in every *fucking* way. Tell me, Claire, why is it that people gravitate to him when he's *nothing*? I have more money than him too, you fucking whore. Is that why you spread your legs for him and not me? You wanted someone to buy your pussy. I've paid for better than yours! I've sliced up better than yours."

"I don't need anyone to buy me, Tyler." I tried to sound soothing, amicable, but mostly I just sounded terrified. *Oh, God, another girl's blood is on my wall.* If he was so rich, why did he work in that office? The thought was nearly crazed, but nothing I was thinking or feeling made any sense. With sickening certainty, I realized it was to give him access to women who trusted him and relied on his guidance. *Molding young minds*, was what he called it.

A tear slipped down my cheek. I stepped backward, hoping to run, but he aimed the gun at me. "I'll blow your fucking brains out and fuck the hole in your skull if you don't get in here and shut the door right *now!*" he screamed so loud that in a normal building people might have paid attention, be concerned about me; unfortunately fights broke out here all the time, and no one paid any mind to what words they used. That's exactly how he smashed the place up, getting nothing more than a tongue lashing from Mrs. Jones.

I did as he said, stepping inside and shutting the door behind me with a quiet and resounding thud. That was it: no more chance of someone coming to my rescue. I would be dead or gone long before Lawrence came to check on me. My voice shook pathetically. "Tyler, what do you want from me?"

"What I want is for you to sit the *fuck* down and shut the *fuck* up!" I held my hands up as I sank to the floor, and stared up at the man intent on ending my life, cutting me apart in the same fashion he did to the girl whose blood painted my wall.

He stood and strode toward me, a gruesome smile on his face at finally having me where he wanted me. He ran a hand softly over my hair and cheek, tipped my chin up so I had to meet his eyes. "Are you fucking *crying*?" he asked disgustedly.

"No, I'm-"

Smack. His palm came down so hard on my cheek I saw stars. My body flew out of the seated position, sprawling across the floor at the force of the impact. I pushed up on my hands and he leaned down to scream directly in my face. "I courted you like a perfect fucking *gentleman* while you spread your cunt for *Mason Sharp*, and *you're* the one crying?! You should be happy!"

I worked hard to keep the rest of the tears inside. My cheek throbbed and my eye swelled shut by the second. He turned from me, pacing back and forth with furious agitation. I returned to my seated position, leaning my throbbing head against the wall.

"Tyler, I didn't even know you liked me. I am so sorry I upset you." I put my hands up in supplication. Ignoring what he said about cutting women up and sticking with the idea that he had been *courting* me.

"Like you? You stupid bitch." He charged toward me, his shoulders curled in rage, to hover in my face. "I don't like you, but you are *mine*." He fisted my blouse in his hands, popping off the top two buttons and exposing my cleavage. "*MINE*!" His spit hit my face as he screamed and his eyes roved hungrily over me. I thought back to the date we went on and how he sprayed me with spit then too. How many of this man's fluids would I be forced to endure?

"We only went on one date," I pleaded.

He turned bright red with his anger. "It wasn't supposed to ever go that far. I didn't need a date to know what's mine. Not *only* did you ruin my plans, but you also *humiliated* me. You posted an ad on the internet asking strangers to fuck you, but my dick wasn't good enough? You're a fucking whore, Claire. Tell me how that makes any sense!"

"How did you find out about the ad?"

"I told you, you're stupid. You leave your computer logged on. I did nothing other than look. I know everything. All those filthy emails you sent, how wet it made you when all those horny fucks begged for your cunt. You're *disgusting*. You put them all in a book like being a hole to fill was a point of *pride* for you."

"Then please, just leave me alone. You're right, Tyler. I am a disgusting whore. Why bother with someone like me?"

"It doesn't matter what you do, Claire. You were marked the first time I saw you. The thing inside me, it likes you, it wants to see you in pieces. You think you can deny me, *us*? You're fucking delusional. I'm going to fuck every one of your holes, drill another one in your skull, maybe your guts too. I'm going to fuck them both too, and leave you here for your precious Mason to find."

Sweat beaded up on my spine, pure terror raced through me. I was not getting out of this, but I wasn't ready to roll over and let him fuck my corpse. "You're going to get caught. Am I worth your freedom?"

"You're not the first useless whore I killed. You're not even the tenth." He hiked a thumb over his shoulder, pointing to the word on the wall. "She was, and she loved every single thing I did to her." A satisfied look crossed his face as he relived the memories, but it darkened again as he regained his focus on me.

"You're not special, you are a piece of shit. No one will search for you. I told you, I have money, enough that any of my little *side projects* are easily swept away. I would have killed you that first night. Fucked you once, cut you up, and fucked the pieces, but you had to make things *interesting*. I had to take my time hunting you, and now, everything is going to be so much worse for you."

"But you took me home. You could have killed me when you took me home." I pleaded, begging for what he was saying not to be true.

"I do blood and guts. I don't do *vomit*." He sneered at me. "You weren't going anywhere. I had more than enough time to circle back to you."

"That can't be true! You lied to everyone. You told them all I slept with you! Why would you do that if you wanted to kill me?"

He seemed impressed by the question, but that didn't hamper the enjoyment he got from my denial. "That's not all I told them. You followed me, Claire, and stole things from my office. You were completely obsessed with me and I couldn't care less about you. I never killed a coworker before. I figured if they found your body and the cops came asking, it would be in my best interest to have twenty people who would tell them exactly that." His idea was sick, but he was right. Every last one of them would have defended him. "I would have disappeared if I needed to, but the situation never would have come to that."

"Who have you killed?"

"Students mostly, I traveled awfully far at times, but each time has been worth the trouble. But you, you just dropped onto my lap, exactly my type and too irresistible to pass up."

Time was the only chance I had of getting away, and he was enjoying his grandstanding. Tyler loved talking about himself, and I wanted answers. "Why not kill me some other time then? You followed me, broke into my apartment, you wrecked the place-"

"Your work too," he interrupted, "even watched you fuck yourself in your office and take pictures." The evil satisfaction on his face intensified as added fear and realization flitted across my own: he was the shadow under the skylight.

"Then, why wait?"

His brown eyes crinkled around the edges. "I already told you. This has been the most satisfying hunt I've ever been on. I've never played with my dinner this long, and let me tell you, it's been scrumptious. I blew more loads to your nervous glances than a teenage boy discovering porn."

"You don't have to do this, Tyler. Please, please don't do this. My family-"

"Are you going to tell me your family will miss you? They won't. You don't have anyone but your mother, and she doesn't even answer your phone calls. We're both only children, remember? No one will notice you're gone but Mason, and don't worry, Claire, he fucks around so much he won't miss your cunt before he's stuffed into the next one."

A wretched sob escaped my throat, and he smiled in response. "Did you think he loved you, Claire? I knew you were stupid and pathetic but look at you smashing your own glass ceiling. Don't fret, I'm going to take it all away." He shoved the gun in his pocket as he opened the button and zipper on his pants to pull out his penis. I whimpered in terror as I realized how hard he was, and how thoroughly he enjoyed each moment of this.

He grabbed the foul appendage roughly in his fist and started pumping himself with a sickening, fleshy sound. He dragged the gun back out, aiming at me. "Spread your legs. I'm going to obliterate every one of your holes, starting with your ass."

"You mean you're going to rape me!" I spat at him, unsure what weapon he meant to destroy me with first.

"To-may-to, to-mah-to." He shrugged, the heat in his eyes blurred by the tears streaming from my good eye.

He took another step toward me and I sealed my eyelid shut as tightly as the one he'd beaten, silently preparing myself to endure the torture he would inflict before he not-so-mercifully ended my life. I didn't believe in an afterlife, and for the first time, I didn't envy people who had faith. I would rather be nothing than remember what was about to happen.

The door burst open, straight off the hinges, and my one good eye flew wide open. Was I wrong? Was there a heaven? I must be dead already for what I saw to be true. Mason stood furious, like an avenging angel with a gun in his hand trained on Tyler. His angry expression changed to one of confusion for the briefest moment as he realized who was standing there. He was wrong, and if I weren't so terrified and so grateful for his arrival I would have said, 'I told you so'.

"Put the gun down, Sharp. I'll happily blow a hole or two in her." Tyler's gun trained on me, and that was the only reason Mason left him breathing. He was so close to me, only a few feet between us, with his miserable penis in his hand. Mason glanced between the two of us, assessing the situation. He placed the gun on the floor, and I shook my head at him. He needed to stay armed. So what if I died? I wasn't taking Mason with me.

"What's this about, Charles? Still mad I took your girlfriend and her virginity?" *Charles*, what the fuck?

He gave Mason a sickening smile as he stepped back toward the wall. "Rebecca? I'll admit, her choosing you over me stung, but I expect not as much as my blade stung her when I cut that bitch into pieces." He shrugged, dropping his erection, but making no move to put it away. "Let's just say I have a thing for breaking your toys. I would have killed Claire here, hard and fast if it weren't for the fact you seemed to like her. Imagine my surprise when you came along, eyeing up my prize."

The look on Mason's face was perfectly blank, but I understood him well enough to sense the emotions boiling under the surface. It was his fault Rebecca disappeared, but not for the reasons he imagined. He would never forgive himself for what happened to her, or what was happening here. "Where's her body, Charles?"

"There's nothing left of her, so forget your noble ideas of bringing her home to mommy."

"Trust me, Charles, I have no noble ideas at the moment."

"Your name is Tyler." I squeaked, without a speck of reason left in my fear-addled mind.

"You think I use my real name at that shit hole office? God, you are one stupid bitch."

The muscle in Mason's jaw ticked furiously at the insult and the stress of the situation. "Charles, I always knew you were a fucked-up son of a bitch. Your mommy never loved you much, huh? That's why she-"

"Shut the fuck up!" His gun twitched away from me, pointed slightly off toward the corner.

Mason's eyes trained on his hand. "Mommy liked to fuck the staff and make you watch? Rebecca told me all about it. Sick bitch, that one. No wonder she birthed such a fucked-up pup." Tyler shook, the gun pointed at the floor near my feet as he was sucked back to another memory, one far less enjoyable than killing the girl from my wall.

At that moment of weakness, Mason pulled a second gun out of his waistband. Tyler's hand jerked up for only a flash before Mason fired. Two bangs filled the air, canceling out all other sounds. The bullet hit Tyler dead center in his forehead, blowing his brains out, further bathing the word written in blood, and ruining my peace of mind forever. Tyler slumped, sliding down the wall, leaving a trail of gore behind him.

I let out a choking gasp, not understanding what was happening: I couldn't feel anything, but cold. My palms slid down my stomach and I gasped again when I found warm wetness. Mason only shot Tyler once, but there were two gunshots. I lifted my blood-covered hands and gaped down at the wound in my stomach. This was too much blood; I was going to die.

Mason turned to me, the anger on his face switching to a look of pure agony. It felt like minutes since he killed Tyler, but only seconds passed. Mason raced to my side, laying me flat as my vision blurred around the edges. "I love you." I gurgled out before everything went black.

Chapter Twenty-Two
MASON

"I love you..." Claire's sweet voice trailed off in a broken whisper, gurgled up on bubbles of blood and shattered promises. I dropped to my knees beside her, frantically patting her bruised face, trying to wake her up, to have another moment of her attention, but I was too late. The room stunk of gunpowder and blood. Unnatural heat clung to the air like the devil stood watching in glee at the destruction he wrought.

"I love you too! I love you too!" I shouted, hoping the desperation in my plea would bring her back to me, but she remained silent, growing paler by the second. Pushing up her blouse, I found the bullet wound. I needed to stem the bleeding. Rivers of crimson poured from her, leaving a puddle beneath her. I shoved my jacket off my shoulders and into the pool of her blood. Ripping off my dress shirt, I bundled it and pushed it against her stomach. I let out a wretched wail when she didn't flinch in pain.

Someone came up beside me, "Sir, the ambulance is here."

"Could they take any fucking longer?!" I shouted, practically crazed.

"Sir, it's been four minutes. Their response time was above average." Tears pricked my eyes, but I held them back. I wanted to beat James to a bloody pulp for defending the ambulance driver, but loyalty was hard to find and it wouldn't help me or Claire to take my frustration out on him. A flurry of color filled the room as two EMTs brought in a stretcher and bags of medical supplies.

I stepped back, feeling like the separation might kill me, while they loaded her onto the stretcher and worked over her.

"Cops?" I muttered.

"All ours." He gestured to the men working over her. Plenty of public service members were indebted to or in the pocket of the crime ring secretly running this city. Getting the right one where you wanted them was easy if you knew who to call.

"I'll ride with you." I told the pair of men prodding at the love of my life.

"Sorry, sir. There is not enough room. Meet us at North Central." I wanted to argue, to fight them, but I understood what they suggested though couldn't say. She's dead, and we don't want to be in a small space with Mason Sharp when he realizes his girl is gone. They were right, they didn't. The world was not ready for what I would become without her.

They wheeled her out, and I turned around to face the pathetic sack of shit that took the light out of my existence. The tiny hole in his forehead and the much larger wound in the back were not sufficient. Nothing would ever be enough. His lips settled into a peaceful expression, somewhere near a smile, and I was surer than ever the devil stood over me watching in twisted satisfaction. If an afterlife existed, Charles sat with his maker now, regaling each other with their stories of murdering innocents. I would sit at their table one day, but not today.

"You should leave." I barked out, not checking if James listened. My hand reached for my gun of its own volition, emptying the clip into Charles' gut, blowing his organs apart much like he did to *my* Claire. I kicked his limp body to the ground and stomped on his skull until he was unrecognizable blood and bits. The mess coated the bottom of my shoes, and probably the rest of me too, but I didn't care. Nothing in the world mattered without her.

I sat on the shitty linoleum floor for an indeterminable amount of time when I sensed a presence over my shoulder. "Sir, we're going to need to clean this up, and we need backup."

"Call whoever you want. I don't give a fuck anymore." Loaded silence settled between us, filled with the warning he wanted to give. This debt would be too large to pay back easily. Was this what I really wanted? Did I need to ruin his skull and fill his gut with bullets when I should have claimed self-defense? None of it mattered, not without Claire.

"Sir, the EMTs called. Ms. Green is at the hospital and is going into surgery now."

"She's dead." I barked out, unwilling to let the hope winding in my gut crush me further.

"They revived her, and she's in surgery, sir. It's touch and go, but you should get down there."

I shifted off the ground. "Switch shoes with me." The blood on my clothes would be easy enough to explain, but the skull and brains coating my shoes would be another matter. James slipped his off without question, and I pushed my feet in, satisfied we wore the same size.

Being in debt with the Syndicate is not a place anyone wants to be unless they have a death wish.

Which I did until a few moments earlier. A debt with no number attached is just a fancy way to spin indentured servitude. Jump when we say so until your knee caps are too busted and you have no value left. Now that I knew Claire might make it, I had only one way out of this mess: up through the ranks, until I owned my own fucking debt.

※ ※

3 days later

"Sir, you need to leave. Visiting hours are over." I shot the doctor a disgusted look, and if he was anyone other than the man who pulled the bullet out of Claire's stomach and sewed her back up, I would have done a lot worse. The nurse already told me the same thing, but after I told her to fuck off, she scurried out like a frightened mouse. I couldn't blame her. My best behavior and I parted ways three days ago.

"I'm not going anywhere." I didn't spare him a glance. My eyes stayed immovable, focused on the center of my world, lying in a hospital bed with monitors beeping on every side of her. Each tiny blip signaling her beating heart soothed like a treasured gift and stung like a biting curse, all at the same time. She lived, but her broken body needed constant medical supervision.

I paid for a private room for her on the top floor where senators came to die of heart attacks and strokes. She laid in a wider and plusher bed than the typical cot, and the chair I sat in was about a thousand times nicer than the regular hospital room. Apparently, the price for some fucking peace was steeper.

"Sir, I'll call security." I looked at him, and something in my expression made him take a step back. I almost laughed at the thought of the security guard he would sic on me.

"No, you're going to turn around and forget I'm here. Tell the nurses not to bother me." I waved him off. He left the room, and I took a deep breath, wondering what to do if he actually called security. My explosive temper concerning Claire caused no shortage of problems lately. I always believed my past would come calling, and loving her would forever be my greatest weakness. The past came calling, but in the way I *least* expected.

I inched my chair closer to the bed and dragged my fingers along the back of Claire's perfect but icy hand. Needles and tubes stuck into her skin, with tape and sticky pads holding them in place. I carefully avoided anything that might cause her discomfort, though she was unconscious and had been for the last three miserable days.

She lost a lot of blood. She needs time. It's better she's asleep. She would be in too much pain right now. The nurses' platitudes ran through my head as I lifted Claire's gown to check if her bandage needed to be changed. It looked clean and tightly placed, so I lowered the fabric and tried to take a deep breath. The thought of what lay beneath the gauze twisted in my gut as if my own organs contorted to match hers.

My gaze drifted over her perfect face. Her eyes lay shut. One swelled to twice its normal size with a dark purple bruise. A cherry on top of the shit sundae of this entire ordeal. The edges were yellowing ever so slightly, and it would take weeks to fade entirely. I clenched my hands, my knuckles whitening as I flexed them open and closed, trying to quell the ineffectual rage burning through me.

Red, violence, and death were the only things I saw for so long. After I put that life behind me, it haunted my every step. Violent memories and urges cropping up in clean corporate offices were part of my normal. I enjoyed keeping fat cats honest, encouraging them to pay their taxes and do things the right way. Corporate law was a good use of my skills and a slap in the face to my father who went down for embezzlement.

There was a lot more to the situation than that, including a couple of snitches and shit so big even David Sharp couldn't escape entirely unscathed. The tremors of those events would rock this city long after the earthquake ended. The few years David Sharp served in prison were a minor inconvenience compared with what he did to the parties responsible when he got out.

My mind drifted out of the hospital room and to the darkest places I'd been, places he bred me to thrive. Visiting those places wouldn't help Claire, and I pushed them out with the thought of her eyes wide and mischievous. Big and brown, like melted chocolate with such warmth and sweetness. A thick fringe of curled lashes surrounding them, fanning over her cheeks. That girl made everything better.

I forced my eyes open, needing to see her. One time, I told Claire how guilty the things I did as a young moron under my father's heel made me feel. I didn't lie to her about the regret plaguing my every move and driving me to build a better life. All of that was true, and at times, I pretended I succeeded, that I atoned for my sins in some way. What a fantasy that was! I would never forgive myself for a single drop of innocent blood I spilled. When I left this world and sat at the devil's table, he would smile at me. *'You did good, my son.'*

The truth I kept from her was that I relished the power and the pain. I enjoyed hurting people, and no amount of atonement or distance would wash that filth off of my soul. I never tried to lay down roots before, knowing a sickness crept along beside me like a second shadow, made of something so dark it would steal the light of anything foolish enough to touch it.

Then I met Claire, and all I saw or dreamt of were roots and family. The blazing radiance coming off her shined so brightly, I only dimmed her by a fraction with my nearness. Those roots I wanted to lay with her seemed so possible, but they twisted through broken glass and crumbled tombstones. Pain and revenge marred every step we took.

After all the heinous things I did, of course, the straight and narrow life I built would eventually come crashing down. Charles Gains cropping up first to take everything from me was a cosmic joke. I would have laughed if anything filled me other than pure venom and bile. My days as Mason Dubois were always numbered, but I never would have guessed this is what they ticked down to.

My father never made a secret of how he crept over my shoulder, waiting for a moment of weakness to strike and bring me back into the fold. He didn't mind me becoming a lawyer. The knowledge and public station could only help his pursuits. He would win either way, by taking my life or ruining it, but I never imagined Mason Dubois would end at the hands of a serial killer with an old grudge and a flash of uncontrollable rage.

This one was not entirely on me, although I could have handled things better. From what my men discovered, Charles stalked her and planned to hurt her before we went on our first date. He had a job at the office she got fired from under a fake name, all to find young women to murder. He didn't discover us until he watched me bring her home, and yet serendipity needed to fuck me in the ass and make that my fault as well. *I have a thing for breaking your toys,* he said. The muscles in my jaw strained so hard it was a miracle my teeth didn't break.

Poor Rebecca. I dropped my head into my hands, thinking of the many ways she suffered in the end. Asking my old acquaintances for simple favors was worth the risk in order to keep Claire safe, more than a reasonable price to pay to avoid history repeating itself. Asking people to check into old feuds and squabbles wouldn't force me into a situation I couldn't escape. *Put an ear to the ground. See who's trying to come after me.* That was fine. I would have handled it. Until I made a catastrophic mess of Charles' remains and he needed to disappear.

Claire wouldn't like what the situation demanded now, but she would stick by me all the same. This thing between us was too powerful to be ignored, and I imbedded myself as deeply in her as she did in me.

The doctor popped into the doorway with a hulking security guard at his side. *Well, fuck.* I was going to need to hurt someone. At that moment, Claire's hand twitched, and she made a little sound of pain. The doctor flew to her, forgetting my presence. "Wh-, where am I?" she croaked.

It took every bit of self-control I had to stay seated and let the doctor do his job, checking her bandaging and vitals. "You're at North Central Hospital, Ms. Green. Do you remember what happened?"

"I, uh, no. I don't think so..." she muttered, her pretty eyes searching the room, resting when they found me. I let out a ragged breath at the sight. I worried I would never bathe in the light of her glances again. She lied. Claire was an open book, at least for me. The haunted look in her eye meant she remembered everything, or most of it anyway.

The doctor checked her over, poking and prodding. She made little noises of pain, and I nearly vomited. I killed people, tortured them, and the slightest ache from her was enough to turn my stomach. "Everything looks good," he told her with a small, satisfied smile. Then he turned to leave, nodding to the security guard. "Escort him out, please."

"What? No! Please, you can't make him go!" Claire wailed, gasping in shock and pain when the exertion pressed on her injured organs, not realizing how torn apart she was.

"Ms. Green, please calm down. Visiting hours are over." He put his hands up, trying to placate her.

"Please, please, I need him to stay." Miserable tears fell down her cheeks as she whimpered the words, barely possessing the energy to push them out.

With an annoyed and tired sigh, he muttered. "Tonight, only. Do not expect me to make another exception." She nodded frantically to him, willing to accept whatever he said. I would be all too happy to kill the prick myself, but again, he saved her.

Once they left, I walked to her side, leaning down and kissing along her hairline. I saved her lips for last, touching mine gently to hers. "Do you remember what happened?"

"Everything." She confirmed with a slightly drugged slur to her speech.

"I love you too." The words raced out of me as I traced my forefinger over her jaw. I tried to tell her back in her apartment, but she lost consciousness too quickly. It nearly killed me to think she would die without me telling her I loved her and I couldn't stand another minute of her not knowing. I kept my feelings for her in for so long, not wanting to scare her off or chase her away.

"You don't have to. Just because I almost died, doesn't mean..."

I put the same finger over her lips. "Claire, I love you. I have loved you since we sat in that park and I told you about my mom. You are *it* for me, and if you think for one *fucking* minute I would tell you I love you because I feel bad or some other self-hating bullshit, then you don't know me at all."

Her pale cheeks flooded with color, and guilt swamped me. *Fuck, she just woke up. I need to calm down.* I reminded myself.

"I love you too..." she answered, but she wouldn't look at me. Tears slid from her undamaged eye. "You weren't the one on the phone, were you?"

"What are you talking about, Claire?" Something thick and black tightened in my stomach, reminding me of fear, but after I watched her nearly bleed out in front of me, nothing scared me anymore, except losing her.

"I overheard Gavin talking to someone. I thought, well, I thought it was you. That's why I went home. I thought you were my stalker. I am so unbelievably sorry." Tears streamed down her face. "I ruined everything."

It took me a moment to respond. It felt like she kicked me in the stomach. Typical Claire, blaming herself for shit wildly out of her control.

"Baby, what did he say to make you so upset, and why did you think it was me?" I got to her in time by sheer chance. Lawrence called her to ask if she would go to lunch soon, and when she didn't answer, he called me straight away.

"He said, Mr. Sharp." I barely heard her through the tears, but after a lot of coaxing and calming, she told me everything. The murderous rage in my gut threatened to spill over.

"Gavin was talking to my father." I let the words hang in the air between us, not sure how to continue. She stared up at me, hurt and confused. "I promise you, Claire, I will fix all of this."

She nodded her head and tried to wipe away her tears. She winced when her tube-covered hand met her injured eye. "Why didn't you warn me about Gavin? You were always at the library. You must have known something." She sniffled, and what remained of the fractured thing beating in my chest broke further.

I breathed out a heavy sigh. "When I involved myself in my father's business, Gavin was a nobody. I warned you when we went to dinner. The library has a sordid history, but I didn't think I needed to be any more specific than that. I would never expect them to contact one another directly."

"Why would your father know who I am? Why would he care?" Her strength faded fast.

I had a lot of ideas, but she was hurt, and this was not the right time for this conversation. "I don't know, baby, but I will find out."

"Mason, I don't want to lose my job. I love my job." Fat tears blubbered down her cheeks, and I was sure the drugs in her system affected her enough that the details of our exchange would be hazy. We would talk again when she would remember. If she wanted to keep her job, that was fine. There wasn't a place on earth we could run to and avoid this anyway. This problem needed to be solved head-on. The library was small potatoes and there wasn't a single part of this city left untouched by my father's influence.

"You don't have to." I assured her, running my fingers through her curly brown hair, twisting one of the curls around my finger possessively. "We're going to get you all better and figure everything out. Let me handle Gavin and my father."

"You shouldn't. You shouldn't be involved with them." Her good eye drifted closed and I ran my hand across her undamaged cheek, savoring the feel of her being alive and talking to me.

"Everything will be okay, I promise. I will take care of everything." I crooned the words like she was a small child. Not being able to hold her while she cried made me want to pull Charles out of the river and kill him again but slow this time. I couldn't tell her yet, but my involvement was cemented. If my father had his sights set on her, I would need to get my hands dirtier than she could imagine before all of this ended.

I let her cry herself out and held her hand until she fell asleep. Leaving her side felt as if it might kill me, but with the information she gave me, I had no other choice. I stalked out of the hospital like an animal on the hunt. The cold air crashed against me, chilling my skin, but stoking the fire within me.

It was nearly midnight, and my first stop was Gavin Wolfe's office downtown. It wasn't far from the hospital, and I used the walk there to wrangle the rage burning inside me. I needed control, not a wild ball of fury. Gavin and the rest of the board of directors for the library, along with many of the city's movers and shakers, had offices in the same high-rise.

I could find his home address easily enough without the theatrics of breaking in, but I wanted to send a message. The rotating door moved beneath my hand. How fortunate, this building remained unlocked twenty-four seven. I found Gavin's name on the directory hanging on the wall. Riding the elevator up to the fifteenth floor, I achieved the control I searched for.

I approached his office, taking one deep breath before I kicked the thing off the hinges. The little man on the other side yelped in fear, before hardening his face and putting on a show of bravery. How convenient. I didn't expect to find him there so late. "Mason, what are you doing here?" He tried to keep his voice steady, but it broke like a pubescent boy.

"I'm here because you made the piss poor choice of working for my father, and you're letting your lapse in judgment affect my girl." I stopped directly in front of him, staring down at the pitiful bastard.

"No, I'm not—" he opened his mouth to continue bullshitting me, but I pulled out my gun, and he quickly shut up.

"Let me clarify things for you, Gavin. You will keep going exactly as you have been, but when daddy dearest calls, the information you give him will be exactly what I tell you to say. You will protect the librarian with your fucking life. If you don't, if you double-cross me, I'm going to make what happened to Charles Gains look like an island retreat. Do you understand me?"

He laughed at me with a disparaging expression. "We all know you've gone soft, baby Sharp. No way am I backing a losing horse."

I took the few steps separating us, picked up my gun and smashed the metal into his face. His head flew to the side, blood poured from his mouth, down his chin, staining the suit a man such as him could only afford with the dirty money lining his pockets. He made a miserable whimpering sound as he cupped his cheek.

I slapped his hand away, squeezing his jaw, painfully forcing it open. I shoved my gun in so hard I'm sure I cracked some of his teeth. "Remember, Gavin, I was my father's heir apparent. Anything he can do to you, I will do better, with youthful exuberance. Do you understand?"

He nodded his head, his eye already blackening. Spit and blood dripped from his chin. I ripped the gun out of his mouth, pulled his handkerchief out of his pocket, and wiped off the barrel before dropping the used cloth back on him.

"Why bother? Why not kill me now?" he spat through the blood.

"Oh, Gavin! Why would I kill you? We're friends! I've got big plans for you." I left him bloodied and slobbering, unconcerned with cops or cameras. He wouldn't call them. I rode the elevator to the bottom floor and stepped out into the cool night to return to my girl. I took my phone out of my pocket and dialed one of the two guys whose loyalty I was certain of. "Watch that prick, start a tap on his phone, hack his systems. I want to know if he takes a shit."

"Yes, Mr. Sharp."

"Thanks, and James?"

"Yes, Mr. Sharp?"

"Welcome back."

<u>The End</u>

The Illicit Library Collection book 2 coming in July 2022 preorder now!

https://www.amazon.com/dp/B09RQGTZYM

Follow Aurelia

Join Aurelia's mailing list for updates, book recommendations, and a free novelette coming soon!

Website:

https://www.Aureliaknight.com

Facebook:

https://www.facebook.com/aureliaknightauthor

Instagram:

https://www.instagram.com/aureliaknightauthor/

Tik Tok:

https://www.tiktok.com/@aureliaknightauthor

About the Author

Aurelia Knight is a hot mess, doing her best to keep it together most days. Words are the greatest love of her life second only to her husband and sons. If she's not typing away, getting lost in her own world, she's reading and slipping away into the worlds of other writers. A caffeine addict who believes sleep is secondary to the endless promise of "just one more chapter".

Acknowledgements

I would be remiss if I did not take a moment to thank the people I love; they have supported me in ways I can scarcely begin to describe.

My husband, who has forgiven my distractions, cooked for the kids, and endured my constant imagination induced turmoil, and generally uplifted me in everyway. I would be half the person I am today without you.

My friend and future coauthor, S.A. Hurst, this book would be a forgotten, abandoned mess without you. Thank you for seeing the potential in it and encouraging me to fight for it. You push me to be better everyday and I cannot put into words how much your friendship means to me.

My editor, Kemely Adames Parfrey, thank you for your hard work, kindness, and plethora of ideas.

Printed in Great Britain
by Amazon